THE

*Translated by
Sonia Pitt-Rivers and Irina Morduch*

THE SQUARE

TEN-THIRTY ON A SUMMER NIGHT

THE AFTERNOON OF MONSIEUR ANDESMAS

Marguerite Duras

JOHN CALDER
LONDON

First published in Great Britain by John Calder (Publishers) Ltd., 1977
Originally published in French by Editions Gallimard as follows:
Le Square; 1955. *Dix heures et demie du soir en été*; 1960
L'Après-midi de Monsieur Andesmas; 1962
The Square translated by Sonia Pitt-Rivers and Irina Morduch first published 1959 by John Calder (Publishers) Ltd.,
Ten-Thirty on a Summer Night translated by Anne Borchardt first published by John Calder (Publishers) Ltd., 1962
The Afternoon of Monsieur Andesmas translated by Anne Borchardt first published by John Calder (Publishers) Ltd., 1964

©Marguerite Duras 1977

ALL RIGHTS RESERVED

This translation of *The Square* ©John Calder (publishers) Ltd., 1959,1977
This translation of *Ten-Thirty on a Summer Night* ©John Calder (Publishers) Ltd., 1962,1977
This translation of *The Afternoon of Monsieur Andesmas* ©Anne Borchardt, 1964, 1977

Reprinted 1999

ISBN 07145 3602 4 Paperback Edition

British Library Cataloguing in Publication Data is available.
Library of Congress Cataloguing in Publication Data is available.

No part of this publication may be reproduced, stored in a retrieval system, or transmitted in any form by any means, electronic, photocopying, mechanical or otherwise, except brief extracts for review, without the prior written permission of the Copyright owner and publisher.

Printed and bound in England by Redwood Books.

THE child came over quietly from the far side of the Square and stood beside the girl.

'I'm hungry,' he announced.

The man took this as an opportunity to start a conversation.

'I suppose it is about tea-time?'

The girl was not disconcerted: on the contrary she turned and smiled at him.

'Yes, it must be nearly half-past four, when he usually has his tea.'

She took two sandwiches from a bag beside her on the bench and handed them to the child, then skilfully knotted a bib around his neck.

'He's a nice child,' said the man.

The girl shook her head as if in denial.

'He's not mine,' she remarked.

The child moved off with his sandwiches. It was afternoon and the Park was full of children: big ones playing hide-and-seek, small ones playing in the sandpits, while smaller ones still sat patiently waiting in their prams for the time when they would join the others.

'Although,' the girl continued, 'he could be mine

and, indeed, is often taken for mine. But the fact is he doesn't belong to me.'

'I see,' said the man. 'I have no children either.'

'Sometimes it seems strange, don't you think, there should be so many children, that they are everywhere one goes and yet none of them are one's own?'

'I suppose so, yes, when you come to think of it. But then, as you said, there are so many already.'

'But does that make any difference?'

'I should have thought that if you were fond of them anyway, the opposite might also be true? If you enjoyed just watching them, it matters less.'

'Probably. I expect it depends on one's nature: I think that some people are quite happy with the children who are already there, and I believe I am one of them. I have seen so many children and I could have had children of my own and yet I manage to be quite satisfied with the others.'

'Have you really seen so many?'

'Yes. You see, I travel.'

'I see,' the girl said in a friendly manner.

'I travel all the time, except just now of course when I'm resting.'

'Parks are good places to rest in, particularly at this time of year. I like them too. It's nice being out of doors.'

'They cost nothing, they're always gay because of

the children and then if you don't know many people there's always the chance of starting a conversation.'

'That's true. I hope you don't mind my asking, but do you sell things when you travel?'

'Yes, you could call that my profession.'

'Always the same things?'

'No, different things, but all of them small. You know those little things one always needs and so often forgets to buy. They all fit into a medium-sized suitcase. I suppose you could call me a commercial traveller if you wanted to give what I do a name.'

'Like those people you see in markets selling things from an open suitcase?'

'That's right. I often work on the outskirts of markets.'

'I hope you don't think it rude of me to ask, but do you manage to make a living?'

'I've nothing to complain of.'

'I'm glad. I thought that was probably the case.'

'I don't mean to say that I earn a lot of money because that would not be true. But I earn something each day and in its way I call that making a living.'

'In fact you manage to live much as you would like?'

'Yes, I think I live about as well as I want to: I don't mean that one day is always as good as another.

No. Sometimes things are a little tight, but in general I manage well enough.'

'I'm glad.'

'Thank you. Yes, I manage more or less and have really nothing to worry about. Being single with no home of my own I have few worries and the ones I have are naturally only for myself – sometimes for instance I find that I have run out of toothpaste, sometimes I might want for a little company. But on the whole it works out well. Thank you for asking.'

'Would you say that almost anyone could do your work? I mean is it the kind of work which practically anybody could take up?'

'Yes indeed. I would even go so far as to say that simply through being what it is it is one of the ways of earning a living most open to everybody.'

'I should have thought it might need special qualifications?'

'Well I suppose it is better to know how to read, if only for the newspaper in the evenings at the hotel, and also of course to know which station you are at. It makes life a little easier but that's all. It's not much of a qualification as you can see, and yet one can still earn enough money to live.'

'I really meant other kinds of qualification: I would have thought your work needed endurance, or patience perhaps, and a great deal of perseverance?'

'I have never done any other work so I could hardly say whether you are right or not. But I always imagined that the qualifications you mention would be necessary for any work; in fact that there could hardly be a job where they are not needed.'

'I am sorry to go on asking you all these questions but do you think you will always go on travelling like this? Or do you think that one day you might stop?'

'I don't know.'

'I'm sorry. Forgive me for being so curious, but we were talking. . . .'

'Of course and it's quite all right. But I am afraid I don't know if I will go on travelling. There really is no other answer I can give you: I don't know. How does one know such things?'

'I only meant that if one travelled all the time as you do, I would have thought that one day one would want to stop and stay in one place. That was all.'

'It's true I suppose that one should want to stop. But how do you stop doing one thing and start another? How do people decide to leave one job for another, and why?'

'If I've understood you, the fact that you travel depends only on yourself, not on anything else?'

'I don't think I have ever quite known how such things are decided. I have no particular attachments.

In fact I am a rather solitary person and unless some great piece of luck came my way I cannot really see how I could change my work. And somehow I can't imagine where any luck would come from: there doesn't seem much about my life which would attract it. Of course I don't mean that some luck could not come my way – after all one never knows – nor that if it did I would not accept it very gladly. But for the moment I must confess I cannot see much luck coming my way and helping me to a decision.'

'But couldn't you just simply want it? I mean just decide you wanted to change your work?'

'No, I don't think so. Each day I want to be clean, well fed and sleep well, and I also like to feel decently dressed. So you see I hardly have time for wanting much more. And then, after all, I don't really dislike travelling.'

'Can I ask you another question? How did all this start?'

'How could I begin to tell you? Things like that are so long and so complicated, and sometimes I really think they are a little beyond me. It would mean going so far back that I feel tired before I start. But on the whole I think things happened to me as they do to anyone else, no differently.'

A wind had risen, so light it seemed to carry the summer with it. For a moment it chased the clouds away, leaving a new warmth hanging over the city.

'How lovely it is,' the man said.

'Yes,' said the girl, 'almost the beginning of the hot weather. From now on it will be a little warmer each day.'

'You see I had no special aptitude for any particular work or for any particular kind of life. And so I suppose I will go on as I am. Yes, I think I will.'

'So really your feelings are only negative? They are just against any particular work or any particular life?'

'Against? No. That's too strong a word. I can only say that I have no very strong likes. I really just came to be as I am in the way that most people come to be as they are: there is nothing special about my case.'

'But between the things that happened to you a long time ago and now, wasn't there time for you to change – almost every day in fact – and start liking things? Anything?'

'I suppose so. I don't deny it. For some people life must be like that and then again for others it is not. Some people must get used to the idea of never changing and I think that really is true of me. So I expect I will just go on as I am.'

'Well, for me things will change: they will not go on being the same.'

'But can you know already?'

'Yes, I can, because my situation is not one which

can continue: sooner or later it must come to an end, that is part of it. I am waiting to marry. And as soon as I am married my present life will be quite finished.'

'I understand.'

'I mean that once it is over it will seem so unimportant that it might as well never have been.'

'Perhaps I too – after all it's impossible to foresee everything, isn't it? – might change my life one day.'

'Ah, but the difference is that I want to change mine. What I do now is hardly a job. People call it one to make things easier for themselves, but in fact it is not. It's something different, something with no meaning outside itself like being ill or a child. And so it must come to an end.'

'I understand, but I've just come back from a long journey and now I'm resting. I never much like thinking of the future and today, when I'm resting, even less: that's why I am so bad at explaining to you how it is I can put up with my life as it is and not change it, and what is more, not even be able to imagine changing. I'm sorry.'

'Oh no, it is I who should apologize.'

'Of course not. After all we can always talk.'

'That's right. And it means nothing.'

'And so you are waiting for something to happen?'

'Yes. I can see no reason why I should not get

married one day like everybody else. As I told you.'

'You're quite right. There is no reason at all why you should not get married too.'

'Of course with a job like mine – one which is so looked down upon – you could say that the opposite would be more true and that there is no reason at all why anyone should want to marry me. And so somehow I think that to make it seem quite ordinary and natural, I must want it with all my might. And that is how I want it.'

'I am sure nothing is impossible. People say so at least.'

'I have thought about it a great deal: here I am, young, healthy and truthful just like any woman you see anywhere whom some man has settled for. And surely it would be surprising if somewhere there isn't a man who won't see that I am just as good as anyone else and settle for me. I am full of hope.'

'I am sure it will happen to you. But if you were suggesting that I make the same sort of change, I can only ask what I would do with a wife? I have nothing in the world but my suitcase and it is all I can do to keep myself.'

'Oh no, I did not mean to say that you need this particular change. I was talking of change in general. For me marriage is the only possible change, but for you it could be something else.'

'I expect you are right, but you seem to forget

that people are different. You see, however much I wanted to change, even if I wanted it with all my might, I could never manage to want it as much as you do. You seem to want it at all costs.'

'Perhaps that is because for you a change would be less great than it would for me. As far as I am concerned I feel I want the greatest change there could be. I might be mistaken but it still seems to me that all the changes I see in other people are simple and easy beside the one I want for myself.'

'But don't you think that even if everyone needed to change, and needed it very badly indeed, that even so they would feel differently about it according to their own particular circumstances?'

'I am sorry but I must explain that I am quite uninterested in particular circumstances. As I told you I am full of hope and what is more I do everything possible to make my hopes come true. For instance every Saturday I go to the local Dance Hall and dance with anyone who asks me. They say that the truth will out and I believe that one day someone will take me for what I am, a perfectly marriageable young woman who would make just as good a wife as anyone else.'

'I don't think it would help me to go dancing, even if I wanted to change, and wanted it less than you do. My profession is insignificant: in fact it can hardly even be called a profession since it only just provides enough for one person, or perhaps it would be nearer the truth to say a half-person. And so I couldn't, even for an instant, imagine that anything like that would change my life.'

'But then perhaps, as I said before, it would be enough for you to change your work?'

'Yes, but how? How does one change a profession, even such a miserable one as mine? One which doesn't even allow me to marry? All I do is to go with my suitcase through one day to the next, from one night to another and even from one meal to the next meal, and there is no time for me to stop and think about it as perhaps I should. No, if I were to change then the opportunity must come to me: I have no time to meet it half way. And then again I should, perhaps, explain that I never felt that anyone particularly needed my services or my company – so much so that quite often I am amazed that I occupy any place in the world at all.'

'Then perhaps the change you should make would be just to feel differently about things?'

'Of course. But you know how it is. After all one is what one is and how could anyone change so radically? Also I have come to like my work, even if it could hardly be called that: I like catching trains, and sleeping almost anywhere no longer worries me much.'

'You must not mind my saying this, but it seems

to me that you should never have let yourself become like this.'

'You could perhaps say I was always a little predisposed to it.'

'For me it would be terrible to go through life with nothing but a suitcase full of things to sell. I think I should be frightened.'

'Of course that can happen, especially at the beginning, but one gets used to little things like that.'

'I think that in spite of everything I would rather be as I am, in my present position rather than in yours. But perhaps that is because I am only twenty.'

'But you mustn't think that my work has nothing but disadvantages. That would be quite wrong. With all the time I have on my hands for instance, on the road, in trains, in Squares like this, I can think of all manner of things. I have time to look around and even time to work out reasons for things.'

'But I thought you said you had only enough time to think of yourself? Or rather of managing to keep yourself and of nothing else?'

'No. What I lack is time to think of the future, but I have time to think of other things or perhaps I should say I make it. Because, after all, if one can face struggling a little more than others do, just to get enough to eat, it is only possible on condition that once a meal is over one can stop thinking about the whole problem. If immediately one meal was finished you had to start thinking about the next one it would be enough to drive you mad.'

'I imagine so. But you see what would drive me mad would be going from city to city as you do with no other company than a suitcase.'

'Oh one is not always alone you know. I mean so alone that one might go mad. No, there are boats and trains full of people to watch and observe and then, if one ever feels one is really going mad, there is always something to be done about it.'

'But what good would it do me to make the best of things since all I want is to finish with my present position? In the end all your attitude does for you is to give you more reasons for not finishing with yours.'

'That is not completely true, because should an opportunity arise for me to change my work I would certainly seize it: no, my attitude helps me in other ways. For example it helps me to see the advantages of my profession, such as travelling a great deal and possibly of becoming a little wiser than I was before. I am not saying I am right. I could easily be wrong and, without realizing it, have become far less wise than I ever was. But then, since I couldn't know, it doesn't really matter, does it?'

'And so you are continually travelling? As continually as I stay in one place?'

'Yes. And even if sometimes I go back to the same places they can be different. In the spring for instance cherries appear in the markets. That is really what I wanted to say and not that I thought I was right in putting up with my life as it is.'

'You're right. Quite soon, in about six weeks, the first cherries will be in the markets. I am glad for your sake. But tell me what other things you see when you travel?'

'Oh, a thousand things. One time it will be spring and another winter; either sunshine or snow, making the place unrecognizable. But I think it is really the cherries which change things the most: suddenly there they are, and the whole market place becomes scarlet. Yes, they will there in about six weeks. You see, that is what I wanted to explain, not that I thought my work was entirely satisfactory.'

'But apart from the cherries and the sunshine and the snow, what else do you see?'

'Sometimes nothing much: small things you would hardly notice, but a number of little things which added together seem to change a place. Places can be familiar and unfamiliar at the same time: a market which once seemed hostile can, quite suddenly, become warm and friendly.'

'But sometimes isn't everything exactly the same?'

'Yes. Sometimes so exactly the same that you can only think you left it the night before. I have never understood how this could happen because after all it would seem impossible that anything could remain so much the same.'

'Tell me more about other things you see.'

'Well, sometimes a new block of flats which was half built when last I was there is finished and lived in: full of people and noise. And the odd thing is that although the town had never seemed overcrowded before, there it suddenly is – a brand new block of flats, completed and inhabited as if it had always been utterly necessary.'

'All the things you describe and the changes you notice are there for anyone to see, aren't they? They are not things which exist for you alone, for you and for no one else?'

'Sometimes there are things which I alone can see, but only negligible things. In general you are right: the things I notice are mostly changes in the weather, in buildings, things which anyone would notice. And yet sometimes, just by watching them carefully, such things can affect one just as much as events which are completely personal. In fact it feels as though they were personal, as if somehow one had put the cherries there oneself.'

'I see what you mean and I am trying to put myself in your place, but it's no good, I still think I should be frightened.'

'That does happen. It happens to me sometimes when I wake up at night. But on the whole it is only at night that I feel frightened, although I can also feel it at dusk – but then only when it's raining or there's a fog.'

'Isn't it strange that although I have never actually experienced the fear we are talking about, I can still understand a little what it must be like.'

'It is not the kind of fear you might feel if you said to yourself that when you died no one would care. No, it's another kind of fear, a general one which affects everything and not just you alone.'

'As if you were suddenly terrified of being yourself, of being what you are instead of different, almost instead of being some quite other kind of thing.'

'Yes. It comes from feeling at the same time like everyone else, exactly like everyone else, and yet being oneself. In fact I think it is just that: being one kind of thing rather than another. . . .'

'It's complicated, but I understand.'

'As for the other kind of fear – the fear of thinking that no one would notice if you died – it seems to me that sometimes this can make one happier. I think that if you knew that when you died no one would suffer, not even a dog, it makes it easier to bear the thought of dying.'

'I am trying to follow you, but I am afraid I don't understand. Perhaps because women are different from men? All I do know is that I could not bear to live as you do, alone with that suitcase. It is not that

I would not like to travel, but unless there was someone who cared for me somewhere in the world I don't think I could do it. In fact I can only say that I would prefer to be where I am.'

'But could you not think of travelling while waiting for what you want?'

'No. I don't believe you know what it is to want to change one's life. I must stay here and think about it, think with all my might, or else I know I will never manage to change.'

'Perhaps. I don't really know.'

'How could you know? Because, however modest a way of life you have, it is at least yours. So how could you know what it is like to be nothing?'

'Am I right in thinking that no one would particularly care if you died either?'

'No one. And I've been twenty now for two weeks. But one day someone will care. I know it. I am full of hope. Otherwise nothing would be possible.'

'You are quite right. Why shouldn't someone care about you as much as about anyone else?'

'That's just it. That's just what I say to myself.'

'You're right, and now I'd like to ask you a question. Do you get enough to eat?'

'Yes thank you, I do. I eat as much as and even more than I need. Always alone, but one eats well in my job since after all one does the cooking; and good things too. Even if I have to force myself I always eat a great deal because sometimes I feel I would like to be fatter and more impressive so that people would notice me more. I think that if I were bigger and stronger I would stand a better chance of getting what I want. You may say I'm wrong but it seems to me that if I were radiantly healthy people would find me more attractive. And so you see, we are really very different.'

'Probably. But in my own way I am also someone who tries. I must have explained myself badly just now. I assure you that if I should ever want to change, why then I would set about it like everyone else.'

'You know, it is not very easy to believe you when you say that.'

'Perhaps, but you see while I have nothing against hope in general, the fact is that there has never seemed much reason for it to concern me. And yet I feel that it would not take a great deal for me to feel that hope is as necessary to me as it is to others. It might only need the smallest bit of faith. Perhaps I lack the time for it, who knows? I don't mean the time I spend in trains thinking of this or that, or passing the time of day with other people, no, I mean the other kind of time: the time anyone has, each day, to think of the one that follows. I just lack the time to start thinking about that particular subject and so discovering that it might mean something to me too.'

'And yet it seems to me, as I think you yourself said, that there was a time when you were like everyone else?'

'Yes, but almost so much so that I was never able to do anything about it. I could never make up my mind to choose a profession. No one can be everything at once or, as you said, want everything at once, and personally I was never able to get over this difficulty. But after all I have travelled, my suitcase takes me to a great many places and once I even went to a foreign country. I didn't sell much there but I saw it. If anyone had told me some years ago that I should want to go there I would never have believed them, and yet you see one day when I woke up I suddenly felt I would like to visit it and I went; and although very little has happened to me in my life at least I managed that – I went to that country.'

'But aren't people unhappy in this country of yours?'

'Yes.'

'And there are girls like me, waiting for something to happen?'

'I expect so, yes.'

'So what is the point of it?'

'Of course it's true that people are unhappy and

die there and there are probably girls like you waiting hopefully for something to happen to them. But why not know that country as well as just this one where we are, even if some things are the same? Why not see another country?'

'Because ... and I am sure I am wrong, and I am sure you will tell me I am, but the fact is that it is a matter of complete indifference to me.'

'Ah but wait. There for instance the winters are less harsh than here: in fact you would hardly know it was winter.'

'But what use is a whole country to anyone, or a whole city or even the whole of one warm winter? It's no use, you can say what you like but you can only be where you are, when you are and so what is the point?'

'But exactly: the town where I went ends in a big square surrounded by huge balustrades which seem to go on for ever....'

'I am afraid I simply don't want to hear about it.'

'The whole town is built in white limestone: imagine, it is like snow in the heart of summer. It is built on a peninsula surrounded by the sea.'

'And the sea I suppose is blue. It is blue isn't it?'

'Yes, very blue.'

'Well I am sorry, but I must tell you that people who talk of how blue the sea is make me sick.'

'But how can I help it? From the Zoo you can see it surrounding the whole town. And to anybody it must seem blue. It's not my fault.'

'No. For me, without those ties of affection I was talking about, it would be black. And then, although I don't want to offend you in any way, you must see that I am much too preoccupied with my desire to change my life to be able to go away or travel or see new things. You can see as many towns as you like but it never gets you anywhere. And once you have stopped looking, there you are, exactly where you were before.'

'But I don't think we are talking about the same thing. I'm not talking of those huge events which change a whole life, no, just of the things which give pleasure while one is doing them. Travelling is a great distraction. Everyone has always travelled, the Greeks, the Phoenicians: it has always been so, all through history.'

'It's true that we're talking of different things. Travel or cities by the sea are not the things I want. First of all I want to belong to myself, to own something, not necessarily something very wonderful, but something which is mine, a place of my own, maybe only one room, but mine. Why sometimes I even find myself dreaming of a gas stove.'

'You know it would be just the same as travelling. You wouldn't be able to stop. Once you had the gas stove you would want a refrigerator and after that something else. It would be just like travelling, going from city to city. It would never end.'

'Excuse me, but do you see anything wrong in my wanting something further perhaps after I have the refrigerator?'

'Of course not. No, certainly not. I was only speaking for myself, and as far as I am concerned I find your idea even more exhausting than travelling and then going on travelling, moving as I do from place to place.'

'I was born and grew up like everyone else and I know how to look around me: I look at things very carefully and I can see no reason why I should remain as I am. I must start somehow, anyhow, to become of consequence. And if at this stage I began losing heart at the thought of a refrigerator I might never even possess the gas stove. And anyway, how am I to know if it would weary me or not? If you say it would, it might be because you have given the matter a great deal of thought or perhaps even because at some time you very much disliked one particular refrigerator.'

'No it is not that. Not only have I never possessed a refrigerator, but I have never had the slightest chance of doing so. No, it's only an idea, and if I talked of refrigerators like that it was probably only because to someone who travels they seem especially heavy and immobile. I don't suppose I would have made the same remarks about another object. And yet I do understand, I assure you, that it would be impossible for you to travel before you had the gas stove, or even perhaps, the refrigerator. And I expect I am quite wrong to be so easily discouraged at the mere thought of a refrigerator.'

'It does seem very strange.'

'There was one day in my life, just one, when I no longer wanted to live. I was hungry, and as I had no money it was absolutely essential for me to work if I was to eat. It was as if I had forgotten that this was as true of everyone as of me. That day I felt quite unused to life and there seemed no point in going on living because I couldn't see why things should go on for me as they did for other people. It took me a whole day to get over this feeling. Then, of course, I took my suitcase to the market and afterwards I had a meal and things went on as they had before. But with this difference, that ever since that day I find that any thought of the future – and after all thinking of a refrigerator is thinking of the future – is much more frightening than before.'

'I would have guessed that.'

'Since then, when I think about myself, it is simply in terms of one person the more or one the less, and so you see that a refrigerator more or less can hardly seem as important to me as it does to you.'

'Tell me, did this happen before or after you went to that country you liked so much?'

'After. But when I think about that country I feel pleased and I think it would have been a pity for one more person not to have seen it. I don't mean that I imagine I was especially made to appreciate it. No, it just seems to me that since we are here, it is better to see one country more rather than one less.'

'I can't feel as you do and yet I do understand what you are saying and I think you are right to say it. What you really mean is that since we are alive anyhow it is better to see things than not to see them? It was that you meant wasn't it? And that seeing them makes the time pass quickly and more pleasantly?'

'Yes, it is a little like that. Perhaps the only difference between us is that we feel differently about how to spend our time?'

'Not only that, because as yet I have not had the time to become tired of anything, except of waiting of course. I don't mean that you are necessarily happier than I am, but simply that if you were unhappy you could imagine something which would help, like moving to another city, selling something different, or even ... even bigger things. But I can't start thinking of anything yet, not even the smallest thing. My life has not begun except, of course, for the fact that I am alive. There are times, in summer for example when the weather is fine, when I feel that something might have begun for me even without there being any proof of it, and then I am frightened. I become frightened of giving in to the fine weather and forgetting what I want even for a second, of losing myself in something unimportant. I am sure that if at this stage I started thinking of anything except the one big thing, I would be lost.'

'But it seemed to me for instance that you were fond of that little boy?'

'It makes no difference. If I am I don't want to know it. If I started finding consolations in my life, if I was able, to however small a degree, to put up with it then I know I would be lost. I have a great deal of work to do, and I do it. Indeed I am so good at my work that each day they give me a little more to do, and I accept it. Naturally it has ended by them giving me the hardest things to do, dreadful things, and yet I do them and I never complain. Because if I refused it would mean that I imagined that my situation, as it stands, could be improved, that it could be made somehow bearable, and then, of course, it would end up one day by becoming bearable.'

'And yet it seems strange to be able to make one's life easier and refuse to do so.'

'I suppose so, but I must do whatever they ask. I have never refused anything although it would have been easy at the beginning and now it would be easier still since I am asked to do more and more. But for as long as I can remember it has always been like this: I accepted everything quite quietly so that one day I would be quite unable to accept anything any more. You may say that this is a rather childish way of looking at things, but I could never find another way of being sure that I would get what I wanted. You see, I know that people can get used to anything and all around me I see people who are still where I am, but ten years later. There is nothing people cannot get accustomed to, even to a life like mine, and so I must be careful, very careful indeed, not to become accustomed to it myself. Sometimes I am frightened, because although I am aware of this danger, it is still so great that I am afraid that even I, aware as I am, might give in to it. But please go on telling me about the changes you see when you travel, apart from the snow, the cherries and the new buildings?'

'Well, sometimes the hotel has changed hands and the new owner is friendly and talkative where the old one was tired of trying to please and never spoke to his clients.'

'Tell me, it is true isn't it that I must not take things for granted: that each day I must still be amazed to be where I am or else I shall never succeed?'

'I think that everyone is amazed, each day, to be still where they are. I think people are amazed quite naturally. I doubt if one can decide to be amazed at one thing more than at another.'

'Each morning I am a little more surprised to find myself still where I am. I don't do it on purpose: I just wake up and, immediately, I am surprised. Then I start remembering things ... I was a child like any other: there was nothing to show I was different. At cherry time we used to go and steal fruit in the orchards. We were stealing it right up to the last day, because it was in that season that I was sent into service. But tell me more about the things you see when you travel?'

'I used to steal cherries like you, and there was nothing which seemed to make me different from other children, except perhaps that even then I loved them very much. Well, apart from a change of proprietor in an hotel, sometimes a wireless has been installed. That's a big change, when a café without music suddenly becomes a café with music: then of course they have many more customers and everyone stays much later. And that makes an evening to the good.'

'You said to the good?'

'Yes.'

'Ah, I sometimes think if only we had known. . . . My mother simply came up to me and said, 'Well, you must come along now.' And I just let myself be led away like an animal to the slaughterhouse. If only I had known then, I promise you I would have fought. I would have saved myself. I would have begged my mother to let me stay. I would have persuaded her.'

'But we don't know.'

'The cherry season went on that year like all the others. People would pass under my window singing and I would be there behind the curtains watching them, and I got scolded for it.'

'I was left free to pick cherries for a long time....'

'There was I behind the window like a criminal and yet my only crime was to be sixteen. But you? You said you went on picking them for a long time?'

'Longer than most people. And yet you see....'

'Tell me more about your cafés full of people and music.'

'I like them very much. I don't really think I could go on living without them.'

'I think I would like them too. I can see myself at the bar with my husband, listening to the wireless. People would talk to us and we would make conversation. We would be with each other and with the others. Sometimes I feel how nice it would be to go and sit in a café, but if you are a single young woman you can hardly afford to do so.'

'I forgot to add that sometimes someone looks at you.'

'I see, and comes over?'

'Yes, they come over.'

'For no reason?'

'For no particular reason, but then the conversation somehow becomes less general.'

'And then?'

'I never stay longer than two days in any town. Three at the most. The things I sell are not so essential.'

'Alas.'

The wind, which had died down, rose again scattering the clouds, and once more the sudden warmth in the air brought thoughts of approaching summer.

'But the weather is really wonderful today,' the man said again.

'It is nearly summer.'

'Perhaps the fact is that one never really starts anything: perhaps things are always in the future?'

'If you can say that, it is because each day is full enough for you to prevent you thinking of the next. But my days are empty, a desert.'

'But don't you ever do anything of which you could say later that at least it was something to the good?'

'No, nothing. I work all day, but I never do anything of which I could say what you have just said. I cannot even think in those terms.'

'Please don't think I want to contradict you, but you must see that whatever you do, this time you are living now will count for you one day. You will look back on this desert as you describe it and discover that it was not empty at all, but full of people. You won't be able to escape it. We think nothing has started and yet it has. We think we are doing nothing, but all the time we are doing something. We think we are going towards some solution and then we pause and turn around, and there the solution is, behind us. It was like that with that city. At the time I did not appreciate it for what it was. The hotel was indifferent, they had let the room I had reserved, it was late, and I was hungry. Nothing was waiting for me in that city except the city itself, vast: and try and imagine what a vast city, utterly absorbed in its own occupations, can be like for a tired traveller seeing it for the first time.'

'I cannot imagine it.'

'Nothing is waiting for you except a nasty room giving onto a noisy, dirty, courtyard. And yet, looking back on it, I know that that voyage changed me, that much of what I had seen and done before led up to it and so became clear and understandable. It is only afterwards that we know whether we have been in such or such a city: you should be aware of that.'

'If you mean things in that sense, perhaps you are right. Perhaps things have begun for me, and that they began on that particular day when I wanted them to.'

'Yes, you see we think nothing happens and yet, take your case, it seems to me that perhaps the most important thing that will have happened in your life is just this decision you have made not to begin living yet.'

'I understand you, I really do, but you must also try and understand me. Even if the most important part of my life is over, I can't know it as yet and I haven't the time to understand it. I hope one day I will know, as you did with your journey, and that when I look back everything behind me will be clear and fall into place. But now, at this moment, I am too involved to be able even to guess at what I might feel one day.'

'I know. And I know that probably it is impossible for you to understand things you have not yet felt, but all the same it is hard for me not to try and explain them to you.'

'You are very kind, but I am afraid that I am not very good yet at understanding the things I am told.'

'Believe me that I do understand all you have said, but even so, is it absolutely necessary to do all that work? Of course I am not trying to give you any advice, but don't you think that someone else would make a little effort and still manage, without quite so much work, to have as much hope for the future as before? Don't you think that another person would manage that?'

'Are you frightened that one day, if I have to wait too long and go on working a little more each day without complaining, I might suddenly lose patience altogether?'

'I admit that your kind of will power is a little frightening, but that's not why I made my suggestion. It was just because it is difficult to accept that someone of your age should live as you *do*.'

'But I have no alternative, I assure you. I have thought about it a great deal.'

'Can I ask you how many people there are in the family you work for?'

'Five.'

'And how big is the house?'

'Average.'

'And rooms?'

'Eight.'

'It's too much.'

'But no. That's not the way to think. I must have explained myself very badly because you haven't understood.'

'I think that work can always be measured and

that, no matter what the circumstances, work is always work.'

'Not my kind. It's probably true of the kind of work of which it is better to do too much than too little. But if in my kind of work there was time over to think or start enjoying oneself then one would really be lost.'

'And you're only twenty?'

'Yes, and as they say I've not yet had time to do any wrong. But that seems beside the point to me.'

'On the contrary I have a feeling that it is not and that the people you work for should remember it.'

'After all it's hardly their fault if I agree to do all the work they give me. I would do the same in their place.'

'I should like to tell you how I went into that town, after leaving my suitcase at the hotel.'

'Yes I should like to hear that. But you mustn't worry on my account: I would be most surprised if I let myself become impatient. I think all the time of the risk I would run if that should happen and so, you see, I don't think it will.'

'I did not manage to leave my suitcase until the evening....'

'You see people like me do think too. There is nothing else for us to do, buried in our work. We think a great deal, but not like you. We have dark thoughts, and all the time.'

'It was evening, just before dinner, after work.'

'People like me think the same things of the same people and our thoughts are always bad. That's why we are so careful and why it's not worth bothering about us. You were talking of jobs, and I wonder if something could be called a job which makes you spend your whole day thinking ill of people? But you were saying it was evening, and you had left your suitcase?'

'Yes. It was only towards the evening, after I had left my suitcase at the hotel, just before dinner, that I started walking through that town. I was looking for a restaurant and of course it's not always easy to find exactly what one wants when price is a consideration. And while I was looking I strayed away from the centre and came by accident to the Zoo. A wind had risen. People had forgotten the day's work and were strolling through the gardens which, as I told you, were up on a hill overlooking the town.'

'But I know that life is good. Otherwise why on earth should I take so much trouble.'

'I don't really know what happened. The moment I entered those gardens I was a man overwhelmed by a sense of living.'

'How could a garden, just seeing a garden, make a man happy?'

'And yet what I am telling you is quite an ordinary experience and other people will often tell you similar things in the course of your life. I am a person for whom talking, for example, feeling at one with other people, is a blessing, and suddenly in that garden I was so completely at home, so much at my ease, that it might have been made specially for me although it was an ordinary public garden. I don't know how to put it any better, except perhaps to say that it was as if I had achieved something and become, for the first time, equal to my life. I could not bear to leave it. The wind had risen, the light was honey-coloured and even the lions whose manes glowed in the setting sun were yawning with the pure pleasure of being there. The air smelt of lions and of fire and I breathed it as if it were the essence of friendliness which had, at last, included me. All the passers-by were preoccupied with each other, basking in the evening light. I remember thinking they were like the lions. And suddenly I was happy.'

'But in what way were you happy? Like someone resting? Like someone who is cool again after having been very hot? Or happy as other people are happy every day?'

'More than that I think. Probably because I was unused to happiness. A great surge of feeling overwhelmed me, and I did not know what to do with it.'

'A feeling which hurt?'

'Perhaps so, yes. It hurt because there seemed to be nothing which could ever appease it.'

'But that, I think, is hope.'

'Yes that is hope, I know that really is hope. And of what? Of nothing. Just the hope of hope.'

'You know if there were only people like you in the world, no one would get anywhere.'

'But listen. You could see the sea from the bottom of each avenue in that garden, every single one led to the sea. Actually the sea really plays very little part in my life, but in that garden they were all looking at the sea, even the people who were born there, even it seemed to me, the lions themselves. How can you avoid looking at what other people are looking at, even if normally it doesn't mean much to you.'

'The sea couldn't have been as blue as all that since you said the sun was setting?'

When I left my hotel it was blue but after I had been in that garden a little while it became darker and calmer.'

'But you said a wind had come up: it couldn't have been as calm as all that?'

'But it was such a gentle wind, if you only knew, and it was probably only blowing on the heights: on the town and not on the plain. I don't remember exactly from which direction it came, but surely not from the open sea.'

'And then again, the setting sun couldn't have illuminated all the lions. Not unless all the cages faced the same way on the same side of the garden looking into the sun?'

'And yet I promise you it was like that. They were all in the same place and the setting sun lit up each lion without exception.'

'And so the sun did set first over the sea?'

'Yes, you're quite right. The city and the garden were still in sunshine although the sea was in shade. That was three years ago. That's why I remember it all so well and like talking about it.'

'I understand. One thinks one can get by without talking, but it's not possible. From time to time I find myself talking to strangers too, just as we are talking now.'

'When people need to talk it can be felt very strongly, and strangely enough people in general seem to resent it. It is only in Squares that it seems quite natural. Tell me again, you said there were eight rooms where you worked? Big rooms?'

'I couldn't really say since I don't suppose anyone else would see them in quite the same way as I do. Most of the time they seem big, but perhaps they're not as big as all that. It really depends. On some days they seem endless and on others I think I could stifle they seem so tiny. But why did you ask?'

'It was only out of curiosity. For no other reason.'

'I know that I must seem stupid to you, but I can't help it.'

'I would say you are a very ambitious person, if I have really understood you, someone who wants everything that everyone else has, but wants it so much that one could almost say your desire is heroic.'

'That word doesn't frighten me, although I had not thought of it in that way. You could almost say I have so little that I could have anything. After all I could want to die with the same violence as I want to live. And is there anything, any one little thing in my life to which I could sacrifice my courage? And who or what could weaken it? Anyone would do the same as I do: anyone I mean who wanted what I want as much as I do.'

'I expect so. Since everyone does what he has to do. Yes I expect there are cases where it is impossible to be anything else but heroic.'

'You see if just once I refused the work they give me, no matter what it was, it would mean that I had begun to manage things, to defend myself, to take an interest in what I was doing. It would start with one thing, go on to another, and could end anywhere. I would begin to defend my rights so well that I would take them seriously and end by thinking they existed. They would matter to me. I wouldn't be bored any more and so I would be lost.'

There was a silence between them. The sun, which had been hidden by the clouds, came out again. Then the girl started talking once more.

'Did you stay on in that town after being so happy in that garden?'

'I stayed for several days. Sometimes I do stay longer than usual in a place.'

'Tell me, do you think that anyone can experience the feelings you had in that garden?'

'There must be some people who never do. It's an almost unbearable idea but I suppose there are such people.'

'You don't know for certain do you?'

'No. I can easily be mistaken. The fact is I really don't know.'

'And yet you seem to know about these things.'

'No more than anyone else.'

'There's something else I want to ask you: as the sun sets very quickly in those countries, surely, even if it set first on the sea, the shade must have reached the town soon afterwards? The sunset must have been over very soon, perhaps ten minutes after it had begun.'

'You are quite right and yet I assure you it was just at that moment that I arrived: just at the moment when everything is alight.'

'Oh, I believe you.'

'It doesn't sound as though you do.'

'But I do, completely. And anyway you could have arrived at any other moment without changing all that followed, couldn't you?'

'Yes, but I did arrive then, even if that moment only lasts for a few minutes a day.'

'But that isn't really the point?'

'No, that isn't really the point.'

'And afterwards?'

'Afterwards the garden was the same, except that it became night. A coolness came up from the sea and people were happy for the day had been hot.'

'But even so, eventually you had to eat?'

'Suddenly I was no longer very hungry. I was thirsty. I didn't have dinner that evening. Perhaps I just forgot about it.'

'But that's why you had left your hotel, to eat I mean?'

'Yes, but then I forgot about it.'

'For me, you see, the days are like the night.'

'But that is a little because you want them to be like that. You would like to emerge from your present situation just as you were when you entered it, as one wakes up from a long sleep. I know, of course, what it is to want to create night all around one but it seems to me that however hard one tries the dangers of the day break through.'

'Only my night is not as dark as all that and I

doubt if the day is really a threat to it. I'm twenty. Nothing has happened to me yet. I sleep well. But one day I must wake up and for ever. It must happen.'

'And so each day is the same for you, even though they may be different?'

'Tonight, like every Thursday night, there will be people for dinner. I will eat chicken all alone in the kitchen.'

'And the murmur of their conversation will reach you the same way? So very much the same that you could imagine that each Thursday they said exactly the same things.'

'Yes, and as usual, I won't understand anything they talk about.'

'And you will be all alone, there in the kitchen, surrounded by the remnants of food in a sort of drowsy lull. And then you will be called to take away the meat plates and serve the next course.'

'They will ring for me, but they won't waken me. I serve at table half-asleep.'

'Just as they waited on, in absolute ignorance of what you might be like. And so in a way you are quits: they can neither make you happy nor sad, and so you sleep.'

'Yes. And then the guests will leave and the house will be quiet till the morning.'

'When you will start ignoring them all over

again, while trying to wait on them as well as possible.'

'I expect so. But I sleep well! If you only knew how well I sleep. There is nothing they can do to disturb my sleep. But why are we talking about these things?'

'I don't know, perhaps just to make you remember them.'

'Perhaps it is that. But you see one day, yes one day, I shall go into the drawing-room and I shall speak.'

'Yes, you must.'

'I shall say: "this evening I shall not be serving dinner." Madam will turn round in surprise. And I will say: "why should I serve dinner since as from this evening ... as from this evening" ... but no, I cannot even imagine how things of such importance are said.'

The man made no reply. He seemed only attentive to the softness of the wind, which once more, had risen. The girl seemed to expect no response to what she had just said.

'Soon it will be summer,' said the man and added with a groan, 'We really are the lowest of the low.'

'It's said that someone has to be.'

'Yes, indeed and that everything has its place.'

'And yet sometimes one wonders why this should be so.'

'Yes. Although sometimes, in cases like ours, one
'Why us rather than others?'
wonders whether it's being us or someone else
makes any difference. Sometimes one just wonders.'

'Yes and sometimes, in certain instances, that is a consoling thought.'

'Not for me. That could never be a consoling thought. I must believe that I myself am concerned rather than anyone else. Without that belief I am lost.'

'Who knows? Perhaps things will soon change for you. Soon and very suddenly: perhaps even this very summer you will go into that drawing-room and announce that, as from that moment, the world can manage without your services.'

'Who knows indeed? And you could call it pride, but when I say the world, I really mean the whole world. Do you understand?'

'Yes I do.'

'I will open the door of that drawing-room and then, suddenly, everything will be said and for ever.'

'And you will always remember that moment as I remember my journey. I have never been on so wonderful a journey since, nor one which made me so happy.'

'Why are you suddenly so sad? Do you see anything sad in the fact that one day I must open that door? On the contrary doesn't it seem the most desirable thing in the world?'

'It seems utterly desirable to me, and even more than that. No, if I felt a little sad when you talked of it – and I did feel a little sad – it was only because once you have opened that door it will have been opened for ever, and afterwards you will never be able to do it again. And then, sometimes, it seems so hard, so very hard to go back to a country which pleased me as well as that one did, that occasionally I wonder if it would not have been better never to have seen it at all.'

'I wish I could, but you must see I cannot understand what it is like to have seen that city and to want to go back to it, nor can I understand the sadness you seem to feel at the thought of waiting for that moment. You could try as hard as you liked to tell me there was something sad about it, I could never understand. I know nothing, or rather I know nothing except this: that one day I must open that door and speak to those people.'

'Of course, of course. You mustn't take any notice of what I say. Those thoughts simply came into my mind when you were talking, but I didn't want them to discourage you. In fact quite the opposite. I'd like to ask you more about that door. What special moment are you waiting for, to open it? For instance why couldn't you do it this evening?'

'Alone I could never do it.'

'You mean that being without money or education you could only begin in the same way all over again and that really there would no point to it?'

'I mean that and other things. I don't really know how to describe it, but being alone I feel as if I had no meaning. I can't change by myself. No. I will go on visiting that Dance Hall and one day a man will ask me to be his wife. Then I will open that door. I couldn't do it before that happened.'

'How do you know if it would turn out like that if you have never tried?'

'I have tried. And because of that I know that alone ... I would be, as I said, somehow meaningless. I wouldn't know any more what it was to want to change. I would simply be there, doing nothing, telling myself that nothing was worth while.'

'I think I see what you mean: in fact I believe I understand it all.'

'One day someone must choose me. Then I will be able to change. I don't mean this is true for everyone. I am simply saying it is true for me. I have already tried and I know. I don't know all this just because I know what it is like to be hungry, no, but because when I was hungry I realized I didn't care. I hardly knew who it was in me who was hungry.'

'I see all that: I can see how one could feel like

that: in fact I can guess it although personally I have never felt the need to be singled out as you want to be; or perhaps I really mean that if such a thought ever did cross my mind I never attached much importance to it.'

'You must understand: you must try to understand that I have never been wanted by anyone, ever, except of course for my capacity for housework; and that is not choosing me as a person but simply wanting something impersonal which makes me as anonymous as possible. And so I must be wanted by someone, just once, and even if only once. Otherwise I shall exist so little even to myself that I would be incapable of knowing how to want to choose anything. That is why, you see, I attach so much importance to marriage.'

'Yes I do see and I follow what you are saying, but in spite of all that, and with the best will in the world, I cannot really see how you hope to be chosen when you cannot make a choice for yourself?'

'I know it seems ridiculous but that is how it is. Because you see, left to myself, I would find any man suitable: any man in the world would seem suitable on the one condition that he wanted me just a little. A man who so much as noticed me would seem desirable just for that very reason, and so how on earth would I be capable of knowing who would suit me when anyone would, on the one condition that they wanted me? No, it's impossible. Someone else must decide for me, must guess what would be best. Alone I could never know.'

'Even a child knows what is best for him.'

'But I am not a child, and if I let myself go and behaved like a child and gave in to the first temptation I came across – after all I am perfectly aware that it is there at every street corner – why then I would follow the first person who came along, the first man who just wanted me. And I would follow him simply for the pleasure I would have in being with him, and then, why then I would be lost, completely lost. You could say that I could easily make another kind of life for myself, but as you can see I no longer have the courage even to think of it.'

'But have you never thought that if you leave this choice entirely to another person it need not necessarily be the right one and might make for unhappiness later?'

'Yes I have thought of that a little, but I cannot think now, before my life has really begun, of the harm I might possibly do later on. I just say one thing to myself and that is: if the very fact of being alive means that we can do harm, however much we don't want to, just by choosing or making mistakes, if that is an inevitable state of affairs, why then, I too will go through with it. If I have to, if everyone has to, I can live with harm.'

'Please don't get so excited: there will be someone one day who will discover that you exist both for him and for others, you must be sure of that. And yet you know one can almost manage to live with this lack of which you speak.'

'Which lack? Of never being chosen?'

'If you like, yes. As far as I am concerned I should be so surprised if anyone chose me, that I should simply laugh.'

'While I should be in no way surprised. I am afraid I would find it perfectly natural. It is just the contrary which astonishes me, and it astonishes me more each day. I cannot understand it and I never get used to it.'

'It will happen. I promise you.'

'Thank you for saying so. But are you saying that just to please be, or can people tell these things? Can you guess it already just from talking to me?'

'I expect such things can be guessed, yes. To tell you the truth I said that without thinking much, but not at all because I thought it would please you. It must have been because I could see it.'

'And you? How are you so sure the opposite is true of you?'

'Well I suppose it is because. . . . Yes, just because

I am not surprised. I think it must be that. I am not at all surprised that no one has chosen me, while you are so amazed that you have not yet been singled out.'

'In your place you know I would force myself to want something, however hard it might be. I would not remain as you are.'

'But what can I do? Since I don't feel this same need it could only come to me. . . . Well, from the outside. How else could it be?'

'You know you almost make me wish I was dead.'

'Is it I in particular who has that effect, or were you just speaking in general?'

'Of course I was only speaking in general. In general about us both.'

'Because there is another thing I would not really like, and that is to have provoked in anyone, even if only once, a feeling as violent as that.'

'Oh I'm sorry.'

'It doesn't matter.'

'And I would like to thank you too.'

'But for what?'

'I don't really know. For your niceness.'

The child came over quietly from the far side of the Park and stood beside the girl.

'I'm thirsty,' he announced.

The girl took a thermos and a mug from the bag beside her.

'I can well imagine,' said the man, 'that he must be thirsty after eating those sandwiches.'

The girl uncorked the thermos. Warm milk gleamed in the sunshine.

'But as you see,' she said, 'I have brought him some milk.'

The child drank the milk greedily, then gave the mug back to the girl. A milky cloud stayed round his lips. The girl wiped them. The man smiled at the child.

'If I said what I did,' he remarked, 'it was only to try and make myself clear. For no other reason.'

Completely indifferent the child contemplated this man who was smiling at him. Then he went back to the sand pit. The girl's eyes followed him.

'His name is James,' she said.

'James,' the man repeated.

But he was no longer thinking of the child.

'I don't know if you've noticed,' he went on, 'how a trace of milk stays round a child's mouth when he has drunk it? It's strange. In some ways they are so grown up: they seem to talk and walk like everyone else and then when it comes to drinking milk, one realizes....'

'He doesn't say "milk", he says "my milk".'

'When I see something like that milk I suddenly feel full of hope although I could never say why. As if some pain was deadened. I think perhaps that watching these children reminds me of the lions in that Garden. I see them as minute lions, but lions all the same.'

'Yet they don't seem to give you the same kind of happiness as those lions did in their cages facing the sun?'

'They give me a certain happiness but you are right, not the same one. Somehow children always make one feel obscurely worried, and it is not that I particularly like lions: it would be untrue to say that. It was just a way of putting things.'

'I wonder if you attach too much importance to that town with the result that the rest of your life suffers by comparison? Or is it just that never having been there I can hardly be expected to understand the happiness it gave you?'

'And yet it is probably to someone like you that I should most like to talk about it.'

'Thank you. It was kind of you to say that. But you know I didn't want to imply that I was particularly unhappy, more unhappy I mean than anyone else would be in the same position. I was speaking of something quite different, something which I am afraid could not be solved by seeing any country, anywhere in the world.'

'I'm sorry. You see when I said that I should like to talk most about that country to someone like you I did not mean for a second that you were unhappy without knowing it, and that telling you certain things would make you feel better. I simply meant that you seemed to me to be a person who might understand what one was trying to say better than most people. That's all. But I expect I have talked too much about that town and it is natural that you should have misunderstood.'

'No, I don't think it is that. All I wanted was to put you right in case you had made the mistake of thinking I was unhappy. Of course there are times when I cry, naturally there are, but it's only from impatience or irritation. I am not old enough yet to be profoundly sad about my life. That stage is to come.'

'Yes, I really do see, but don't you think it is just possible that you might be wrong, that you don't know which stage you have reached?'

'No, that would not be possible. Either I shall be

unhappy in the same way as everyone else is, or I shall not be unhappy at all. I want to be exactly like everyone else and I shall go on trying as much as I can. I want to find out for myself if life is terrible. I shall die as I mean to and someone will care. But let's forget all that. Please tell me more of how you felt in that town.'

'I am afraid I will tell it badly. I had no sleep and yet I was not tired.'

'And. . . .'

'I did not eat and I wasn't hungry.'

'And then. . . .'

'All the minor problems of my life seemed to evaporate as if they had never existed except in my imagination. I thought of them as belonging to a distant past and laughed at them.'

'But surely you must have wanted to eat and sleep in the end? It would have been impossible for you to go on without feeling tired or hungry.'

'I expect so, but I didn't stay long enough there for those feelings to come back to me.'

'And were you very tired when they did come back?'

'I slept for a whole day in a wood by the roadside.'

'Like a tramp?'

'Yes, just like a tramp with my suitcase beside me.'

'I understand.'

'No, I don't think you can, yet.'

'I mean I am trying to understand and one day I will. One day I shall understand what you have been saying to me completely. After all, anybody could couldn't they?'

'Yes. I think one day you will understand them as completely as possible.'

'Ah, if only you knew how difficult the things I was telling you about can be. How difficult it is to get for yourself, completely by yourself, just the things which are common to everyone. I think I really mean how hard it is to fight the apathy which comes from wanting just the ordinary things which everyone else seems to have.'

'I expect it is just that which prevents so many people from trying to achieve them. I admire you for being as you are.'

'Ah, if only will power were enough! There have been men who found me attractive from time to time, but so far none of them has asked me to be his wife. There is a great difference between liking a young girl and wanting to marry her. And yet that must happen to me. Just once in my life I must be taken seriously. I wanted to ask you something: if you want a thing all the time, at every single moment of the day and night, do you think that you necessarily get it?'

'Not necessarily, no. But it still remains the best way of trying and the one with the greatest chance of success. I can really see no other way.'

'After all, we're only talking. And as you don't know me or I you, you can tell me the truth.'

'Yes that's quite true, but really and truly I can see no other way. But perhaps I haven't had enough experience to answer your question properly.'

'Because I once heard that quite the opposite was true. That it was by trying not to want something that it finally happened.'

'But tell me, how could you manage not to want something, when you want it so much?'

'That is exactly what I say to myself, and to tell you the truth I never felt that the other was a very serious idea. I think it must apply to people who want little things, to people who already have something and want something else, but not to people like us – I didn't mean that, I mean not to people like me who want everything, not just a part of something but ... I don't know how to say it....'

'A whole.'

'Perhaps it is that. But please tell me more about your feelings for children. You said you were fond of them?'

'Yes. Sometimes when I have no one else to talk to I talk to them. But you know how it is, one can't really talk to children.'

'Oh, you're right. We are the lowest of the low.'

'But you mustn't think either that I am unhappy

simply because sometimes I need to talk so badly that I talk to children. That's not true, because after all I must in some way have chosen my life or else I am just a madman indulging in his folly.'

'I'm sorry. I didn't mean what I said. I simply saw the fine weather and the words came out of their own accord. You must try to understand and not mind, because sometimes fine weather makes me doubt everything: but it never lasts for more than a few seconds. I'm sorry.'

'It doesn't matter. When I sit in Squares like this it is generally because I have been for some days without talking: when there have been no opportunities for conversation except with the people who buy my goods and they have been so rushed or standoffish that I could say nothing to them except the things that go with the sale of a reel of cotton. Naturally you mind this after some time and suddenly you want to talk and be listened to so badly that it can even produce a feeling of illness like a slight fever.'

'I know how you feel. You feel you could do without everything else, without eating, sleeping, anything rather than be silent. But in that town you were telling me about you didn't have to talk to children?'

'Not in that town, no. I was not with children then.'

'That is what I thought.'

'I used to see them in the distance. There were lots of them in the streets: they are left very free there and from about the age of the one you look after they cross the whole town on their own to visit the Zoo. They eat at any hour and sleep in the shadow of the lions' cages. Yes, I saw them in the distance sleeping in the shadow of those cages.'

'Children have all the time in the world and they'll talk to anyone and always be ready to listen, but one hasn't very much to say to them.'

'That's the trouble. It's true they don't despise solitary people: in fact they like almost anyone but then, as you said, there is so little to say to them.'

'But tell me more.'

'Oh, as far as children go one person is as good as another provided they talk about airplanes and trains. There is never any difficulty in talking to children about those sort of things. It can become a little monotonous but that's how it is.'

'They can't understand other things, unhappiness for example, and I don't think it does much good to mention them.'

'If you talk to them of things that don't interest them they simply stop listening and wander off.'

'Sometimes I have conversations on my own.'

'That has happened to me too.'

'I don't mean I talk to myself. I speak to a

completely imaginary person, not just anybody, but to my worst enemy. You see although I haven't any friends yet, I invent enemies.'

'And what do you say to them?'

'I insult them: and always without the slightest explanation. Why do I do this?'

'Who knows? Probably because an enemy never understands one and I think you would be hard put to it to accept being understood and to give in to the particular comfort it brings.'

'After all, my insults are a form of talking aren't they? And I never mention my work.'

'Yes, it is talking; and since no one hears you and it gives you some satisfaction it seems better to go on.'

'When I spoke of the unhappiness which children cannot understand I was talking of unhappiness in general, the unhappiness everyone knows about, not of a particular kind of personal unhappiness.'

'I knew that. The fact is we could not bear it if children could understand unhappiness. Perhaps they are the only people we cannot stand to see unhappy.'

'There are not many happy people are there?'

'I don't think so. There are some who think it important to be happy and believe that they are, but at bottom are not really as happy as all that.'

'And yet I thought it was a duty for people to be

happy, an instinct like going to the sun rather than to the dark. Look at me for instance; at all the trouble I take over it.'

'But of course it's like a duty. I feel that too. But if people feel the need for the sun it is because they know how sad the dark can be. No one can live always in the dark.'

'I make my own darkness but since other people seek the sun, I do so too, and that is what I feel about happiness. Everything I do is for my happiness.'

'You are right and that is probably why things are simpler for you than for other people: you have no alternative, while people who have a choice can long for things they know nothing about.'

'You would think the gentleman where I am in service would be happy. He is a business man with a great deal of money and yet he always seems distracted as if he were bored. I think sometimes that he has never looked at me, that he recognizes me without ever having seen me.'

'And yet you are a person people would look at.'

'But he doesn't see anyone. It is as if he no longer used his eyes. That is why he sometimes seems to me less happy than one might think. As if he were tired of everything, even of looking.'

'And his wife?'

'His wife too. One could take her for being happy but I know she is not.'

'Do you find that the wives of such men are easily frightened and have the tired, shaded look of women who no longer dream?'

'Not this one. She has a clear look and nothing catches her off her guard. Everyone thinks she has everything she could want and yet I know it is not so. You learn about these things in my work. Often in the evening she comes into the kitchen with a vacant expression which doesn't deceive me, as if she wanted my company.'

'It is just what we said: in the end people are not good at happiness. They want it of course but when they have it they eat themselves away with dreaming.'

'I don't know if it is that people are not good at happiness or if they don't understand what it is. Perhaps they don't really know what it is they want or how to make use of it when they have it. They may even get tired of trying to keep it. I really don't know. What I do know is that the word exists and that it was not invented for nothing. And just because I know that women, even those who appear to be happy, often start wondering towards evening why they are leading the lives they do, I am not going to start wondering if the word is meaningless. That is all I can say on the subject.'

'Of course it is. And when I said that happiness is difficult to stand I didn't mean that because of that it should be avoided. I wanted to ask you: is it around six o'clock when she comes into your kitchen?'

'Yes always around that time. I know what it means believe me. I know it is a particular time of day when many women long for things they haven't got: but for all that I refuse to give up.'

'It's always the same: when everything is there for things to go right people still manage to make them go wrong. They find happiness sad.'

'It makes no difference to me. I can only say again that I want to experience that particular sadness.'

'If I said what I did, it was for no special reason. I was only talking.'

'One could say that without wanting to discourage me you were, all the same, trying to warn me.'

'Oh hardly at all. Or only in the smallest degree, I promise you.'

'But since my work has already shown me the other side of happiness you need not worry. And in the end what does it matter if I find happiness or something else as long as it is something real I can feel and deal with. Since I am in the world I too must have my share of it. There is no reason why I should not. I will do just as everyone else does. You see I cannot imagine dying without having had the look that my employer has in her eyes when she comes to see me in the evening.'

'It is hard to imagine you with tired eyes. You may not know it, but you have very fine eyes.'

'They will be fine when they need to be.'

'I can't help it, but the thought that one day you might have the same look as that woman is sad, that's all.'

'Who can tell how things will turn out? And I will go through whatever is necessary. That is my greatest hope. And after my eyes have been fine they will become clouded like everyone else's.'

'When I said that your eyes were fine I meant that they had a wonderful expression.'

'I am sure you are wrong and even if you were right I couldn't be satisfied with it.'

'I understand and yet I find it hard not to tell you that for other people your eyes are very beautiful.'

'Otherwise I would be lost. If for one moment I was satisfied with my eyes as they are I would be lost.'

'And so you said this woman comes into the kitchen?'

'Yes, sometimes. It is the only moment of the day when she does and she always asks the same thing, how am I getting on?'

'As if things could go differently for you from one day to another?'

'Yes, as if they could.'

'Such people have strange illusions about people

like us. What else can you expect? And perhaps it is part of our job to preserve their illusions.'

'Have you ever been dependent on a boss? It seems as if you must have to understand so well.'

'No. But it is a threat which hangs over people like us so constantly that it is easier to imagine than most things.'

There was a silence between the girl and the man and one would have thought them distracted, attentive only to the softness of the air. Then once again the man started to speak. He said:

'We really agree, you know. You see, when I talked of this woman and of people who managed not to be entirely happy I did not mean that it was a reason for not following their example, for not trying in one's own turn and in one's own turn failing. Nor that one should deny longings such as you have for a gas stove, which would be to reject in advance all that might follow from it, such as a refrigerator or even happiness. I don't doubt the truth of your hopes for a moment. On the contrary I think they are exactly what they should be. I really do.'

'Must you go? Is that why you said all that?'

'No, I have no need to go. I just didn't want you to misunderstand me, that's all.'

'The way you talked like that, all of a sudden drawing conclusions from everything we had said, made me think that perhaps you had to go.'

'No, I have nothing to go for. I just wanted to say that I understood you and like everything about you. And I was going to add that if there was one thing I didn't quite understand, and I hate being a bore on this subject, it is still the fact that you take on so much extra work and that you always agree to do whatever they ask. Don't blame me for coming back to it, but I can't agree with you on this point even if I do understand your reasons. I am afraid.... What I am really afraid of is that you might feel that if you accept all the worst things that come your way you will one day have earned the right to be finished with them for ever....'

'And if that was the case?'

'Ah no. I cannot accept that. I don't believe that anything or anyone exists whose function it is to reward people for their personal merits, and certainly not people who are obscure or unknown. We are abandoned.'

'But if I told you it was not for that reason but so that I should never lose my horror for my work, so that I should go on feeling all the disgust I felt for it as much as ever.'

'I am sorry but even then I could not agree. I think you have already begun to live your life and even at the risk of repeating this endlessly to you and becoming a bore I really must say that I think things have already started for you, that time passes for you as much as for anyone else, and that even now you can waste it; as you do when you take on work which anyone else in your place would refuse.'

'I think you must be very nice to be able to put yourself into other people's places and think for them with so much understanding. I could never do that.'

'You have other things to do; if I can think about other people it is only because I have the time for it, and as you said yourself, it is not the best kind of time.'

'Perhaps you're right. Perhaps the fact that I have decided to change everything is a sign that things have begun for me. And the fact that I cry from time to time is probably also a sign and I expect I should no longer hide this from myself.'

'Everyone cries, and not because of that, but simply because they are alive.'

'But one day I checked up on my position and I discovered that it was quite usual for maids to be expected to do most of the things I have to do. That was two years ago. For instance there's no reason why I shouldn't tell you that sometimes we have to look after very old women, as old as eighty-two, weighing fifteen stone and no longer quite right in their minds, making messes in their clothes at any hour of the day or night and whom nobody wants to bother about.'

'Did you really say fifteen stone?'

'Yes, I am looking after one now; and what's more, last time she was weighed she had gained. And yet, I would have you appreciate the fact that I haven't killed her, not even that time two years ago after I had found out what was expected of me. She was fat enough then and I was eighteen. I still haven't killed her and I never will, although it becomes easier and easier as she gets older and frailer. She is left alone in the bathroom to wash and the bathroom is at the far end of the house. All I would have to do would be to hold her head under water for three minutes and it would be all over. She is so old that even her children wouldn't mind her death, nor would she herself since she hardly knows she is there any more. But I look after her very well and always for the reasons I explained, because if I killed her it would mean that I could imagine improving my present situation, making it bearable, and that would be contrary to my plan. No, no-one can rescue me except a man. I hope you don't mind my telling you all this.'

'Ah, I no longer know what to say to you.'

'Let's not talk about it any more.'

'Yes, but still! You said it would be easy to get rid of that old woman and no-one, not even she herself, would mind. I am still not giving you advice but it seems to me that in many cases other people could do something of that nature to make their lives a little easier and still be able to hope for their future as much as before?'

'It's no good talking to me like that. I would rather my horror became worse. It is my only chance of getting out.'

'After all we were only talking. I just wondered whether it might not be almost a duty to prevent someone from hoping so much.'

'There seems no reason why I shouldn't tell you that I know someone like me who did kill.'

'I don't believe it. Perhaps she thought she had killed someone but she couldn't really have done it.'

'It was a dog. She was sixteen. You may say it is not at all the same thing as killing a person, but she did it and says it is very much the same.'

'Perhaps she didn't give it enough to eat. That's not the same as killing.'

'No, it was not like that. They both had exactly the same food. It was a very valuable dog and so they had the same food: of course it was not the same as the things the people in the house ate and she stole the dog's food once. But that wasn't enough.'

'She was young and longed for meat as most children do.'

'She poisoned the dog. She stayed awake a long time mixing poison with its food. She told me she didn't even think about the sleep she was losing.

The dog took two days to die. Of course it is the same as killing a person. She knows. She saw it die.'

'I think it would have been more unnatural if she had not done it.'

'But why such hatred for a dog? In spite of everything he was the only friend she had. One thinks one isn't nasty and yet one can do something like that.'

'It is situations like that which should not be allowed. From the moment they arise the people involved cannot do otherwise than as they do. It is inevitable, quite inevitable.'

'They knew it was she who killed the dog. She got the sack. They could do nothing else to her since it is not a crime to kill a dog. She said that she would almost have preferred them to punish her, she felt so guilty. Our work, you know, leads us to have the most terrible thoughts.'

'Leave it.'

'I work all day and I would even like to work harder but at something else: something in the open air which brings results you can see, which can be counted like other things, like money. I would rather break stones on the roads or work steel in a foundry.'

'But then do it. Break stones on the road. Leave your present work.'

'No, I can't. Alone, as I explained to you, alone

I could not do it. I have tried, without success. Alone, without any affection, I think I should just die of hunger. I wouldn't have the strength to force myself to go on.'

'There are women roadmenders. I have seen them.'

'I know. I think about them every day. But I should have started in that way. It's too late now. A job like mine makes you so disgusted with yourself that you have even less meaning outside it than in it. You don't even know that you exist enough for your own death to matter to you. No, from now on my only solution is a man for whom I shall exist; only then will I get out.'

'But do you know what that is called . . .?'

'No. All I know is that I must persist in this slavery for some time longer before I can enjoy things again, things as simple as eating.'

'Forgive me.'

'It doesn't matter. I must stay where I am for as long as I have to. Please don't think that I lack good will because it is not that. It is just that it is not worth while trying to make me hope less – as you put it – because if I tried to hope less than I do I know that I would no longer hope at all. I am waiting. And while I wait I am careful not to kill anything, neither a person nor a dog, because those are serious things and could turn me into a nasty person for the rest of my life. But let's talk a little more about you: you who travel so much and are always alone.'

'Well, yes, I travel and I am alone.'

'Perhaps one day I will travel too.'

'You can only see one thing at a time and the world is big, and you can only see it for yourself with your own two eyes. It is little enough and yet most people travel.'

'All the same, however little you can see, I expect it is a good way of passing the time.'

'The best I think, or at least it passes for the best. Being in a train absorbs time as much as sleeping. And a ship even more: you just look at the furrows following the ship and time passes by itself.'

'And yet sometimes time takes so long to pass that you feel almost as if it was something which had been dragged out of your own insides.'

'Why not take a little trip for eight days or so? For a holiday. You need only want to. Couldn't you do that? While still waiting of course?'

'It's true that waiting seems very long. I joined a political party, not because I thought it would help my personal problems but I thought it might make the time pass more quickly. But even so it is very long.'

'But that is it exactly! Since you are already doing something outside your job, and you go to this Dance Hall, since in fact you are doing everything you can to be able to leave your present job one day, then surely you could also make a short journey while waiting for your life to take the turning you want it to?'

'I did not mean anything more than I said: that sometimes things seem very long.'

'All you need to do is change your mood just a fraction and then you could take a little voyage for eight days or so.'

'On Saturday when I come back from dancing I cry sometimes as I told you. How does one make a man desire one? Love cannot be forced. Perhaps it is the mood that you were talking about which makes me so undesirable: a feeling of rancour, and how could that please anyone?'

'I meant nothing more about your mood than that it prevented you from taking a holiday. I wouldn't advise you to become like me, a person who finds hope superfluous. But you must see that from the moment you decided it was best to let that old woman live out her days, and that you must do everything they ask of you, so as one day to be free to do something quite different, then it seems to me that as a kind of compensation you could take a short holiday and go away. Why. even I would do it.'

'I understand, but tell me what would I do with a holiday? I wouldn't know what to do with myself.

I would simply be there looking at new things without them giving me any pleasure.'

'You must learn, even if it is difficult. From now on as a provision against the future you must learn that. Looking at new things is something one learns.'

'Yes, but tell me again: how could I ever manage to learn how to enjoy myself in the present when I am worn out with waiting for the future? I wouldn't have the patience to look at anything new.'

'It doesn't matter. Forget about it. It wasn't very important.'

'And yet if you only knew, I would so much like to be able to look at new things.'

'Tell me, when a man asks you to dance with him, do you immediately think he might marry you?'

'Yes. You see I'm too practical. All my troubles come from that. But how could I be anything else? It seems to me that I could never love anyone before I had some freedom and that can only come to me through a man.'

'And another question: if a man doesn't ask you to dance do you still think he might marry you?'

'I think less then because I am at the Dance. When I dance I get carried away by the movement and the excitement and at those moments I think a man might most easily forget who I am, and even if he did find out he would mind it less under those circumstances than at any other time. I dance well. In fact I dance very well and when I am dancing I feel quite different from my usual self. Ah, sometimes I don't know what to do any more.'

'But do you think about it while you are at the Dance Hall?'

'No. There I think of nothing. I think before or afterwards. There it is as if I were asleep.'

'Everything happens, believe me. We think that nothing will ever happen but it does. There is not a man among all the millions who exist, not a single one, who hasn't known the things you are waiting for.'

'I am afraid you don't really understand what it is I am waiting for.'

'I am talking, you see, not only of the things you know you want but also of the things you want without knowing. Of something less immediate, something of which you are still unaware.'

'Yes I follow what you are saying. And it is true that there are things I don't think of now. But all the same I would so like to know how those things happen.'

'They happen like anything else.'

'Just as I know I am waiting?'

'Exactly. It is difficult to talk to you of things you know so little. I think that those things either come about suddenly, all at once, or else so slowly that one scarcely notices them. And when they have happened and are there they don't seem at all surprising: it feels as if they had always been there. One day you will wake up and there it will all be. And it will be the same for the gas stove: you will wake up one day and not even be able to explain how it came to be there.'

'But what about you? You who are always travelling and who seem, if I have understood you, to attach so little importance to events.'

'But the same things can happen anywhere without any warning. In places like trains. And the only difference between the things which happen to me and those you want for yourself are that in my case they are without a future: there is nothing one can do with them.'

'I don't know what to say but I think it must be very sad to live as you do, always with events which can have no future. I think that from time to time you must cry too.'

'But no. One gets used to it like everything else. And good gracious me everyone has cried at least once, every single one of all the millions of people on earth. That proves nothing in itself. Perhaps I should also explain that as far as I am concerned the tiniest thing can make me happy. I like waking up in the morning for instance and quite often I find myself singing while I shave.'

'Oh but surely singing proves nothing to someone who talks as you do?'

'But you must understand: I like being alive and I should have thought that was the one point on which no one could make a mistake.'

'I don't know what it feels like. Perhaps that is why I understand you so badly.'

'Whatever the cause of your unhappiness – and I really can find no other word for it – you must, you really must, show a little goodwill.'

'But I am worn out with waiting and yet I go on waiting. It is more than I can do to wash that old woman and yet I go on washing her. I do all the things which are really too much for me. What more do you ask?'

'By good will I mean that you could, perhaps, wash her as you would wash anything else – a saucepan for example.'

'No, I tried that but it was no good. She smiles, she smells bad. She is human.'

'Alas. What can one do?'

'Sometimes I don't know myself. I was sixteen when this life began for me. At the beginning I didn't pay much attention and now look where I am. I am twenty and nothing has happened to me, nothing, and that old woman never manages to die and is still there. And nobody has asked me to be his wife. Sometimes I even think I must be dreaming, that somehow I must be inventing so many difficulties.'

'Why not work for another family? One where there are no old people? Find a place with some advantages – although naturally I know they could only be relative.'

'That wouldn't help. Whatever the family was like it would always treat me as something apart. In my kind of work changing jobs means nothing, since the only real change would be for such jobs to be abolished. If I did manage to find a family such as you describe I wouldn't really be able to put up with them any better than I do with my present one. And then just through changing and changing, without changing anything I would end by believing in, I hardly know what, some sort of fate and that would be worse than anything. No, I must stay where I am right up to the moment when I can leave for ever. Sometimes I believe in it so much. I can hardly tell you how much. As much as I know I am sitting here.'

'Well, then, while staying where you are, you could still take that little journey. I believe you could.'

'Yes perhaps. Perhaps I could make that journey.'

'Of course you could.'

'But from all you said that city you talked about must be very far away. Immensely far.'

'I reached it by little stages, taking fifteen days in all, stopping off here and there for a day at a time. But someone who could afford to do so could reach it by one night in the train.'

'You can be there in a night?'

'Yes, and already it is full summer there. Of course I couldn't be certain that someone else would find it as beautiful as I did. I suppose it is quite possible that someone else might not like it at all. I imagine I didn't see it with the same eyes as a person who found nothing there but the place itself.'

'But if one knew in advance that another person had been happy there I think one would look at it with different eyes. We're only talking....'

'Yes.'

They were silent. Imperceptibly the sun was sinking and once more a memory of winter lay over the city. It was the girl who started the conversation again.

'What I meant,' she began, 'was that something of that happiness must remain in the air. Don't you agree?'

'I don't know.'

'I would like to ask you something more. Could you tell me more about those things we were discussing – the things that could take place in a train for example?'

'Not really. They happen, that's all. You know,

few people would put up with a commercial traveller of my status.'

'But I am only a maid and I still hope. You mustn't talk like that.'

'I am sorry. I explained myself badly. You will change but I don't think I will, or rather I don't think so any more. And whichever way you look at it there is nothing to be done about it. Even if I could have wished that things had been different I can never forget the commercial traveller I have become. When I was twenty I was smart and gay and played tennis. That is how my life started. I mean a life can begin anyhow – a fact we do not appreciate enough. And then time passes and we discover that life has very few solutions: and things become established until one fine day we find they are so established that the very idea of changing them seems absurd.'

'That must be a terrible moment.'

'No. It passes unnoticed as time passes. But you mustn't be sad. I am not complaining about my life and to tell you the truth I don't think about it much. The least thing amuses me.'

'And yet you give the impression of not having told the whole truth about your life.'

'I assure you I am not someone to be pitied.'

'I too know that life is terrible. I am not as stupid as that. I know it is as terrible as it is good.'

Once more a silence fell between the man and the girl. The sun was sinking even lower.

'Although I only took the train in small stages,' the man said, 'I don't think it can be very expensive.'

'I spend very little money,' said the girl, 'in fact the only expenses I have are connected with dancing. So you see even if the train was expensive I could still afford the journey if I wanted to. But I am afraid that wherever I was I would feel I was wasting my time. I would say to myself: what are you doing here instead of being at that Dance Hall? For the moment your place is there and nowhere else. Wherever I was I would think of it. If it interests you the Dance Hall is called the Mecca: by the station. A lot of soldiers go there and unfortunately they never think of marrying, but there are other people too and one never knows.'

'Thank you. But you know they also have dances in that town and if you did decide to make the journey you could go to them. And no one would know who you were there.'

'Are they held in the Garden?'

'Yes, in the open air. On Saturdays they last all night.'

'I see. But then I would have to lie about what I am. I know you will say that it's not my fault that I have to do the job I do, but it still makes me feel as if I had a crime to conceal.'

'But since you want to change so much surely concealing it would only be a half-lie?'

'I think I could only lie about something for which I was responsible, but not about anything else. And although it sounds strange I feel almost as if I had chosen that particular Dance Hall and that what I want must happen there. It's a small one but it suits me as I really have no illusions about what I am or what I might become. I would feel strange and out of place anywhere else. If you were to come there we could have a dance while waiting for someone else to ask me. I mean if you would like to, of course. I dance well and I've never been taught.'

'I dance well too.'

'Don't you find that strange? Why should we dance well? Why us rather than anyone else?'

'Us rather than the people who dance badly you mean?'

'Yes, I know some. If you could only see them. They have no idea at all. It's double dutch to them....'

'But you're laughing.'

'What else can I do? People who dance badly always make me laugh. They try, they concentrate and there's nothing to be done about it: they simply can't manage.'

'It must be because dancing is something which

cannot entirely be learned. Do the ones you know hop or shuffle?'

'She hops and he shuffles with the result . . . I can hardly describe it to you. And yet it's obviously not their fault.'

'No it's not their fault. And yet it's difficult not to feel that somehow there is a certain justice in the fact that they can't dance.'

'We may be wrong.'

'Yes, we may be and after all it doesn't matter so much whether one dances well or badly.'

'No it's of no great importance. Yet all the same it's as if we had a secret strength concealed in us. Oh nothing very much of course. . . . And yet don't you think I'm right?'

'But they could just as easily have been good dancers?'

'Yes, that's true, but then there would be something else, although I can't imagine what, which we would have and they would not: I don't know what it would be but it would be something.'

'I don't know either, but I think you're right.'

'I love dancing. It is probably the only thing I do now which I would like to go on doing for the rest of my life.'

'I feel the same. I think everyone likes dancing, even people like us, and perhaps we would not be such good dancers if we didn't enjoy it so much.'

'But perhaps we don't know exactly how much we do enjoy it? How could we know?'

'I don't think it matters. If it suits us so well we should go on not knowing.'

'But the dreadful part is that when the Dance is over I start remembering. Suddenly it's Sunday and I mutter "Old Bitch" as I wash her. I don't think I'm a nasty person, but of course I have no one to reassure me on this point and so I can only believe myself. When I say "Bitch" she smiles.'

'I can tell you that you are not a nasty person.'

'But when I think about the people I work for my thoughts are so evil, if you only knew, just as if my wretchedness was their fault. I try to reason with myself but I can never manage to think in any other way.'

'Don't worry about those thoughts. You are not a nasty person.'

'Do you really think so?'

'I do. One day you will be very giving, with yourself and with your time.'

'You really are nice.'

'But I didn't say that out of niceness.'

'But you, what will happen to you?'

'Nothing. As you can see I am no longer very young.'

'But you. . . . You who once thought of killing yourself – because you did say that.'

'Oh that was only laziness at the thought of having to go on feeding myself: nothing serious really.'

'But that's impossible. Something will happen to you or else it will only be because you don't want anything to happen.'

'Nothing happens to me except the things that happen to everyone, every day.'

'You say that, but in that town?'

'There I was not alone. And then, afterwards, I was alone again. I think it was just luck.'

'No. When someone is without any hope at all, as you are, it is because something happened to him: it's the only explanation.'

'One day you will understand. There are people like me, people who get so much pleasure from just being alive that they can get by without hope. I sing while I shave – what more do you want?'

'But were you unhappy after you left that town?'

'Yes.'

'And did you think of staying in your room and never leaving it again?'

'No, not then. Because then I knew that it is possible not to be alone, even if only by accident.'

'Tell me what else you do, apart from singing while you shave?'

'I sell my goods, then I eat, then I travel, then I read the newspapers. I can't tell you how much I enjoy the newspapers. I read them from cover to cover including the advertisements. I get so absorbed in a newspaper that when I put it down I have to think for a minute who I am.'

'But I meant other things: what do you do apart from all the obvious things, apart from shaving and selling your goods and taking trains and eating and reading the newspapers? I mean those things which no one appears to be doing, but which everyone is doing all the same.'

'I see what you mean. . . . But I really don't know what I do apart from the things I mentioned. I don't deny that sometimes I do wonder what I am doing, but just wondering doesn't seem to be enough. I probably don't wonder hard enough and I think it's perfectly possible that I shall never know. You see I believe that it is quite usual to be like me and that a great many people go through life without ever exactly knowing why.'

'But it seems to me that one could try to know a little harder than you do.'

'But I hang by a thread. I even hold on to myself by the merest thread. So you see life is easier for me than it is for you, which explains everything. And then too I can manage to live without having to know certain things.'

Once more they were silent. Then the girl went on:

'I still can't understand. Forgive me for going

back to the subject, but I still can't understand how you came to be as you are, nor even how you came to do the work you do.'

'But as I told you, little by little. My brothers and sisters are all successful people who knew what they wanted. And I can only say once again that I didn't know. They can't understand either how I managed to come down so much in the world.'

'That seems an odd way of putting it: I would rather say how did you come to be so discouraged. And it's still beyond me to understand how you came to do such wretched work.'

'Perhaps it comes from the fact that the idea of success was always a little vague in my mind. I never quite understood what it had to do with me. And after all I don't find my work quite so wretched.'

'I am sorry to have used that expression, although I thought it would have been all right from me since my own work can hardly even be described as work. I only said that to try and make you tell me more. I wanted you to see that I found you mysterious, not that I was blaming you.'

'I understood that and I'm sorry I took you up. I know there are people in the world who can judge what I do on its own merits and not necessarily despise it. I didn't mind anything you said. To tell you the truth I was only half aware of what I was saying myself. I am afraid it always bores me to talk of myself in the past.'

Again they were silent. This time the memory of winter became insistent. The sun would no longer reappear: it had reached the stage where it was hidden by the mass of the city's buildings. The girl remained silent. The man started to talk to her again:

'I wanted to say,' he went on, 'that I would be very unhappy if you thought, even for an instant, that I was trying to influence you in any way. Even when we talked about that old woman we were, after all, only talking....'

'Please let's not talk about me any more.'

'All right.'

'But I wanted to ask you something. What happened after you left that town...?'

The man was silent and the girl did not try to break his silence. Then, when she no longer seemed to expect a reply, he said:

'I told you. I was unhappy.'

'But how unhappy?'

'I believe as unhappy as it is possible to be. I thought I had never been unhappy before.'

'Did that feeling go eventually?'

'Yes, in the end.'

'You were never alone in that town?'

'Never.'

'Neither during the day nor the night?'

'Never, not by day nor by night. It lasted eight days.'

'And then you were alone again. Completely alone?'

'Yes. And I have been alone ever since.'

'I suppose it was tiredness that made you sleep all day in the wood with your suitcase beside you?'

'No, it was unhappiness.'

'Yes, you did say you were as unhappy as it was possible to be. Do you still believe that?'

'Yes.'

It was the girl's turn to be silent.

'Please don't cry, I beg you,' the man said, smiling.

'I can't help myself.'

'Things happen like that. Things that cannot be avoided, that no one can avoid.'

'Oh, it is not that. Those things hold no terrors for me.'

'You want them too?'

'Yes I want them.'

'You are right, because nothing is so worth living as the things which make one so unhappy. Don't cry.'

'I'm not crying any more.'

'You will see. Before the summer is out you will open that door and it will be for ever.'

'Sometimes it almost doesn't seem to matter any more.'

'But you will see. You will see. It will happen quite quickly.'

'It seems to me you should have stayed in that town. You should have tried to stay by all possible means.'

'I stayed as long as I could.'

'No. I don't believe you did everything. I cannot believe it.'

'I did everything I thought could be done. Perhaps I didn't go about it in the right way. Don't think about it any more. You will see, before the summer is out things will have turned out all right for you.'

'Perhaps. Who knows? Sometimes I wonder if it is all worth so much trouble.'

'Of course it is. And after all as you said yourself since we are here – we didn't ask to be but here we are – we must take the trouble. There is nothing else we can do, and you will do it. Before the summer is out you will have opened that door.'

'Sometimes I think I will never do it. That when I am ready to open it I will draw back.'

'No. You will open it.'

'If you say that it must be because you think I have chosen the best way of getting what I want, of ending my present life and finally becoming something?'

'Yes I do think so. I think the way you have chosen is the best for you.'

'If you say that it must be because you think there are other ways which other people would have taken?'

'I expect there are other ways but I also believe they would suit you less well.'

'Are you sure of what you are saying?'

'I believe what I am saying, but neither I nor anyone else could tell you with complete certainty.'

'I ask because you said you understood things through travelling and seeing so many different places and people.'

'Perhaps I understand less well where hope is concerned. I think that if I understand anything it's probably more the small, ordinary things of everyday life: little problems rather than big ones. And yet I can say this: even if I am not absolutely and entirely sure of the means you have chosen, I am absolutely and entirely sure that before this summer is out you will have opened that door.'

'Thank you all the same, very much. But tell me once again, what about you?'

'Spring is on its way and the fine weather. I will be off again.'

They were silent one last time. And one last time it was the girl who took up the conversation:

'What was it that made you get up and start off again after sleeping in the wood?'

'I don't really know. Probably simply that one just had to get up and go on.'

'A short while ago you said it was because from then on you knew it was possible not to be alone, even if only by accident?'

'It was later that I knew that. Some days later. At the time it was different. I knew nothing at all.'

'You see how different we really are. I think I should have refused to get up.'

'But of course you would not. What or who would you have refused?'

'Nothing or no-one. I would have simply refused.'

'You're wrong. You would have done as I did. It was cold, I was cold, and I got up.'

'But we are different all the same.'

'Oh doubtless we are different in the way we take our troubles.'

'No, I think we are even more different than that.'

'I don't think so. I don't think we are more different than anyone is different from anyone else.'

'Perhaps I am mistaken.'

'Since we understand each other? Or at least we try to. And we both like dancing. You said you went to the Mecca?'

'Yes. It is a well-known place. A lot of people like us go there.'

THE child came over quietly from the far side of the Square and stood beside the girl.

'I'm tired,' he announced.

The man and the girl looked around them. It was darker than it had been. It was evening.

'It is true, it is late,' said the girl.

This time the man made no comment. The girl wiped the child's hands, picked up his toys and put them into her bag, all without rising from the bench. Tired of playing, the child sat down at her feet to wait.

'Time seems shorter when one is talking, 'said the girl.

'And then afterwards, suddenly, much longer.'

'Yes, like another kind of time. But it does one good to talk.'

'Yes it does one good. It is only afterwards that it is rather sad: after one has stopped talking. Then time becomes too slow. Perhaps one should never talk.'

'Perhaps,' said the girl after a pause.

'Only because of the slowness afterwards: that was all I meant.'

'And perhaps because of the silence to which we are both returning.'

'Yes, it is true that we are both returning to silence. It seems as though we are already there.'

'No one will talk to me again this evening: I will go to bed in silence. And I am only twenty. What have I done to the world that my life should be like this?'

'Nothing. There are no answers to be found in thinking in that direction. You should be thinking rather of what you will do to the world. Yes, perhaps one should never talk. When one starts it is like picking up a delightful habit one had abandoned: even if it is a habit one had never quite acquired.'

'Yes, that is right. As if we knew how wonderful it was to talk. It must be a very deep instinct to be so strong.'

'And to be talked to is as deep and as natural an instinct.'

'I expect so, yes.'

'Later you will understand how much. At least for your sake I hope that you will.'

'I have talked so much that I feel ashamed.'

'Oh that is the very last thing you should worry about, if indeed there is any need for you to worry at all.'

'Thank you.'

THE SQUARE

The girl rose. The child got up and took her hand. The man remained seated.

'It is getting quite cold,' the girl said.

'Yes, it is not yet summer although sometimes, during the day, one has the illusion that it is already here.'

'Yes one forgets that it is still too soon. It is rather like going back into silence after talking.'

'Yes, it is the same thing.'

The child tugged at the girl's hand.

'I'm tired,' he repeated.

The girl did not seem to have heard the child.

'I really must go back,' she said at last.

The man made no move. His eyes rested vaguely on the child.

'And you, are you not leaving?' asked the girl.

'No. I will stay here until the Square closes and go then.'

'Have you nothing to do this evening?'

'No. Nothing in particular.'

'I must go back,' said the girl after a moment's hesitation.

The man rose slightly from the bench, and very lightly blushed.

'Could you not, just for once I mean, go back a little later?'

For a space the girl hesitated, and then she pointed at the child:

'I wish I could, but I cannot.'

'I only meant that it seems to me that it does you good to talk. Particularly you. That was all I meant.'

'Oh, I understood that, but I cannot stay. I am late already.'

'Well then, I must say good-bye. You said it was on Saturdays that you went to that Dance Hall?'

'Yes. Every Saturday. If you came there we could have a dance together. If you would like to, I mean.'

'Yes perhaps we could. If you would allow me to invite you?'

'I simply meant for the fun of it.'

'That is how I understood you. Well, perhaps we shall meet again. On Saturday perhaps, one never knows.'

'Perhaps. Well, good-bye.'

'Good-bye.'

The girl took two steps and then turned back:

'I wanted to say ... all I wanted to say was, why don't you go for a walk ... instead of sitting there waiting for the Square to close.'

'It is kind of you, but I think I would prefer to remain here until it shuts.'

'But just a little walk, for no particular reason. Just to look at things.'

'No thank you. I really prefer to remain here. A walk means nothing to me.'

'It is going to become colder ... and if I am so insistent it is only because ... because perhaps you do not know what Squares are like towards closing time, how sad they can be....'

'I do know. But I would rather stay here.'

'Do you always do that? Always wait for Squares to close?'

'No. Generally I am like you: it is a moment I avoid. But today I want to wait for it.'

'Perhaps you have your own reasons,' said the girl reflectively.

'I am a coward, that is why.'

The girl moved back a step towards him.

'Oh, if you say that,' she said, 'it must be because of me, because of what I said.'

'No. It is because somehow this time of day always makes me want to recognize and to speak the truth.'

'Please don't say things like that.'

'But surely my cowardice was clear in every word I said, ever since we started talking.'

'No. It is not the same thing as saying it all at once, in one word. You are wrong.'

The man smiled.

'Believe me, it is not such a very serious matter.'

'But I cannot understand why the fact that a Square is closing should suddenly make you discover that you are a coward.'

'Because I do nothing to avoid ... despair. On the contrary.'

'But in that case what difference could a walk make?'

'To do anything to avoid it would be courageous. To create any diversion, however small.'

'I beg of you. Just take a little walk.'

'No. It would not be possible. My whole life is like this.'

'But try just once! Try.'

'No. I don't want to start to change.'

'Ah! I see that I have talked far too much.'

'On the contrary. It was the great pleasure I had in listening to you that made me understand so well what I am really like: how submerged in cowardice. It is not your fault: I am no worse than I was yesterday, for example, and no better.'

'I am afraid I do not understand cowardice very well, but I know that yours suddenly seems to make my courage a little despicable.'

'And to me, you see, your courage makes my cowardice appear more dreadful still. That is what it means to talk.'

'It is as if, after knowing you, courage became slightly useless, a thing which, finally, one could do without.'

'In the end we only do what we can, you with

your courage and me with my cowardice, and that is all that matters.'

'You are probably right, but why is it that courage seems so unattractive and cowardice so appealing? For it is like that isn't it?'

'It is all cowardice. If you only knew how facile it was.'

The little boy pulled at the girl's hand.

'I'm tired,' he said again.

The man raised his eyes and seemed troubled.

'Do you think I am wrong?'

'Inevitably.'

'I am sorry.'

'Ah, if only you knew how little it mattered. It is as if someone other than I were involved.'

The waited a few moments in silence. The Square was emptying. At the ends of the streets the sky showed pink.

'It is true,' the girl said, and her voice was almost the voice of sleep, 'that we do what we can, you with your cowardice and I with my courage.'

'And yet we manage to earn our livings. We have at least managed that.'

'Yes, that is true, we have managed that as well as anyone else.'

'And from time to time we even manage to talk.'

'Yes, even if it makes us unhappy afterwards.'

'Everything, no matter what, makes one unhappy. Sometimes even eating.'

'You mean eating after one has been hungry for too long?'

'Yes, just that.'

The child started to whimper. The girl looked at him as though for the first time.

'I must go,' she said.

She turned again to the child.

'Just for once,' she said to it gently, 'just for once you must be good.'

And she turned again to the man.

'And so I will say good-bye.'

'Good-bye. Perhaps we will meet again at that Dance Hall.'

'Perhaps. You do not know yet if you will go there?'

The man made an effort to reply.

'Not yet, no.'

'How strange that is.'

'If you only knew what a coward I am.'

'But you mustn't let going to the Dance Hall depend on your cowardice. If you go, let it be for fun; for no other reason.'

The man made a further effort to reply.

'It is very difficult for me to know yet whether I will go. I cannot, no I cannot know now whether I will or not.'

'But you do go dancing from time to time?'

'Yes, without knowing anyone.'

It was the girl's turn to smile.

'But just for the fun of it, that is all you must think of. And you will see how well I dance.'

'Believe me, if I went it would be for fun.'

The girl smiled even more. But it was a smile the man could ill support.

'I thought, if I understood you correctly, that you reproached me for allowing too little place for pleasure in my life?'

'It was true, yes.'

'You said I should be less suspicious of it than I am?'

'You know so little about it, if you only knew how little.'

'You must excuse me for saying this, but I have the feeling that perhaps you know less about it than you imagine. I was talking of the pleasure of dancing of course.'

'Yes, of dancing with you.'

The child started whimpering again.

'We are going,' the girl said to him, and to the man, 'I must say good-bye. Perhaps then we shall meet again this coming Saturday?'

'Perhaps, yes, perhaps. Good-bye.'

The girl turned and went off rapidly with the child. The man watched her going, watched her as hard as he could. She did not turn back. And he took this as a sign of encouragement to go to that Dance Hall.

TEN-THIRTY
ON A SUMMER NIGHT

*Translated by
Anne Borchardt*

I

'His name is Paestra. Rodrigo Paestra.'
'Rodrigo Paestra.'
'Yes. And the man he killed is Perez. Toni Perez.'
'Toni Perez.'
On the square, two policemen were walking by in the rain.
'When did he kill Perez?'
The customer didn't know exactly, at the beginning of the afternoon that was coming to an end. At the same time that he killed Perez, Rodrigo Paestra had also killed his wife. Both victims had been found two hours earlier, at the back of a garage belonging to Perez.

In the café, it was already getting dark. Candles had been lit on the wet counter in the back, and their yellow light mingled with the blueness of the dying day. The shower stopped suddenly, as it had started.

'How old was she, Rodrigo Paestra's wife?' Maria asked.
'Very young. Nineteen.'
There was a look of regret on Maria's face.
'I would like another glass of manzanilla,' she said.
The customer ordered it for her. He was also having a manzanilla.

'I wonder why they haven't caught him yet,' she went on, 'the town is so small.'
'He knows the town better than the police. Quite a man, Rodrigo.'

The bar was full. Everyone was talking about Rodrigo

Paestra's crime. They all agreed about Perez, but about his young wife they didn't. A child. Maria was drinking her manzanilla. The customer looked at her with surprise.

'Do you always drink like that?'

'It depends,' she said, 'more or less, yes, almost always like that.'

'Alone?'

'At the moment, yes.'

The café wasn't directly on the street but on a square arcade, divided, split right through by the town's main avenue. This arcade was bordered by a stone balustrade, with a top that was wide and strong enough to hold children who sometimes jumped over it and sometimes lay flat on it while watching the rain come down or the police walk by. Among them was Judith, Maria's daughter. Leaning against the balustrade, she was looking at the square, with only her head showing above it.

It must have been between six and seven in the evening.

Another shower started and the square became empty. A group of palmettos in the middle of the square were bending under the wind, crushing the flowers between them. Judith came back from the arcade and huddled against her mother. But her fear had vanished. The strokes of lightning came so close together that they seemed like one, and the noise in the sky was continuous. It was a noise that sometimes burst like metal fireworks, but which would immediately rise again, its modulation less and less defined as the shower let up. In the arcade there was silence. Judith left her mother and went to take a closer look at the rain, and the square that was dancing in the streaks of rain.

'This will last all night,' the customer said.

All of a sudden the shower stopped. The customer left the

counter and pointed at the dark blue sky, patched with large spots of dark gray, and so low that it brushed the rooftops.

Maria wanted to go on drinking. He ordered the manzanillas without saying anything. He was also going to have one.

'It's my husband who wanted us to spend our vacation in Spain. I would have preferred somewhere else.'

'Where?'

'I haven't thought about it. Everywhere at once. Including Spain. Don't pay attention to what I say. Actually, I'm quite happy to be in Spain this summer.'

He picked up her glass of manzanilla and handed it to her. He paid the waiter.

'You got here around five, didn't you?' the customer asked. 'Weren't you in the little black Rover that stopped on the square?'

'Yes,' Maria answered.

'It was still very light,' he went on. 'It wasn't raining yet. There were four of you in the black Rover. There was your husband, driving. Were you next to him? Yes? And in the back there was a little girl,'—he pointed at her—'that one. And another woman.'

'Yes. We had been running into thunderstorms since three o'clock, out in the country, and my daughter was afraid. That's why we decided to stop here instead of going on to Madrid.'

During the conversation, the customer was watching the square, and the police who had come out again with the end of the rain; and, through the noise of the storm, he listened hard to the whistles which rang out from every street corner.

'My friend was also afraid of the storm,' Maria added.

The sun set at the end of the main avenue. The hotel was in that direction. It wasn't quite as late as it seemed. The storm had scrambled the hours, pushed them on, but here they were again, reddening the sky.

'Where are they?' the customer asked.

'At the Hotel Principal. I must go and join them.'

'I remember. A man, your husband, got half out of the black Rover and asked some young people how many hotels there are in town. And you left in the direction of the Hotel Principal.'

'There were no rooms left, naturally. Already, there were none left.'

The sunset was covered again. A new phase of the storm was getting ready. The afternoon's dark blue, ocean-like mass moved slowly over the town. It was coming from the east. There was just enough light left to see its threatening color. They must still be at the threshold of the balcony. There, at the end of the avenue. Look, now your eyes are blue, Pierre is saying, this time because of the sky.

'I can't go back yet. Look what's coming.'

Judith, this time, wasn't coming back. She was watching children playing barefoot in the gutter around the square. The water that ran between their feet was filled with clay. The water was dark red, like the stones of the town and the earth around it. All the young people were outside, on the square, under the lightning and the constant grumbling of the sky. You could hear songs whistled by some youngsters, so sweet they pierced the thunder.

Another shower. The ocean spilled onto the town. The square disappeared. The arcades filled with people. In the café they had to talk louder to be heard. Some screamed at times. And the names of Rodrigo Paestra and Perez.

'Leave Rodrigo Paestra alone,' the customer said.

He pointed at the police who had taken shelter in the arcade and who were waiting for the shower to end.

'He was married six months,' the customer went on. 'He found her with Perez. Who wouldn't have done the same. He'll be acquitted, Rodrigo.'

Maria kept on drinking. She made a face. The time of day had come when liquor turned her stomach.

'Where is he?' she asked.

The customer leaned toward her. She could smell the thick, lemony odor of his hair. His lips were smooth, beautiful.

'On one of the roofs.'

They smiled at each other. He moved away. She could still feel the warmth of his voice on her shoulder.

'Drowned?'

'No', he was laughing, 'I'm just repeating what I heard. I don't know.'

At the back of the café, a very noisy argument about the crime had started, which made the other conversations stop. Rodrigo Paestra's wife had thrown herself into Perez's arms, was it Perez's fault? Can you push away a woman who falls into your arms like that?

'Can you?' asked Maria.

'It's hard. But Rodrigo had forgotten that.'

Perez had some friends who were mourning him that night His mother was there, alone, next to his body in the town hall. And Rodrigo Paestra's wife? Her body was also in the town hall. But she didn't come from here. No one was with her tonight. She came from Madrid, she had come here for the wedding, in the autumn.

The shower was over and with it the nerve-racking noise of the rain.

'Once she was married, she wanted every man in the village. What was there to do? Kill her?'

'What a question,' Maria said—she pointed to a spot on the square, a big, closed door.

'That's where it is, that's right,' said the customer, 'that's the town hall.'

A friend came back into the café. Again they talked about the crime.

Once more, with the end of the shower, the square filled with children. It was hard to see the end of the avenue, where the town ends, and the white shape of the Hotel Principal. Maria noticed that Judith was among the children in the square. She inspected the paving carefully and finally stepped into the red, muddy water. The customer's friend offered Maria a manzanilla. She accepted. How long had she been in Spain? Nine days, she said. Did she like Spain? Of course. She knew it from before.

'I have to go back,' she said. 'With this storm, you don't know where to go.'

'My place,' said the customer.

He was laughing. She laughed, but not as much as he would have liked.

'One more manzanilla?'

No, she didn't want to drink any more. She called Judith who came in with red boots dyed onto her by the muddy water.

'Will you be back? Tonight?'

She didn't know, it was possible.

They took the sidewalk leading to the hotel. Stable smells and smells of hay were blowing through the town. The night was going to be good, sea-like. Judith was walking in the puddles of red water. Maria let her. They met the police who were guarding every street corner. It was nearly night. There was still no electricity, and there probably wouldn't be any for some time. On the rooftops there was the glimmering of the sunset for those who could see it. Maria took Judith's hand and talked to her. Judith, as usual, was not listening.

They were there, sitting opposite each other, in the dining room. They smiled at Maria and Judith.

'We waited for you,' Pierre said.

He looked at Judith. On the road, she too had been very afraid of the storm. She had cried. She still had rings under her eyes.

'The thunderstorm hasn't stopped yet,' Pierre said. 'It's a shame. We could have been in Madrid tonight.'

'It was to be expected,' said Maria. 'They still have no rooms? No one dared to leave?'

'None. Not even for the children.'

'Tomorrow will be much less hot,' Claire said, 'that's one consolation.'

Pierre promised Judith they would stay.

'We shall eat,' Claire told her. 'And they'll put blankets in the halls for little girls like you.'

There wasn't one free table in the dining room.

'And they're all French,' Claire said.

In the candlelight her beauty was even more obvious. Had someone told her he loved her? She was there, smiling, ready for a night that wouldn't happen. Her lips, her eyes, her uncombed hair, her hands spread apart, open, loose in anticipation of happiness growing closer, none of this proved that tonight they had set aside for the silent fulfilment of the promise of approaching happiness.

The rain again. It made so much noise on the skylight above the dining room that the guests had to shout their orders. Children were crying. Judith hesitated, did not cry.

'What rain,' Claire said—she stretched with impatience—'it's crazy how it's raining, crazy, crazy; listen, Maria, how it's raining.'

'Remember how afraid you were, Claire?'

'Yes.'

Everything in the hotel had been up side down. It hadn't been raining yet, but the storm was always present, threatening. When Maria had joined them, they were in the hotel lobby. They were talking, next to each other in the hotel lobby. She stopped, filled with hope. They hadn't seen Maria. That's when she noticed their hands, discreetly linked together, their bodies close. It was early. You might have thought that evening had come, but it was the storm darkening the sky. There wasn't a trace of fear left in Claire's eyes. Maria had decided that she had enough time—enough time—to go to the square, to the cafe they had seen when they arrived.

So as not to look at Pierre, they watched the waiters juggling trays of manzanilla and other sherries. Claire caught a waiter on his way by and asked him for manzanillas. You had to shout because of the noise of the rain on the skylight. They shouted louder and louder. The dining room door opened every minute. People were still coming in. The storm was huge, very spread out.

'Where were you, Maria?' Pierre asked.

'In a café, with a friend of that man Rodrigo Paestra.'

Pierre leaned toward Maria.

'If you really want to,' he said, 'we can go on to Madrid tonight.'

Claire was listening.

'Claire?' Maria questioned.

'I don't know.'

She almost moaned. Pierre's hands moved toward hers and

then pulled back. Earlier he had made the same gesture, in the car when she was afraid of the storm, the sky rolling over on itself, hanging over the wheatfields; Judith screaming; the day dark like twilight. Claire had become pale, so much so that her paleness was even more surprising than the fear it revealed.

'You don't know, Claire, you don't know this type of inconvenience, sleepless nights spent in hotel corridors.'

'Of course I do. Who doesn't know?'

She was struggling, immersed in the thought of Pierre's hands on her, only a few hours ago under Maria's blinded eyes. Did she grow pale again? Did he notice she was getting pale again?

'We'll stay here tonight,' he said. 'Just this time.'

He smiled. Did he ever smile before?

'Just this time?' Maria asked.

Pierre's hands, this time, reached their goal and touched the hands of his wife, Maria.

'I meant that I wasn't used to these inconveniences enough to be as frightened as you, Maria.'

Maria moved away from the table and, clutching at the chair while speaking, closed her eyes.

'Once, in Verona,' she said.

She didn't see what was going on. It was Claire's voice which, through the noise of the other voices, cut a bright path.

'In Verona? What happened there?"

'We slept badly,' Pierre said.

The meal had started. The smell of the candles was so strong that it overpowered the smell of the food which perspiring waiters were carrying in big loads. There were shouts and complaints. The hotel manager asked that she be forgiven, she was in a difficult spot that night, because of the storm.

'Did I drink,' Maria announced. 'Again, did I drink!'

'It always surprises you,' said Claire.

The rain had stopped. In moments of unforeseen silence, you could hear the gay streaming of rain on the skylight. Judith, who had gone off to the kitchen, was brought back by a waiter. Pierre was talking about Castile. About Madrid. He found out that in this town there were two Goyas in the church of San Andrea. The church of San Andrea is on the square they crossed when they arrived. The waiter brought the soup. Maria served Judith. And Judith's eyes filled with tears. Pierre smiled at his child. Maria gave up hope of getting Judith to eat.

'I'm not hungry tonight,' Claire said, 'you know, I think it's the storm.'

'Happiness,' said Maria.

Claire concentrated on what was going on in the dining room. Behind her suddenly thoughtful expression there was a smile. Pierre, wincing, raised his eyes on Maria—the same eyes as Judith's—and Maria smiled at those eyes.

'Everyone has been waiting so much for this storm, for this coolness,' Maria explained.

'Yes,' Claire said.

Maria was again hoping to get Judith to eat. She succeeded. Spoonful by spoonful, Judith ate. Claire told her a story. Pierre was listening too. The disorder in the dining room was straightening out a little. Yet, you could still hear thunder, more or less loud, depending on whether the storm was coming closer or moving farther away. Every time the skylight was lit up by lightning, a child would cry.

While dinner was being served, people spoke of Rodrigo Paestra's crime. Some laughed. Who would ever have the chance to kill with such simplicity, like Rodrigo Paestra?

Police whistles continued in the night. Whenever they were

heard very close to the hotel, conversations would die down, people would listen. Some were hoping and waiting for Rodrigo Paestra to be captured. A difficult night was ahead.

'He's on the rooftops,' Maria said very softly.

They didn't hear her. Judith was eating fruit.

Maria got up. She walked out of the dining room. They were left alone. She had said she was going to see what the hotel looked like.

There were many corridors. Most of them were circular. Some had a view of the wheat fields. Others, a vista of the avenue which crossed the square. No one was sleeping in the corridors yet. Still others led to balconies overlooking the rooftops of the city. Another shower was in the making. The horizon was lurid. It seemed very far away. The storm had become even bigger. There seemed to be little hope that it would die down during the night.

'Storms go as they come,' Pierre had said. 'Just like that. You mustn't be afraid, Claire.'

That's what he had said. Maria didn't yet know the irresistible perfume of her fear, of her frightened youth. Just a few hours ago.

The rooftops were empty. They would probably always be, whatever hope you might have of seeing them, just for once, filled with people.

The rain was light but it covered the empty rooftops, and the town disappeared. You couldn't see anything any more. There remained only the memory of a dream of loneliness.

When Maria came back to the dining room the manager was announcing the arrival of the police.

'As you probably know,' she said, 'a crime was committed in our town this afternoon. We are very sorry.'

II

No one had to identify himself. The manager vouched for her guests.

Six policemen rushed through the dining room. Three others walked over to the circular corridors surrounding it. They were going to search the rooms off these corridors. They were just going to search these rooms, the manager said. It wouldn't take long.

'I was told he's on the rooftops,' Maria said again.

They heard. She had spoken softly. But they weren't surprised. Maria left it at that. The confusion in the dining room had reached a new peak. All the waiters came from this village and knew Rodrigo Paestra. The policemen also came from the village. They questioned one another. The waiters stopped serving. The manager intervened. Be careful not to say anything bad about Perez. The waiters went on talking. The manager shouted orders that no one heard.

And then, little by little, everything having been discussed by the waiters, the customers slowly regained their wits and asked for the rest of their meal. The waiters went back to work. They spoke to the customers. All the customers listened carefully to what the waiters were saying, watched the police coming and going, worried, gained or lost hope as to the outcome of the search, some were still smiling at Rodrigo Paestra's naïveté. Some women talked about how horrible it is to be killed at nineteen, and to be left like Rodrigo Paestra's wife, alone, so alone, that night, in the town hall, a mere child. But all were eating, more or less heartily, in the midst of the confusion, eating the food brought in by the waiters in the midst of anger and confusion. Doors slammed in the corridors, and the policemen crossed the dining room, with Tommy guns, wearing boots and belts, unalterably serious, giving off a nauseating smell of wet leather and sweat. At the sight of them, children always start to cry.

Two of the policemen must have gone to the corridor, on the left of the dining room, where Maria had just been.

Judith, in a state of terror, stopped eating her fruit. There were no longer any policemen in the dining room. The waiter who had been taking care of them came back to their table shaking with anger; he was muttering insults against Perez and paying tribute to Rodrigo Paestra's lasting patience; and Judith, pieces of orange dripping between her fingers, was listening to him, listening all the time.

They must have reached the balcony at the end of the circular corridor where Maria had just been. It wasn't raining any more, and Maria could hear their footsteps fading away in that corridor alongside the dining room, through the noise of streaming rain on the skylight, of which no one in the dining room seemed to be aware now.

Everything was quiet again. The quiet of the sky. The quiet streaming of the rain on the skylight punctuated by the policemen's steps in that last corridor—once the rooms, the kitchens, the courtyards will have been searched—will they forget him? Some day? No.

If they had reached the balcony at the end of that last corridor, if they had reached the balcony, then it was certain that Rodrigo Paestra was not on the rooftops.

'Why was I told such a thing?' Maria went on again very softly.

They heard. But neither one was surprised.

She had seen these rooftops. A moment before they were stretched out, evenly strewn under the sky, entangled, bare, right under the balcony, bare and consistently empty.

Calls could be heard from outside. From the street? From the courtyard? Very close. The waiters stopped and listened, their hands full of dishes. Nobody complained. The calls went on. They bore gaps of terror into the sudden silence. Listening, you could hear that these calls were always the same. His name.

'Rodrigo Paestra.'

In long, plaintive, rhythmical, nearly tender tones, they begged him to answer, to surrender.

Maria stood up. Pierre took her by the arm and forced her to sit down. She sat down obediently.

'But he is on the rooftops,' she said very softly.

Judith didn't hear.

'It's funny,' Claire said very softly, 'I don't care at all.'

'But,' Maria said, 'it's just that I know.'

Pierre gently called Maria.

'Please, Maria,' he said.

'It's those calls,' she said, 'that get on one's nerves, it's nothing.'

The calls stopped. And another shower began. The police were back. The waiters went back to their work, smiling, their eyes lowered. The manager stayed at the dining room door, she kept an eye on her staff, she smiled too, she too, she knew Rodrigo Paestra. A policeman went into the hotel office and made a phone call. He called the neighboring town to ask for reinforcements. He was shouting because of the noise of the rain on the skylight. He said that the village had been thoroughly surrounded as soon as the crime had been discovered and that there were ten chances out of ten they would find Rodrigo Paestra at dawn, they had to wait, the search was difficult because of the storm and the power failure, but it was probable that the storm, as usual, would end at daybreak, and what they had to do was to guard, all night, the roads leading from the town, for that they needed more men, so that as soon as it was light Rodrigo Paestra would be caught like a rat. The policeman had made himself understood. He was waiting for an answer that came at once. Around ten, in an hour and a half, the reinforcements would be there. The waiter came back to their table, trembling, and spoke to Pierre.

'If they catch him,' he said, 'if they manage to catch him, he won't let them take him to jail.'

Maria was drinking wine. The waiter left. Pierre leaned toward Maria.

'Don't drink so much Maria, please don't.'

Maria raised her arm, pushed away the potential obstacle this voice seemed to be, again and again. Claire had heard Pierre speaking to Maria.

'I'm not drinking much,' Maria said.

'It's true,' Claire said, 'tonight Maria is drinking less than usual.'

'You see,' Maria said.

As for Claire, she wasn't drinking anything. Pierre got up and said that he too was going to take a look at the hotel.

There were no longer any policemen in the hotel. They had left, in single file, by the staircase next to the office. It wasn't raining. The whistling kept on, but far away, and in the dining room the chatter had started again, the complaints, especially about the bad Spanish food which the waiters were still serving to late-comers with triumphant gusto because Rodrigo Paestra had not yet been caught. Judith was calm and started to yawn.

When the waiter came back to their table he spoke to Claire, to Claire's beauty, and stopped to look at her again after speaking.

'One chance they don't catch him,' he said.

'Did she love Perez?' Claire asked.

'Impossible to love Perez,' the waiter said.

Claire laughed and the waiter gave way to laughter also.

'Still,' Claire said, 'what if she loved Perez?'

'Why do you want Rodrigo Paestra to understand?' the waiter asked.

He left. Claire began to nibble some bread. Maria was drinking and Claire let her.

'Pierre isn't coming back?' Maria said.

'I don't know. Any more than you do.'

Maria moved toward the table, straightened up, then leaned very close to Claire.

'Listen, Claire,' Maria said, 'listen to me.'

Claire leaned back in the opposite direction. She looked past Maria, staring at the back of the dining room without seeing it.

'I'm listening to you, Maria,' she said.

Maria fell back into her chair and said nothing. Some time passed. Claire had stopped nibbling bread. When Pierre came back he told them that he had picked the best corridor in the hotel for Judith, he had seen the sky, he had seen the storm petering out little by little; it would probably be nice tomorrow and very early, if they wanted, they could reach Madrid, after looking at the two Goyas in San Andrea. Since the storm had started again, he spoke a little louder than usual. His voice was beautiful, always precise, with a precision, this evening, that was almost oratorical. He was talking about the two Goyas it would be a shame not to see.

'Without this storm, we would have forgotten them,' Claire said.

She said this like anything else and yet she never would have said it like that before this evening. Where, in the half darkness Maria had given them earlier, in what part of the hotel, did they first wonder and then marvel at having known each other so little until then, at the wonderful agreement that had grown between them, and then at last come to light behind this window? or on that balcony? or in this corridor? in this surging warmth of the streets after the showers, behind the sky so dark, Claire, that your eyes, at that very moment, were the very color of rain. How could I have noticed it before? Your eyes, Claire, are gray.

She told him that the light always had something to do with it and that he was probably mistaken that evening because of the storm.

'It seems to me, if I remember correctly,' Maria said, 'that before leaving France we had talked about these two Goyas.'

Pierre remembered. Not Claire. The shower stopped and they could hear one another. The dining room was getting emptier. The humming picked up in the corridors. They were probably dividing up beds. Children were being undressed. The time had come for Judith to go to sleep. Pierre was quiet. Finally Maria said it.

'I'm going to put Judith to sleep in the corridor.'

'We'll wait for you,' Pierre said.

'I'll be back.'

Judith didn't object. In the hall there were many children, some already asleep. Maria didn't undress Judith that night. She wrapped her in a blanket, against the wall, halfway down the corridor.

She waited for Judith to fall asleep. She waited a long time.

III

So much time went by that no trace of twilight was left in the sky.

'Don't expect any electricity tonight,' the manager of the hotel had said. 'Usually around here the storms are so violent that there's no electricity all night.'

There was no electricity. There were going to be more storms, more sudden showers throughout the night. The sky was still low and small, still whipped by a very strong wind, toward the west. The sky could be seen, perfectly arched up to the horizon. And the limits of the storm could be seen too, trying to take over more of the clearer part of the sky.

From the balcony where she was standing, Maria could see the whole expanse of the storm. They remained in the dining room.

'I'll be back,' Maria had said.

Behind her, in the corridor, all the children were now sleeping. Among them was Judith. When Maria turned around she saw her asleep, her body outlined in the soft light of the oil lamps hooked up on the walls.

'As soon as she's asleep, I'll come back,' Maria had told them.

Judith was asleep.

The hotel was full. The rooms, the corridors, and later on this hall, would be still more crowded. There were more people in the hotel than in a whole district of the town. The town, beyond which stretched deserted roads, all the way to Madrid, toward which the storm was moving since five o'clock, bursting here and there, its clouds breaking and then mending again. To the point of exhaustion. Until when? It was going to last all night.

There was no longer a single café open.

'We'll wait for you, Maria,' Pierre had said.

The town was small, it covered about five acres, all of it was crowded into an irregular, but full, neatly outlined shape. Beyond it, whichever way you turned, open country stretched out, bare, rolling (this was hardly noticeable that night, and yet, in the east, there seemed to be a sudden drop). A stream previously dried out, would overflow in the morning.

If you looked at the time it was ten o'clock. In the evening. It was summer.

Policemen were walking under the hotel balconies. They must have been tired from searching. They dragged their feet in the muddy streets. The crime had been committed a long time ago, hours ago, and they were talking about the weather.

'Rodrigo Paestra is on the rooftops.'

Maria remembered. The rooftops were there, they were empty. They were shining dimly under the balcony where she was standing. Empty.

They were waiting for her in the dining room, in the midst of cleared tables, oblivious of her, looking at each other, motionless. The hotel was full. There was no other place for them to look at each other except there.

Whistling started again at the other end of the town, well beyond the square, in the direction of Madrid. Nothing happened. Policemen gathered at the street corner, on the left, stopped, moved off again. It was just a break in the waiting period. The policemen walked by under the balcony, and turned into another street.

It wasn't much later than ten. It was later than when she should have gone back to the dining room, entered, moved in between them, sat down, and told them once more the surprising news.

'I've been told that Rodrigo Paestra is hiding on the rooftops.'

She left the balcony, entered the hall and lay down next to her sleeping child, her own, the body which, among all the other children in the hall, belonged to her. She kissed her hair lightly.

'My life,' she said.

The child didn't wake up. She barely moved, sighed, and fell back into a calm sleep.

And the town was like her, already locked in sleep. Some still talked about Rodrigo Paestra whose wife was found naked next to Perez, both asleep after hours of love. And then dead. The nineteen year old body was in the town hall.

If Maria were to get up, if she were to go to the dining room, she could ask for a drink. She thought of the first sip of manzanilla in her mouth and the peace in her body that would follow. She didn't move.

Beyond the hall, through the yellow and vacillating screen of the oil lamps, you could imagine the rooftops, covered with the moving sky, its darkness deepening. The sky was there, against the frame of the open balcony.

Maria got up, hesitant about going back to the dining room where they would still be immersed in the wonder of their overpowering desire, still alone in the midst of cleared tables and exhausted waiters who were waiting for them to leave, and whom they didn't see.

She walked back to the balcony, smoked a cigarette. The rain hadn't returned yet. It was slow. The sky was still brooding, it would still be a while. In the back of her, there were couples coming into the hall. They were speaking softly because of the children. They lay down. They kept quiet at first, hoping for sleep that did not come, and then they talked again. From everywhere, particularly from the crowded rooms, came the muted sound of voices, regularly interrupted by the fateful passing of the police.

After each passing, the conjugal hum started again, in the rooms, in the circular corridors, the every day sound, slow and tired. Behind the doors, in the twin beds, in the embraces born in the cool of the storm, there was talk of the summer, of this summer storm, and of Rodrigo Paestra's crime.

At last the shower. In a few seconds it filled the streets. The earth was too dry and couldn't drink up so much rain. The trees on the square were twisted by the wind. Maria could see their tops appear and disappear behind the angle of the roofs and, when lightning lit up the town and the open country, in its livid illumination, she could at the same time see Rodrigo Paestra's motionless and drowned shape clutching a dark stone chimney.

The shower lasted a few minutes. Calm returned as the strength of the wind weakened. A vague glimmering, so long hoped for, descended from the appeased sky. And in this glimmering, which increased as you hoped it would, but which you knew would quickly fade with the beginnings of another phase of the storm, Maria could see the indefinite shape of Rodrigo Paestra, Rodrigo Paestra's dazzling, shrieking and indefinite shape.

Again the police started their search. They returned as the storm subsided. They marched through the mud again. Maria leaned over the railing of the balcony and saw them. One of them laughed. At regular intervals, the whole town rang with the sound of whistling. Just more pauses in the waiting period, which was going to last until morning.

In addition to the balcony where Maria was standing, there were others on the north side of the hotel. They were empty, except one, just one, on Maria's right, one flight above. They must have been there for a very short time. Maria hadn't seen them arrive. She moved back slightly into the corridor where people were now asleep.

This must have been the first time they had kissed. Maria put out her cigarette. She could see them fully outlined against the moving sky. While Pierre kissed her, his hands touched Claire's breasts. They were probably talking. But very softly. They must have been speaking the first words of love. Irrepressible, bursting words which came to their lips between two kisses.

The lightning made the town look livid. It was unforeseeable, striking irregularly. But every time it made their kisses livid too, as well as their single, nearly blinding shape. Was it on her eyes, behind the screen formed by the dark sky, that he had first kissed her? How could one know. Your eyes were the color of your fear in the afternoon, the color of rain at that very moment, Claire, your eyes, I could hardly see them, how could I have noticed it before, your eyes must be gray.

Opposite these kisses, a few yards away, Rodrigo Paestra wrapped in his brown blanket was waiting for the infernal night to end. At dawn, it would be all over.

A new phase of the storm was coming up that was going to separate them and prevent Maria from seeing them.

As he did it, so did she, bringing her hands to her lonely breasts, then her hands fell and, useless, grasped the balcony. While she had moved too far out onto the balcony while they were merging into a single, nearly blinding shape, she now moved back a little from the balcony, toward the corridor where the new wind was already sweeping into the lamp chimneys. No, she couldn't help seeing them. She could still see them. And their shadows were on that roof. Now their bodies broke apart. The wind raised her skirt, and, in a flash, they laughed. The same wind that had raised her skirt, again crossed the whole town, bumping up against the edges of the rooftops.

Two more minutes and the storm would come, sweeping over the whole town, emptying the streets, the balconies. He must have stepped back in order to hold her better, to be reunited with her for the first time, their happiness intensified by the suffering he created by holding her far from him. They didn't know, they were still unaware that the storm would separate them for the night.

More waiting. And the impatience of waiting grew so intense it reached its climax, and at last calm set in. One of Pierre's hands was moving all over another woman's body. His other hand held her close against him. It was done now, forever.

It was ten-thirty. And summer.

And then it was a little later. Night had come at last, completely. There was no room that night, in that town, for love. Maria lowered her eyes before this reality: their thirst for love would remain unfulfilled, the town was bulging, in this summer night made for their love. The flashes of lightning kept lighting up the shape of their desire. They were still there, folded in each other's arms, and motionless, his hand now resting on her hip, hers forever, while she, she, her hands unable to move as they clung to his shoulders, her mouth against his mouth, she was devouring him.

The same flashes, at the same time, lit up the roof opposite them and on its top, around a chimney, the shrouded shape of Rodrigo Paestra, the murderer.

The wind increased, swept into the hallway and moved over the sleeping children. A lamp had gone out. But nothing would wake them. The town was dark and asleep. In the rooms there was silence. Judith was good.

They had disappeared from the balcony as suddenly as they had come. He must have led her away without letting go of her—how could he—into the shadow of the sleeping corridor. The balcony was deserted. Maria looked at her watch once again. It was almost eleven. Because of the wind that was still growing stronger, one of the children—it wasn't that one—uttered a cry, isolated, turned over and fell back to sleep.

The rain. And again its ineffable smell, its lifeless smell of muddy streets. Just as it did on the fields, the rain was falling on the dead shape of Rodrigo Paestra, dead of sorrow, dead of love.

Where could they have found a place to be together that night, in that hotel? Where would he take off her light skirt, that very night? How beautiful she is. How beautiful you are, God how beautiful. With the rain, their shapes had vanished from the balcony.

Summer was everywhere, in the rain, in the streets, in the courtyards, in the bathrooms, in the kitchens, summer, everywhere, summer was everywhere for their love. Maria stretched, went back in, lay down in the hallway, stretched again. Was it done now? Perhaps there was no one in another dark, stifling corridor—could anyone know all of them?—the corridor extending from their balcony, for example, right above this one, in this miraculously forgotten corridor, along the wall, on the floor, was it done?

Tomorrow would be there in a few hours. You had to wait. The shower was longer than the previous one. It kept coming down with force. And also on the skylight, echoing horribly throughout the hotel.

'We waited for you, Maria,' Pierre said.

They appeared with the end of the shower. She saw their two shadows move toward her while she was lying next to Judith, two huge shadows. Claire's skirt had risen above her knees, bulging around her hips. The wind in the corridor. Too fast. They hadn't had much time between leaving the balcony and arriving there, next to Maria. They were smiling. So that hope had been foolish. Love hadn't been fulfilled that night in the hotel. More waiting. The rest of the night.

'You said you would be back, Maria,' Pierre said again.

'Well, I was tired.'

She had seen him looking for her on the floor of the corridor carefully, almost walk past her, and stop in front of her; she was the last one, just where the corridor ended, engulfed in the darkness of the dining room. Claire was following him.

'Well,' Maria repeated—she was pointing at Judith—'she would have been afraid.'

Pierre smiled. He stopped looking at Maria and discovered an open window leading onto a balcony at the end of the corridor.

'What weather,' he said.

He brushed away his discovery of the window at the very moment he made it. Was it fear?

'And it will last all night,' he said. 'It will end by daybreak.'

She could have told just from his voice, trembling, shaky, affected by desire for that woman.

Then Claire also smiled at Judith. At the small, lopsided shape, wrapped in a brown blanket. Her hair was still wet from the rain on the balcony. Her eyes in the yellow light of the oil lamp. Your eyes, blue stones. I'll eat your eyes, he was telling her, your eyes. The youthfulness of her breasts showed clearly under her white sweater. Her blue gaze was haggard, paralyzed by frustration, by the very fulfillment of frustration. Her gaze left Judith and moved back to Pierre.

'Did you go back to a café, Maria?'

'No. I stayed here.'

'A good thing we didn't leave for Madrid,' Pierre said. 'You see.'

He turned again toward the open window.

'A good thing, yes.'

In the street alongside the hotel, a whistle rang out. Was it over? There was no second whistle. The three of them waited. No. Once more, just a pause in the waiting period. Steps made heavy by the mud in the streets moved toward the northern part of town. They didn't talk about it.

'She isn't warm tonight,' Claire said.

Maria stroked Judith's forehead.

'Not really. Less than usual. It's comfortable.'

Maria could have told just from Claire's breasts that they were in love. They were going to lie down there, next to her, separated while torn and tortured by desire. And both were smiling, equally guilty, terrified and happy.

'We waited for you,' Pierre repeated.

Even Claire raised her eyes. Then she lowered them and only a vague, indelible smile remained on her face. Maria would have known just from seeing her eyes lowered on that smile. What glory. On what glory were those eyes closing? They must have looked, looked all over the hotel for a spot. It had been impossible. They had had to give up. Pierre had said Maria is waiting for us. What a future ahead of them, the days to come.

Pierre's hands were dangling beside him. For eight years they had caressed her body. Now Claire was stepping into the misfortune that flowed straight from those hands.

'I'm going to sleep,' she announced.

She took a blanket that had been put on a table. She wrapped herself in it, still laughing, and, with a sigh, stretched out below the oil lamp. Pierre did not move.

'I'm sleeping,' Claire said.

Pierre also took a blanket, then lay down next to Maria, on the other side of the corridor.

Did Rodrigo Paestra still exist, there, twenty yards from them? Yes. The police had again walked by in the street. Claire sighed again.

'Ah, I'm already asleep,' she said. 'Good night, Maria.'

'Good night, Claire.'

Pierre lit a cigarette. The sound of regular breathing rose in the freshness of the corridor, in its odor of rain and of Claire.

'It's very pleasant,' Pierre said softly.

Some time went by. Maria should have told Pierre again: 'You know, it's crazy, but Rodrigo Paestra is really there, on the roof. Opposite. And with daybreak, he'll be caught.'

Maria said nothing.

'You're tired, Maria?' Pierre asked even more softly.

'Less than usual. The storm I suppose. It feels better.'

' Yes ' Claire said, 'we're less tired than the other nights.'

She wasn't sleeping. A gust of wind put out the last light. Lightning again at the end of the corridor. Maria turned slightly, but you couldn't see the roof from where they were.

'It will never stop,' Pierre said. 'Do you want me to put the light back on, Maria?'

'It's not worth it. I like it like that.'

'I like it too,' Claire went on again.

She stopped talking. Maria knew it: Pierre was hoping she would fall asleep. He was no longer smoking and lay motionless against the wall. But Claire was talking again.

'Tomorrow,' she said, 'we'll have to reserve rooms in Madrid by noon.'

'We should, yes.'

She yawned. Pierre and Maria were waiting for her to fall asleep. It was raining hard. Can you die if you want to from having to bear the brunt of a storm? Maria seemed to remember that it was Rodrigo Paestra's dead shape that she had seen on the roof.

Maria knew that Pierre wasn't sleeping, that he was aware of her, Maria, his wife, and that the desire he felt for Claire was becoming corrupted by the memory of his wife; that he was becoming gloomy for fear she had guessed something; that he was disturbed at the thought of Maria's new loneliness, tonight, compared to what had been before.

'Are you sleeping?'

'No.'

They had spoken very softly once more. They were waiting. Yes, this time, Claire was asleep.

'What time is it?' Maria asked.

With the end of the rain, there came the policemen whom Rodrigo Paestra must have also heard. Pierre looked at his watch in the light of the cigarette he had just started.

'Eleven twenty. Do you want a cigarette?'

Maria did.

'It's already lighter,' Pierre said. 'Maybe it's clearing up now. Here, Maria.'

He handed it to her. They sat up a little, just long enough for him to light it, then they lay down again. At the end of the corridor, Maria saw the dark blue screen of the balcony.

'Nights like this are so long,' Pierre said.

'Yes. Try to sleep.'

'And you?'

'I would like a manzanilla. But it's impossible.'

Pierre waited before answering. A last cloudburst, very light, fell on Rodrigo Paestra. You could hear singing and laughing in the street. The police, once again. But in the corridor all was quiet.

'Won't you try to drink a little less, Maria? Just once?'

'No,' Maria said. 'No more.'

The earthy smell came up from the street, endless, the smell of tears along with its complement, the smell of wet, fully ripened wheat. Was she going to tell him: 'It's crazy, Pierre, but Rodrigo Paestra is there. There. Right there. And with daybreak he will be caught.'

She said nothing. It was he who spoke.

'You remember? Verona?'

'Yes.'

If he reached out, Pierre would touch Maria's hair. He had spoken of Verona. Of love all night, the two of them, in a bathroom in Verona. A storm too, and it was summer, and the hotel was full. 'Come, Maria.' He was wondering. 'When, when will I have enough of you?'

'Give me another cigarette,' Maria said.

He gave it to her. This time she didn't sit up.

'If I spoke to you about Verona, it's because I couldn't help it.'

The smell of mud and wheat came in whiffs into the corridor. The hotel was bathed in this odor, as well as the town, Rodrigo Paestra and his dead, and the inexhaustible but perfectly vain memory of a night of love in Verona.

Claire was sleeping soundly. Then she turned suddenly and moaned because of the recent stir of Pierre's hands, that night, on her body. Pierre also heard Claire's moan. It was over. Claire grew quiet. And Maria next to Pierre only heard the sound of children breathing, and the police kept marching by more and more regularly as morning came closer.

'You're not asleep?'

'No,' said Maria. 'What time is it?'

'A quarter to twelve'—he was waiting. 'Here, have another cigarette.'

'All right. At what time is dawn in Spain?'

'Very early at this time of year.'

'I wanted to tell you, Pierre.'

She took the cigarette that he was holding out to her. Her hand trembled a little. He waited until he was lying down again before asking her.

'What do you want to tell me, Maria?'

Pierre waited a long time for an answer which didn't come. He didn't insist. Both of them were smoking, lying on their backs because of the tiles that bruised their hips. You had to suffer this bruise as best you could. She couldn't remove the free end of Judith's blanket that was covering her without being exposed to Pierre's look. She could only try to close her eyes between each puff of her cigarette, open them again, without moving at all, keeping quiet.

'Lucky we found this hotel,' Pierre said.

'Lucky, yes.'

He was smoking faster than she. He had finished his cigarette. He put it out in the narrow space between him and Maria, in the middle of the corridor, between the sleeping bodies. The showers lasted only a short length of time now, the length of one of Claire's sighs.

'You know Maria. I love you.'

Maria also was through with her cigarette, she put it out, just like Pierre, on an empty tile in the corridor.

'Yes, I know,' she said.

What was happening? What was in the air? Was this really the end of the storm? Whenever there were showers, it was like pails of water spilled on the skylight and the roofs. A sound of showering that would only last a few seconds. They should have fallen asleep before this phase of the storm. Have accepted the idea of this last night before this moment.

'You must sleep, Maria.'

'Yes. But the noise,' she said.

She could do it, she could turn over and find herself right against him. They would get up. They would go away together far from Claire's sleep whose memory would grow dimmer with the passing of night. He knew it.

'Maria, Maria. You are my love.'

'Yes.'

She hadn't moved. In the street, more whistling announced that dawn was close, always closer. There was no more lightning, except weak and far away. Claire moaned again because of the memory of Pierre's hands clasping her hips. But that too you became accustomed to like the soft scraping noise of the children breathing. And the smell of rain engulfed the uniqueness of Claire's desire, mixing it with the sea of desire which, that night, raged through the town.

Maria sat up quietly, hardly turned toward him, stopped moving and looked at him.

'It's crazy, but I saw Rodrigo Paestra. He is there on the roof.'

Pierre was asleep. He had just fallen asleep, as suddenly as a child. Maria remembered that it had always been like that.

He was sleeping. Her need to be sure was funny. Hadn't she been sure?

She sat up a little more. He didn't move. She got up completely, brushed against his body, freed, lonely, abandoned in its sleep.

When Maria reached the balcony, she looked at the time she

carried with her on her wrist, her time. It was half past midnight. In about three hours, at this time of year, it would be dawn. Rodrigo Paestra, the same statue of death she had seen earlier, was waiting for this dawn, and to be killed.

IV

The sky had risen above the town, but in the distance, it was still flush with the wheat fields. But this was the end. The lightning was weaker. And the rumbling of the thunder was weaker. In two and a half hours it would be dawn whatever the weather. A bad, veiled dawn, a bad dawn for Rodrigo Paestra. Now everyone was asleep in the hotel and in the town, except Maria, and Rodrigo Paestra.

The police whistles had stopped. They were keeping watch around the town, guarding all exits, waiting for the bright daylight when they would catch Rodrigo Paestra. In two and a half hours.

Perhaps Maria would fall asleep. Her desire to drink was so strong. Perhaps it was too much for her to wait for dawn. The time of night had arrived when, already, each hour pushed you into the weariness of the next, unavoidable day. The mere anticipation of its coming weighs down on you. During this next day, their love would grow still stronger. Wait.

Maria stayed on the balcony, even when a new shower split the sky again. The shower was light, and warm.

The pointed roof opposite her was washed by the rain. On top of it, around a square chimney, where the two sides of the roof met, was this thing whose shape had remained identical to what Maria had seen at ten-thirty, in a flash of lightning. The thing was wrapped in darkness. The rain fell on it just as it fell on the roof. Then it stopped. And the shape was there. It fitted the shape of the chimney so perfectly that, if you looked at it long enough, you might doubt it was human. Perhaps it was cement, propping up the chimney, darkened over the years. And yet at the same time, whenever lightning lit up the roof, it was the shape of a man.

'What weather,' Maria said. She had spoken as if she had said it to Pierre. Then she waited.

The shape remained identical. One chance in a lifetime that it was a man. Silent, tired policemen walked by in the street, their boots splashing. Then they were gone.

This time Maria called.

'Rodrigo Paestra.'

The possibility that he might answer, move, abandon this inhuman position was enough to make her imagination leap with joy.

'Hey,' Maria called out. She gestured toward the roof.

Nothing moved. Little by little Maria woke up. She still felt like drinking. She remembered that there was a bottle of brandy in the car. A while ago, when she mentioned it to Pierre, this desire to drink was slight, hardly noticeable, but now it had become violent. She looked into the corridor, and beyond, to see if some light in the dining room would offer her hopes of getting a drink. None. If she asked Pierre, he would do it. Tonight, he would do it, he would go and wake up one of the waiters. But she wasn't going to do it, she wasn't going to wake up Pierre. 'You know, Maria, I love you.' He was sleeping near Claire ever since she left the corridor. So let him sleep near Claire. Let him sleep, let him sleep. If this was Rodrigo Paestra, this night in particular, what luck for Maria. What relief from boredom. This time it was because of Claire.

'Hey there,' Maria shouted again.

Wait. Why should this shape be a man? Once in a lifetime it

was possible that this would be he, a man. But it was possible. Why not then accept this possibility?

'Hey,' Maria shouted again.

Once more the slow, dull sound of the police moving closer toward dawn. Maria was silent. Could it be Rodrigo Paestra? It was within the realm of possibility that it was he. As long as she was Maria. It was in the realm of possibility that he should have happened on her, Maria, that night. Wasn't the proof right there in front of her? The proof was urgent. Maria had just invented that this was Rodrigo Paestra. No one else knew it but this woman who was eleven yards away from him, away from this man wanted by the police, the storm murderer, this treasure, this monument of suffering.

Again the rain fell softly on him. And on everything else too, the other roofs, the wheat, the streets. The shape hadn't moved. It was waiting to be caught, death for the dawn of the coming day. At dawn, little by little, the roofs would be lit. When the storm would have blown over the wheat fields, dawn would be pale red.

'Rodrigo Paestra, Rodrigo Paestra,' Maria called.

Did he want to die? Again the police. Respectful of the people's sleep, they made their rounds without speaking, without calling, sure of themselves. They turned into the swampy streets, on the right, and their footsteps disappeared without echoes. Maria called a bit louder.

'Answer, Rodrigo Paestra. Answer me.'

She was against the iron railing of the balcony. The railing beat. It was Maria's heart. He didn't answer. Hope was getting thinner, became minute, disappeared. She would know at dawn if it was he. But then it would be too late.

'I beg you, Rodrigo Paestra, answer me.'

It wasn't he? Nothing was sure. Except that Maria wanted it.

Someone coughed in the corridor. Moved. Pierre. Yes, Pierre.

Within the next two days, Pierre and Claire would come together. They would devote themselves to this purpose. They would have to find where. What would follow was still unknown, unpredictable, an abyss of time. A length of time not yet known to them, nor to Maria, which was already spreading beyond the storm. Madrid would be its beginning. Tomorrow.

What words should she use? What words?

'Rodrigo Paestra, trust me.'

It was already one in the morning. In two hours Rodrigo Paestra would be trapped like a rat if nothing happened until dawn but the passage of time.

Maria leaning over the balcony was looking at the man. Above him the sky was clear. The rain had to stop now, it had to. It seemed there was some blue, and moons, appearing in the light, endless sky. Around the chimney, nothing, nothing moved. The rain that had already fallen, flowed down, murmuring, from the shape as well as from the roofs. Fire, as well, could burn it. He wasn't going to surrender at dawn. It was certain that he was waiting to be crushed right there by the city's licensed snipers.

Maria, her body bent over the balcony, started to sing. Very softly. A tune from that summer, that he should know, that he should have danced to with his wife on Saturday nights.

Maria stopped singing. She waited. Yes, the sky had cleared. The storm had moved away. Dawn would be beautiful. Pale red. Rodrigo Paestra didn't want to live. The song had brought no change to his shape. To this shape that had become less and less identifiable with anything but him. A shape, without sharp angles, long and supple enough to be human, with this sudden roundness on top, the small surface of the head surging from the mass of the body. A man.

Maria complained for a long time, in the night. It was like dreaming. The shape did not move. It was like dreaming that it did not move from the moment it could be Rodrigo Paestra. To the shape, Maria was complaining about her fate.

The town became abstract like a jail. No longer the smell of wheat. It had rained too much. It was too late. You could no longer talk about the night. But about what then, about what?

'Oh, I beg you, I beg you, Rodrigo Paestra.'

She would have turned him in for a sip of brandy that she didn't go and get. Maybe we can do something, Rodrigo Paestra. Rodrigo Paestra, in two hours it will be light.

She now said words that meant nothing. The difficulty was so great. She called him, called this beastliness of pain.

'Hey there, hey there.'

Without stopping, softly as she would with an animal. Louder and louder. She had closed the balcony windows behind her. Somebody had moaned, then fallen asleep.

Then the police came. There they were. These men had just arrived there, they were probably fresh troops, they were talking. They were talking more than the others. Reinforcements for dawn. There had been a rumor in the hotel that they would come. They talked about the weather. Maria, leaning over the railing of the balcony, could see them, One of them raised his eyes, looked at the sky, didn't see Maria, and said that the storm had definitely vanished from these parts. On the square, in the distance, a light appeared. The truck bringing reinforcements? Or a café that they had had opened that night, so early, because of the murder and so the police could drink and eat there while waiting to surround the town at dawn? They were talking of thirty men, reinforcements that had arrived at the hotel. Rain, from Maria's wet hair, turned into sweat. The patrol had left.

'Hey, hey,' Maria called again as she would call an animal.

The moon disappeared behind a cloud, but it wasn't going to rain again. He didn't answer. It was a quarter past one. She couldn't see him while the cloud moved in the sky. Then the sky freed itself from this cloud. It hadn't rained. There he was again around the chimney, still motionless, unalterable, there for eternity.

'You're an idiot,' Maria shouted.

No one had waked up in the town. Nothing happened. The shape had remained wrapped in its stupidity. In the hotel nothing had moved. But a window lit up in the house next to the hotel. Maria moved back a little. She had to wait. The light went out. No more shouting. The shout had come from the hotel, from a tourist. Therefore people went back to sleep. Again the deadly silence. And in this silence, Maria insulted him again.

'Idiot, idiot,' she now said softly, being careful.

The patrol came again. Maria stopped shouting insults. The patrol passed. They had been talking about their families, about jobs. If Maria had a weapon she would shoot at the shape. So it would be done. The rain which would not dry made Maria'a blouse stick to her shoulders. She must wait for dawn and Rodrigo Paestra's death.

She wasn't calling any more. He knew it. Again she opened the corridor door. She saw, she could see them, the others, sleeping, cruelly separated. She looked at them for a long time. It hadn't been fulfilled yet, this love. What patience, what patience, she didn't leave the balcony. Rodrigo Paestra knew that she was there. He was still breathing, he existed still in this dying night. He was there, in the same place, geographically related to her.

As often happens in summer, a climatic miracle occurred. The fog had disappeared from the horizon and then little by little from the whole sky. The storm dissolved. It no longer existed. Stars, yes stars, in the pre-dawn sky. Such a long time. The stars could make you cry.

Maria wasn't calling any more. She wasn't shouting insults any longer. She hadn't called him ever since she had insulted him. But she stayed on this balcony, her eyes on him, on this shape which fear had reduced to animal idiocy. Her own shape as well.

A quarter of an hour passed, shortening by that much the time that moved toward a green dawn; the dawn which would start by poking its nose into the wheat fields, and then would sweep this roof, opposite her, and would reveal him, and his terror, to the eyes of everyone. No, Maria wasn't calling any more. Time was getting old, buried. She wasn't going to call any more. Never again.

The night moved at a dizzy speed, without ever halting in its course.

Without events acting as relays. None but the bitter duration of failure. Maria recognized it.

There was one chance left. If he could see, through his shroud, that she was still there, at her post, waiting for him. And if, in his turn, he thought he should display a last act of kindness, and signal to her. One chance that he should remember that time was passing while she was waiting uncomfortably, on this balcony, where perhaps she would stay until dawn. One chance that, because of her, he should step for a short instant out of the artlessness of despair, that he should remember certain general principles of human behavior, of war, of flight, of hatred. That he should remember the pale red dawn moving over his land; the ordinary reasons for living, in the long run, until the end, even when these reasons have disappeared.

A blue light now fell from the sky. It wasn't possible that he didn't see this woman's shape leaning toward him—as no other ever had—on the hotel balcony. Even if he wanted to die, even if he wanted this particular fate, he could answer her one last time.

Again the policemen of hell. They went by. Then there was silence. Behind Maria, the blue sky lit up the hallway where Claire and Pierre were sleeping, apart. An indescribable difference brought on by sleep, was keeping them apart for a few more hours. Tomorrow, their love would be fulfilled, unparalleled, screaming, in the hotel, in Madrid. Oh, Claire. You.

Did he lose hope of seeing her again while she had turned?

Something had emerged from the black shroud. Something white. A face? or a hand?

It was he, Rodrigo Paestra.

They confronted each other. It was a face.

The renewal of time asserted itself. They were face to face and looked at each other.

Suddenly, in the street, below, the police went by, already in the talkative, happy mood of the approaching killing.

Maria had fallen prey to happiness. They became bolder. While the police were passing by they kept looking at each other. The waiting finally burst open, released. From every corner of the sky, from all the streets and from those who were lying there. Just from the sky Maria would have guessed that this was Rodrigo Paestra. It was now ten to two. An hour and a half before his death, Rodrigo Paestra had accepted to see her.

Maria raised her hand to say hello. She waited. A slow, slow hand came out of the shroud, rose and also made the gesture, of mutual understanding. Then both of the hands fell down.

At last, the horizon was completely cleared by the storm. Like a blade it was cutting the wheat fields. A warm wind rose and began to dry the streets. The weather was beautiful, just as it would be beautiful during the day. The night was still whole. Perhaps solutions could be found to the problems of conscience. Perhaps.

Serenely Maria raised her hand, again. He answered, again. Oh, how marvellous. She raised her hand to tell him that he must wait. Wait, her hand was saying. Did he understand? He did. His head had completely emerged from the black shroud, as white as snow. They were eleven yards away from each other. Did Rodrigo Paestra understand that she wanted to help him? He had understood. Maria started again, patiently, reasonably. Wait, wait Rodrigo Paestra. Wait a little longer, I'm going down, I'm coming to you. Who knows, Rodrigo Paestra?

The patrol arrived. This time Maria entered the corridor. The head too had heard and had covered itself again with the shroud. But they couldn't see anything from down below. The idea would never occur to them. Again they spoke about their work, about their low pay, of how hard it is to be a policeman. Like the previous patrol. Just wait. They were gone.

On its own the head had again come out of the shroud, and looked toward the balcony where this woman was waiting. Again she signalled that he should wait. The head nodded. Yes, he had understood that he should wait, that she was going down, coming to him.

Everyone in the corridor was sleeping. Maria took off her shoes to walk around the sleeping bodies. Her little girl was there, in a position of blissful tranquility, lying on her back. There was Claire too, asleep. And Pierre. Two steps away from her, wanted by Claire but unaware. Claire, this beautiful fruit of the slow degradation of their love.

Maria had gone beyond the corridor. She was holding her

shoes in her hand. Through the skylight the brightness of the sky shone on the tables and made the tablecloths look blue, as well as the air. The tables were half cleared. Bodies were lying on the benches: the waiters had probably given their rooms to the tourists. The whole staff was still asleep.

Maria again crossed this area of sleep. It was summer. The staff was exhausted. The back doors must have been left open. It had been a crime of passion, just a one-time murderer. Why would they have locked the doors? On the right there was the manager's office, where Claire and Pierre, last night, had at last been alone, without her, for a long time. The office was dark. Maria looked through the glass pane. Nobody was sleeping there. If Maria wanted to leave by this side of the hotel, she would have to cross a short glass-enclosed passage adjoining the corridor.

The door to this passage was locked.

Maria tried again. Sweat covered her face. The door was locked. There was no other exit to the street besides the stairs leading from this passage. The only other way of leaving was through the servants' hall.

Maria walked back through the dining room. Toward the doors in the rear. One of them was open. Leading to the kitchen. First there was a pantry. Then a long, immense kitchen. Everything was in complete disorder. This was noticeable because a big bay window let in more light there than in the dining room. Could it be dawn? It was impossible that it was dawn. Maria looked through the bay window. It was just a lamp in the courtyard where the cars were parked. The heat from the ovens could still be felt, sticky, heavy, nauseating.

There in the kitchen, near the exit, a young man was sleeping on a camp bed.

A door had been left open in the back, where the walls

narrowed, between the bay window and a cupboard. Maria pulled it toward her. The young man turned over and groaned. Then he was quiet and Maria opened the door. The door opened on a spiral staircase. Had Rodrigo Paestra kept on hoping? The stairs were made of wood. They creaked under Maria's footsteps. It was as hot there as during the day. Sweat was running down from Maria's hair. Two floors. The staircase went on for two floors and was completely dark.

The glazed door was unlocked. It opened onto the garage, and the courtyard within the hotel. Maria hadn't thought of that. But probably there was a watchman there too. He couldn't have heard Maria calling Rodrigo Paestra. The courtyard was far from the street. Perhaps there was no one there. And in that case the gate would be locked. Maria looked at her watch. It was five past two. Pierre had driven the car into the garage. Maria didn't know where it was. She went out. The courtyard seemed sandy, white. The cars were in the back, many of them under a shed, in the dark.

Maria was near the door. She closed it. The door made a long, shrill sound, but apparently no one heard it. No one? Wait. No, apparently no one had heard the door complain.

Between this door and the shed, the courtyard was empty, wide and empty. She had to cross this space. A quarter moon lit up the courtyard. In the middle of this courtyard, the shadow of a roof. The roof of the last house in the town, before the wheat fields. Yes, the light which shone in the kitchen through the bay window came from a storm lamp hanging from the shed, very high, and dancing in the light night wind. The cars were shining. There probably was a reliable watchman. But where?

Just as Maria decided to cross the courtyard, the police went by in the street behind the courtyard gate. They were coming straight from the other street, the one where Rodrigo Paestra was. Maria recognized their soft footsteps in the mud of the street: the last one before the wheat fields. They were still talking. She looked at her watch. And noticed that thirteen minutes had gone by since she had left the balcony, in other words, since the previous patrol. She had put her shoes back on before opening the glazed door at the bottom of the staircase. She went on through the courtyard. And she reached the shed. Already the patrol was in the distance.

It was probably best to make a noise. There was the black Rover. Maria opened the door. Then she waited. A familiar perfume came out of the car: Claire's perfume. Maria noisily slammed the door shut.

Someone coughed in the shed. Then someone asked what was the matter. Maria opened the door again, left it open, and walked toward the voice.

The man hadn't moved. He had sat up on his camp bed, against the wall, in the corner of the shed that was farthest away from the gate.

'I'm a guest at the hotel,' Maria said. 'I was looking for the little black Rover.'

She took out her cigarettes from her skirt pocket. She offered him one, lit it for him. He was about thirty. Very casually he took the cigarette. He probably had been asleep. He was covered with the same brown blanket as Rodrigo Paestra.

'You're already leaving for Madrid?'

He was surprised. Maria pointed to the sky.

'No,' she said. 'The weather is so nice. I couldn't sleep in the corridor. I'm going for a ride.'

The man got up completely. He stood in front of her. She smiled at him. There were still men who would look at her. Both of them were smoking and could see each other in the light of their cigarettes.

'I disturbed you, I'm sorry. But it's because of the gate.'

'It doesn't matter. It's not locked. It's the same every summer.'

He pulled himself together. Spoke about the weather, about the coolness which, every night, comes about that same time.

'You should go back to sleep,' Maria said. 'I'll close the gate.'

He lay down on his bed, went on looking at her. And as she moved away, all of a sudden he became bolder.

'You're going for a ride, like that, alone? I could come along if you want. If you don't take too long.' He laughed.

Maria also laughed. She could hear her laughter in the empty courtyard. The man didn't insist.

Maria took her time. She lowered the top, fastened it. The man heard her. He cried out softly, already half asleep.

'The storm is over,' he said. 'Tomorrow will be beautiful.'

'Thanks,' Maria said.

She got into the Rover, backed up, and drove to the gate without headlights. She idled. She had to wait for the next patrol which was due in two minutes. She could see the time.

There it came. The patrol stopped in front of the gate, was silent, and moved on. Tourists, they must have thought, leaving for Madrid at night to take advantage of the cool temperature.

When Maria opened the gate, the patrol had vanished. She had to get out of the Rover again, but this time, very fast. Maria got out, then closed the gate. Still this heat in her hair. Why be so scared? Why?

Once, the surface of a lake had been as calm as this night. The weather was sunny. Maria remembered the reflection of the sun on the lake and, suddenly, from the boat, through the calm water, you could see the depth of the lake shining also. The water was clear. Shapes appeared. Normal shapes, but raped by the sun.

Pierre was in the boat with Maria.

Maria got back into the Rover. The watchman hadn't followed her. She looked at her watch. Dawn would be there in less than an hour and a half. Maria took the brandy bottle and drank. A long, enormous gulp. It burned so much that she had to close her eyes with pleasure.

V

She had to enter the street the patrol had just left. Their paths went in different directions at the end of that street. They had gone to the right, taking the last street in the town, the one along the wheat fields. She would move toward the main square, driving parallel to the front of the hotel. From the balcony she had been able to see clearly the layout of the town. It was possible. Two perpendicular streets bound Rodrigo Paestra's roof.

She started very slowly, up to the turn, a few yards from the gate. Then she had to speed up. Only ten minutes left before the next patrol. Unless her calculations were wrong. If they were, it was probable that Maria would give Rodrigo Paestra to the town police two hours before dawn.

The Rover was making a dull noise, but it drowned out the sound of the patrol's footsteps, dimmed by the mud. Still, she had to move forward. She reached the corner of the two streets from which you could see their whole length. They were still deserted. In just an hour people would be getting up to go to the fields. But these people were still asleep.

The noise of the engine didn't wake anyone at that time of night.

Maria didn't get out of the Rover. Could he hear her? She sang softly.

From where she was, she couldn't see him. She could only see the sky and, in the sky, the clearly outlined mass of the chimney. The section of the roof on Maria's side was plunged in the darkness of night.

She went on singing the song she had been singing earlier, when she was losing hope that he was there. And she went on singing as she got out of the Rover. She opened the back door, put away the numerous objects Judith always picked up wherever they stopped and then left behind on the back seat. There were also newspapers. One of Pierre's jacket. Claire's scarf, even her own scarf, there. Newspapers, more newspapers.

There were about eight minutes left before the next patrol.

A shadow broke up the neat angle of the roofs against the clear sky. It was he. He had gone around the chimney. Maria kept singing. Her voice clutched at her throat. You can always sing. She couldn't stop singing once she had started. He was there.

The warm wind was again blowing all over. It made the palm trees on the square cry out. It alone was moving through the deserted streets.

He had gone around the chimney, still wrapped in the black shroud in which she had seen him earlier. He was down on all fours. He had become a mass more shapeless than before, monstrously inapt. Ugly. He crawled over the tiles while Maria sang.

Probably six more minutes before the police would come by.

He must have been barefoot. He made no noise except a sound like the wind when, in its course, it blows against trees, houses, street corners.

He was slow. Did he know there was so little time left? Did he know? His legs, stiff after such a long wait, were clumsy. His face was exposed and his whole body, enormous, on the ridge of the roof, was spread out like an animal in a butcher's stall. With both hands, while singing, Maria signalled him to roll over, down the slope of the roof. And then she pointed to the Rover. Showing him that he would, at the end of his fall, land in the

Rover. She sang faster, still faster, more and more softly. The wall was blind for twenty yards on this side of the town. Nobody could hear Maria.

He was doing it. He got ready to do it, his legs raised at first and then falling down, and he was doing it. Again his face had disappeared in the black shroud and a bundle of rags worn by time, its color nondescript like soot, moved toward Maria.

Still no one in the streets. He now rolled cleverly, trying not to make the tiles of the roof squeak under him. Maria made more noise with the engine. She was still singing, not realizing that she was singing for nothing. He was there, he was coming, he was getting there. She sang.

He had covered a yard. She was still singing, still the same song. Very softly. Another yard covered. He had covered three yards. In the street, there still was no one, not even the watchman who must have gone back to sleep.

A patrol should have left the square and gone northward, in the direction of the Hotel Principal. That was their route. Voices were coming from there, loud at first, then becoming dimmer. There were probably four minutes left before these voices would burst out at the end of the street alongside the hotel. Rodrigo Paestra had to cover one more yard to reach Maria.

Just as she thought her calculations were wrong because, before the four minutes were up, steps were already echoing that would turn up in the street alongside the hotel balconies, just as she thought that she wasn't hearing right, that it was impossible, Rodrigo Paestra must have thought so too because he covered the one yard that was left and fell into the Rover, rolling more quickly, flexible, his body like a spring. He had hurled himself forward. He had fallen into the Rover. A bundle of soft, black laundry had fallen into the Rover.

That was it. Just as Maria started, the patrol must have turned into the street. He had fallen on the seat. And he must have rolled onto the floor. Nothing moved. And yet he was there, close to her, on the floor, wrapped in his blanket.

A window lit up. Someone shouted.

Whistles rang out through the town, taking turns endlessly. Maria was approaching the main square. When he had fallen from the roof, the gutter had broken under his weight and had made a catastrophic noise, an obscene racket. One window lit up? Yes. Two, three windows lit up. Things crying out. Doors of the night.

Was it the warm wind that had just risen? Was it Rodrigo Paestra? The whistling went on. The patrol on the hotel street had sounded the alarm. But it hadn't seen the Rover taking off fifty yards away, in another street. The wind had carried its noise toward the fields. Those squares of light over the countryside were windows. The electricity still wasn't working and the windows were slow to light up. After making a turn, Maria was about a hundred yards from where the police must have been searching the roofs.

A patrol was coming toward her on the double. She stopped. The patrol slowed down in front of her, looked at the empty car and went on. It stopped further on, under a window, and called out. No one answered. It went on to the end of the street.

She had to go more slowly. Why would the Rover have been where the gutter was still vibrating, broken, in the wind? The black Rover belonged to a guest at the hotel, a guest who was free, alone, disturbed by this difficult night. What should Maria be afraid of?

Was she no longer afraid? Her fear had practically disappeared. It had left only a fresh, just matured, flowering memory of what it had been. Less than a minute had gone by. Fear became as inconceivable as the heart's jumbled adolescence.

Maria had to make up her mind to cross the square. She did it. She knew now that behind her nothing could be seen of Rodrigo Paestra. The seat was empty. It was impossible to leave the town without crossing the square, where the two roads leading out of the town started, one going to Madrid, the other to Barcelona and France.

At that time of night, only one car, it had to start at some point, was driving toward Madrid. The first tourist, people would say.

About twenty policemen were standing opposite the café where Maria had had her manzanillas the day before. They were listening to the whistles, were answering, waiting for orders to move on. One of them stopped Maria.

'Where are you going?'

He looked at the empty car, was reassured, smiled at her.

'I'm staying at the hotel. We didn't get a room and I can't sleep,' she added, 'with all the noise you're making. I'm going for a ride. What's going on?'

Did he believe her? Yes, he looked at her carefully, then glanced away from her and pointed toward the hotel, in the distance. He explained: 'They must have found Rodrigo Paestra on a roof, but I am not sure.'

Maria turned around. Spotlights swept the rooftops just before the hotel. The policeman said nothing else.

She started off slowly. The road to Madrid was right opposite her. You had to turn around a clump of palmettos. She remembered very clearly that it was there, the road to Madrid. There couldn't be any doubt.

The engine of the car worked smoothly. Claire's black Rover took off, then moved in the direction Maria wanted, toward

Madrid. Maria was at the wheel and, carefully and methodically, she drove around the square. The whistling went on in the part of town where the gutter was still yelping. A jackal. The young policeman, puzzled and smiling, watched Maria drive away. She was driving around him, around the square. Was she smiling at him? She would never know. She drove into the main street, the westward extension of the hotel street. She didn't look whether any balconies, adjacent to corridors she knew, were lit up.

It was the road to Madrid. The biggest road in Spain. Straight ahead, monumental.

True, this was still the town. One patrol, two patrols, empty-handed, saw and looked at the black Rover with foreign license plates which was moving toward Madrid so early in the day. But the recent storm, and this sudden youthfulness of the night, made several of them smile.

One called out to the woman who was driving alone.

There were two garages. And then some kind of a shop, quite large, and isolated. And then very small houses. Maria no longer knew what time it was. It was just any time before dawn. But dawn wasn't there yet. It needed its usual amount of time to get there. It wasn't there yet.

After the houses, the shacks, there were the wheat fields. And nothing but wheat under the blue light. Blue was the wheat. It went on and on. Maria was driving slowly, but moving ahead. At some point in the night, at a turn, she saw a sign, clearly lit up by her headlights, and noticed that she was eight miles out of the town she had just left, Rodrigo Paestra's town.

She went on, up to a dirt road that looked dark next to the light wheat field. She turned into it, went on for about a third of a mile, and stopped. On both sides of this road there was the same wheat as before, and the night was just as full. There was no village in sight. And there was total silence as soon as Maria turned off the engine.

When Maria turned around, Rodrigo Paestra was getting out of his shroud.

He sat down on the back seat and looked around him. His face looked blurred in the blue light of the night.

If there were birds in this plain, they were probably still sleeping in the sodden clay, between the blades of wheat.

Maria took some cigarettes out of her pocket. She pulled one out and handed it to him. He pounced on it and when she lit it for him she noticed that Rodrigo Paestra was shivering with cold. He smoked the cigarette with both hands so as not to let it fall. It is cold in Spain, on stormy nights, an hour before dawn.

He was smoking.

He hadn't looked at this woman.

But she was looking at him. His name is Rodrigo Paestra. While looking at the wheat, she could see him.

His hair was glued to his scalp. His clothes were stuck to his body as if he had drowned. He probably was tall and robust. Was he about thirty? He was still smoking. What was he looking at? The cigarette. Most likely, as he looked at it, his eyes were black.

Maria unfolded the blanket next to her and held it out to him. He took it and put it on the back seat. He hadn't understood. He was smoking again. Then he looked at both sides of the car. He was the first to speak.

'Where are we?'

'The road to Madrid.'

He didn't say anything else. Maria didn't either. She turned again, facing the windshield. They were both smoking. He finished first. She gave him another one. He was still shaking. In the light of the match, his expression was vacant, reduced to his concentrating on not shaking.

'Where do you want to go?' Maria asked.

He didn't answer immediately. He was probably looking at her for the first time, from very far away, without caring. Anyway, this was a glance from him. Maria didn't see his eyes, but she saw his glance as clearly as in broad daylight.

'I don't know,' Rodrigo Paestra said.

Again Maria turned to the front. Then, not being able to bear it, she turned back to face him. She intensely wanted to look at him. The haggard expression he had had when he had looked at her had vanished. There were only his eyes now. And, over his eyes, the eyelids opening automatically whenever he raised his cigarette to his mouth. Nothing. Rodrigo Paestra had no strength left except to smoke. Why had he followed Maria this far? Probably just to be nice, a last polite gesture. Someone calls you and you answer. What was Rodrigo Paestra now? Maria devoured him with her eyes, devoured with her eyes this living prodigy, this black flower which had bloomed that night in the licentiousness of love.

He had split her head open with one shot of his gun. And his love was resting, in an improvised morgue in the town hall, dead at nineteen, still naked, wrapped in a brown blanket, identical with the one he had wrapped around himself on the roof. As for him, the other one, the bullet went through his heart. They were separated.

'What time is it?' Rodrigo Paestra asked.

Maria showed him her watch, but he didn't look at it.

'A little after two thirty.'

His eyes looked at the wheat fields again. He was resting against the back seat and it seemed to Maria that she had heard a man sigh in the silence. Then the silence came back. And also the slow passing of time before dawn. Interminable.

It was cold. Had the warm wind blowing on the town before really existed? A gust that had followed the storm and had disappeared. The swelling, ripe wheat, tortured by the showers of the preceding day, remained motionless.

The cold that suddenly surged from the motionless air bit their eyes and their shoulders.

Rodrigo Paestra must have fallen asleep. His head was resting on the back of the seat. And his mouth was slightly open. He was sleeping.

Something changed in the air they were breathing, a pale light blew over the fields. For how long? For how long had he been sleeping? An onslaught began somewhere on the horizon, colorless, uneven, impossible to define. An onslaught began somewhere in her head and in her body a growing uneasiness, unrelated to the memory of any other, searching for its identity. And yet, and yet, the sky was clear and blue if you wanted it that way. It still was. Of course this was only an accidental light, the perfect illusion of a change of mood, happening through a sudden complaisance, coming from far away, from various strains and from the strain of that night. Perhaps?

No. It was dawn.

He was sleeping. Sleeping.

There still wasn't any specific color in the dawn.

Rodrigo Paestra was dreaming. He was so deeply asleep he could dream. Maria had her chin on the back of the seat, and was watching him. Sometimes the sky too, but always him. Very attentively. That is to say she was watching Rodrigo Paestra. Yes, there he was, sleeping soundly, flying over all his troubles with the wings of a bird. You could see it. He was carried well above his troubles, in spite of his new weight, and he consented unconsciously.

Maria was deprived of Rodrigo Paestra's perfectly empty glance while he was sleeping.

He had just smiled in his sleep. Above his slightly open mouth, she could swear that a smile had taken shape, a quivering smile, unmistakably like a smile of life and joy. Other words were banished from dawn.

Between his thighs, next to his sex, there was the shape of his gun. His blanket was on the floor. The car blanket next to him. It was useless to cover him. Anyway she wanted to see all of him and forever. She could see him clearly. And that his sleep was sound, and good.

She had to avoid looking up at the sky.

It wasn't worth it. Dawn was rising upon him. The livid light had covered his whole body, little by little. His body had clear, obvious proportions. He again had a name: Rodrigo Paestra.

The time had come now when he would have been caught like a rat.

Maria spread out, a little like him, on the front seat, and she watched dawn move over him.

Too late, the memory of a child came back to her. She pushed it away. While he was still dreaming just as he had dreamed the day before.

She still had to wait. And later, she would have to call him.

Then he became pink. A steady weariness blew over the countryside and over Maria. Peacefully, the sky took on color. She still had some time. A car going to Madrid drove by on the highway. Maria furtively looked at the sky, on the other side. The pink color that was on him did come from the sky. They had reached the time of the first departures. The car going to

Madrid undoubtedly had come from the hotel. In one of the still dark corridors, stretching painfully after a bad night, Claire must have greeted the day that was rising on their love. And then, she fell asleep again.

He was sleeping. Maria got up and took the brandy out of the door pocket. Because of her empty stomach, the liquor came up in her throat, burning and familiar, with a feeling of nausea that woke her up. The sun. There was the sun on the horizon. All at once it was less cold. Her eyes hurt. He had been sleeping for nearly an hour. The sun swept over his body, entered his slightly open mouth, and his clothes began to let off a cloud of steam that looked like smoke. His hair let off the same smoke. Very tenuous smoke of an abandoned fire. He still couldn't feel the light. His eyes barely trembled. But his eyelids sealed in his sleep. He no longer smiled.

Wouldn't it be better to call him immediately, as soon as possible, so it would be all over?

Again Maria took the brandy, drank, put it back in the door pocket. She was still waiting. She hadn't done it yet. She still hadn't called Rodrigo Paestra.

And yet, it would be best if that moment in Maria's life, when Rodrigo Paestra would wake up in the Rover with this stranger near him in the wheat road, would be over as fast as possible. His memory would come back—predictably—a few seconds after he woke up. He would remain disconcerted just long enough to understand that he had been dreaming. Maria would have to decide to wake Rodrigo Paestra.

The sun was half off the horizon. Two cars, six cars went by on their way to Madrid. Again Maria took the brandy, took another gulp. This time she felt so nauseous she had to close her eyes. Then, afterwards, she began to call softly.

'Rodrigo Paestra.'

He hadn't heard. His eyes trembled then sealed up still tighter. She was still nauseous from the brandy. She felt like vomiting. Maria closed her eyes so she wouldn't have to vomit and to look at him.

'Rodrigo Paestra.'

She fumbled about to replace the brandy in the pocket and she let her head sink back onto the seat.

'Rodrigo Paestra.'

Something must have moved in the back. Then nothing happened. He didn't wake up. Maria sat up and, this time, looked at him.

'Rodrigo Paestra.'

His eyes had blinked. Maria, her nausea gone, started again. She took the brandy, drank some more. This gulp was bigger than the last one. Was she going to faint? No. It just prevents you from seeing, prevents you from speaking calmly, only lets you scream.

'Rodrigo Paestra, Rodrigo Paestra.'

Again Maria buried her head in the back of the front seat.

It must have happened. This must have been his waking. A soft cry, a long moan had come from the back of the car.

When Maria turned he was already past the first moments of waking. He was sitting up on the seat and with rheumy, bloodshot eyes was looking at the wheat fields, his land of wheat fields. Was he surprised? Yes, he was still surprised, but just a little. Then his eyes wandered from the wheat fields. He was sitting up straight now, but no longer looking at anything. He remembered everything.

'I have to get back to the hotel.'

He was silent. Maria handed him a cigarette. He didn't see it. She was holding the cigarette out to him, but he still didn't see it.

He started to look at Maria. When she had told him that she would have to get back to the hotel, he had grabbed his brown blanket and his gesture had stopped abruptly. He had discovered Maria's existence. It was probably by seeing her that he had remembered.

She was trying not to breathe too deeply so as not to vomit. The last gulp of brandy at daybreak, probably, coming up in her throat like a sob that you have to keep holding in.

He was looking at her, looking at her, looking at her. An empty stare, inconceivably disinterested. What else did he notice looking at Maria? From what surprise, exactly, was he returning when he saw Maria? Had he noticed just then that he could expect nothing more from Maria, from Maria or anyone else? That with this dawn a new certainty was exposed which night had kept hidden?

'I have a child at the hotel,' she said, 'that's why I have to get back.'

It was over. His eyes moved away from her. Again she held out to him the cigarette she had kept in her hand; he took it, and she lit it for him. He picked up the brown blanket from the seat.

'Listen,' Maria said.

Perhaps he hadn't heard. She had spoken very softly. He had opened the door, he had got out, and was now standing next to the car.

'Listen,' Maria repeated. 'The border isn't very far. We can try.'

He was standing in the dirt road and again he looked at his land of wheat fields all around him. And then he came back, he remembered, he closed the door. He remembered. In the same way, during the night, he had been willing to answer when his name was called. He had been gracious then. The sun was glaring and forced him to squint.

'We can try,' Maria repeated.

He shook his head, as if to refuse, very slowly, he had no opinion.

'At noon,' Maria said. 'At noon I'll be here, I'll be back. At noon.'

'Noon,' Rodrigo Paestra said after her.

With her fingers, she pointed to the sun and opened her hands wide toward him.

'Noon, noon,' she kept saying.

He nodded, he had understood. Then he turned around and looked for a spot where he could go, where he could settle down, in this wide, in this free expanse of wheat. The sun was completely above the horizon, and was hitting him full blast, his shadow was perfect, a long shadow on the wheat.

He could have found a spot to go to, where he could rest. He went off on the dirt road. Alongside of him, his blanket, which he held in his hand, was dragging. He was barefoot in his rope sandals. He had no jacket, only a dark blue shirt like all the men in his village.

He walked on the road, stopped, hesitated it seemed, then walked into the wheat field, about twenty yards from the Rover, and just dropped as if struck by lightning. Maria waited. He didn't get up.

When she got back on the highway, away from the humid clay of the wheat fields, it was already hot. It would get hotter still, until noon, inevitably, and would stay that way all day until sundown. She knew that.

With the sun on her neck, her nausea came back, throbbing. Maria fought off sleep, her hands gripping the steering wheel. Whenever she felt she had won, she would be engulfed again. However, she was getting closer to the hotel.

She passed the shop.

Then the garages.

There were already a few peasants. But very few cars going toward Madrid.

Just when Maria thought she could no longer fight off sleep, the memory of Judith got her to the outskirts of the town, then to the town. And then, the square.

The police were still there. The ones from the night must have been sleeping. These men, in broad daylight, looked discouraged. They were yawning. Their feet were muddy, their clothes crumpled, but they were still whistling throughout the town. In front of the town hall, wearily, they kept watch over the two victims of the day before.

The hotel gate was open. The young watchman had been replaced by an old man. There was room in the shed. The cars had been coming from the hotel. Maria left through the gate, took the street around the hotel where, during the night, she had met Rodrigo Paestra. She had some trouble walking because she had had so much brandy, but the street was still deserted and nobody saw her.

There was room in the corridor. Her nausea was so strong that she first had to lie down next to her child to gather enough courage to look around. The brown blanket was warm from Judith's body. Somebody had closed the doors leading to the balcony, so that the hall was still cool and quiet. And restful. Judith turned over, still happily sleeping. Maria rested.

They were still there, both of them. They were still sleeping. Two hours had gone by since she had left the corridor. It was very early. Four in the morning. In their sleep, they had moved closer to each other, probably without realizing it. Pierre had Claire's surrendered ankle against his cheek. His mouth was brushing against it. Claire's ankle was resting on Pierre's open hand. If he closed his hand, that woman's ankle would be completely contained in it. Maria kept looking, but it didn't happen. They were sleeping like logs.

VI

'M<small>ARIA</small>.'

Maria woke up. Pierre was calling her. He was amused by such sleepiness. He was leaning against the wall and looking at her.

'It's ten o'clock,' he apologized. 'Everybody has left.'

'Judith?'

'She's playing in the courtyard. She's all right.'

The corridor around Maria was empty. The balcony window was open and the sun was shining obliquely into the corridor. It shone on the red, glaring ground, like the day before, and was reflected on Pierre's face. Maria felt nauseous again. She got up and then lay down again.

'One more minute, and I'll get up.'

At the end of the corridor, waiters were already going back and forth carrying trays of cool drinks. The bedroom doors were open. Women were singing while they made the beds. And the heat was there, already.

'I told them to let you sleep,' Pierre said. 'But in a few minutes the sun would have been shining on you.'

He looked at her insistently. She had taken a cigarette, she tried to smoke it, and threw it away. She smiled at Pierre through her nausea.

'It's hard for me, in the morning,' she said. 'But I'm going to get up.'

'Do you want me to stay?'

'Wait for me in the dining room. When alcoholics wake up they should be alone.'

They both smiled. Pierre left. Maria called him back.

'Claire, where is she?' Maria asked.

'With the child, downstairs.'

When she managed to get up and reach the dining room, the coffee pot was steaming on Pierre's table. Pierre knew what Maria needed on those mornings. He let her drink, drink all the coffee, without speaking. Then stretch, stretch, run her hands through her hair, and finally smoke.

'I feel better now,' she said.

Except for two other tables, they were alone in the dining room, which was once more perfectly neat and orderly. The tables, all white, were already set for lunch. A large, brownish-gray canvas had been hung under the skylight that had been blue during the night, and was filtering the sun. Here the heat was bearable.

'You drank last night, Maria,' Pierre stated.

She moved her hand over her face. It was through her hands on her face that she could feel, that she knew she had been beautiful, but had started to be less so. It was from the way in which she moved her hands on her face, without caution, that she knew she had accepted defeat forever. She didn't answer Pierre.

'It's a question of will power, again,' Pierre went on. 'You could drink less, at night at least.'

Maria gulped down the rest of her coffee.

'Oh, that's all right,' she said. 'One unpleasant hour in the morning, and then it's over.'

'I looked for you last night. The car wasn't there. The watchman told me that you had gone for a ride. I understood.'

He straightened up a little, and this time he stroked her hair.

'Maria, Maria.'

She didn't smile at him. For a moment he left his hand on her hair, and then took it away. He knew why Maria hadn't smiled.

'I'll take a shower,' she said, 'and then, if you want, we can leave.'

There was Claire, holding Judith by the hand. They walked in. Claire was dressed in blue. She looked at Pierre first as she came in. From the moment she came in, her desire for Pierre was noticeable; it accompanied her like a shadow. It seemed as if she were shouting. But she was talking to Maria.

'You went off last night?'

Maria looked for an answer, in vain. She found herself exposed to Claire's gaze.

'They woke us up last night,' Claire went on. 'They thought they had found Rodrigo Paestra. Everybody was at the windows. What confusion! And we kept looking for you.'

What did they do last night when they noticed she was no longer there? Once they noticed that she wasn't coming back, that the Rover wasn't coming, after the children had fallen asleep again, after the hotel had calmed down, first the corridor, and then little by little the whole hotel? Did they . . .?

'I was with the police,' Maria said. 'I drank manzanillas with the police. In the same café as yesterday.'

Claire laughed. Pierre also laughed, but not as much as Claire. Claire kept sighing, 'Maria, Oh, Maria, Maria.'

They loved her. Claire's laughter was not quite the same as usual. It was not impossible that it should have happened. That they should have been on the lookout for the Rover, leaning against each other, in each other's arms while waiting for her in the darkness of the corridor. Who could tell?

'Judith,' Maria said.

She held her at arms length and looked at her. A little girl who had slept well during the night. Blue eyes. The rings of fear had vanished from under her eyes. Maria pushed her away, away from her. He probably was in the wheat fields. He was sleeping. The shade from the stalks was frail and he had begun to feel too warm. Whom would you save, in the end, if you saved Rodrigo Paestra?

'She gobbled up a big breakfast this morning,' Claire said. 'A cool night and she starts gobbling.'

Judith had come back to Maria. Maria took her, looked at her again, then let her go, nearly knocking her over. Judith was used to it. She let her mother look at her, then push her about to her heart's content, then she went off and walked around the dining room, singing.

'We shouldn't get to Madrid too late,' Claire said. 'Before night if possible. To get rooms.'

Maria remembered, and left for the office. The bathrooms were available. The shower felt good. Some time went by like that. Maria looked at her naked body, all by itself. What would you save, in the end, if you took Rodrigo Paestra to France? He was asleep in an ocean of wheat. Water ran benevolently down her breasts and her stomach. Maria waited for time to go by, like the water, inexhaustibly. Of course, the findings would show extenuating circumstances. They would take into account Rodrigo Paestra's being jealous of Perez. What more could be done for Rodrigo Paestra than to take into consideration this jealousy which made him kill?

In the dining room only Claire was left waiting for Maria.

'Pierre went to pay the bill,' she said. 'And then we'll go.'

'How beautiful you are,' Maria said. 'Claire, you are so, so beautiful.'

Claire lowered her eyes. She tried not to, and then she said it. 'After they had looked for this poor man, just a short time after, cars started to leave. Impossible to go back to sleep. I mean it was difficult. But then,'

'What time was it?'

'It was still night, I don't know exactly. There was whistling all over town. There was a noise of falling tiles, over there, the wind I suppose. They really got into a state. We didn't fall asleep again until late.'

'That late?'

'I think the sun was rising. Yes. Lying down, we could see the sky. We talked, Pierre and I, yes I think we talked until dawn.'

Claire waited. Maria didn't insist. Judith came back. Claire loved Judith, Pierre's child.

'There will never be another storm,' Claire told Judith. 'You mustn't be afraid.'

'Never?'

They promised. She went back to her exploration of the hotel corridors. Pierre came back. He was ready, he said. He had filled in the hotel forms. He apologized for making them wait. And then he was silent. Claire wasn't looking at him this morning. She lowered her eyes while smoking. They must not have been together, even before dawn, in the darkness of the corridors. Maria was mistaken. If they no longer looked at each other as they had the day before, if they avoided doing so, it was because they had confessed their love to each other, whispering, when the sky seemed red over the wheat fields and when the memory of Maria, poignant, loathsome because of the very strength of their new love, came back to them with the dawn. What were they to do with Maria?

'We still want to see San Andrea,' Pierre said. 'Three Goyas. If only not to be sorry later.'

Some guests came in. Women. Pierre didn't look any more.

'I'm tired,' Maria said. 'I'll wait for you.'

'What did you drink?' Claire asked.

'The brandy. I'll wait for you in the car. I'll feel better by noon.'

They exchanged looks. They must have talked about that, that also last night, and once more hoped she would change her ways. And at the same time wished, and were satisfied, that she would stay busy away from them, but not with her new unhappiness.

They went down. The pleasant coolness from her shower disappeared and when Maria recognized the courtyard, her weariness came back, like a spell. It would take enormous strength to pull Rodrigo Paestra from his bed of wheat. She would have to tell them, thwarting their dawning desire, giving up Madrid where, at night, their love was to be fulfilled. Maria watched them load the car—she didn't help—and they laughed at having to do this small job which would have made Maria groan.

She sat in front, next to Pierre. In the back, without asking any questions, Claire folded the blanket that was lying on the seat. Maria saw her doing this but gave her no explanation. They made the trip through the city that Maria had made at night. It was eleven. Four policemen were still on guard in the square, exhausted, like Maria, from their night of searching. The church of San Andrea was on the square. As well as the town hall. The murdered bodies must still be there. Guarded.

'They didn't get him,' Pierre said. He parked the car in the shade, opposite the café that had stayed open during the night. Again a church. Again three Goyas. Again a vacation. Why save Rodrigo Paestra, and from what? How would Rodrigo Paestra wake up this time, from what bad sleep? Pull him out of the wheat, get him into the car, while Claire's fierce desire was being thwarted. It was ten past eleven.

'Really,' Maria said, 'I'm so tired, I'm going to stay here.'

Claire got out, followed by Judith. Pierre left the door open and waited for Maria.

'Ten minutes,' he said, 'come on, Maria, come along.'

She didn't want to. He closed the door. The three of them walked over to San Andrea. They went in. Maria could no longer see them.

Noon would come and Rodrigo Paestra would understand that he had been abandoned. Maria closed her eyes for a moment. Did she remember? Yes. She remembered his eyes looking at the wheat fields without recognizing them, and also his eyes when he woke up, in the sun. When she opened her eyes two children were there, fascinated by the Rover. They weren't coming back. They must have seen something else, not only the Goyas, some primitive perhaps. Holding hands they were looking, together, at other landscapes. In the distance valleys could be seen through open windows, and woods, a village, a herd. Woods in the twilight with charming angels, herds, a smoking village on a hilltop, the breeze blowing between the hills was like their love. A lake, in the distance, as blue as your eyes. Holding hands, they were looking at each other. In the dark, he told her, I never noticed this until now, your eyes are even bluer. Like this lake.

Maria felt like moving, like having a manzanilla in the bar right there, there, opposite the car. Her hands had started to shake and she could imagine liquor in her throat and in her body, as strong as a bath. If they didn't come back she would go in that bar.

They came back. Between them, Judith was skipping.

'There weren't just the Goyas,' Pierre said. 'You should have come.'

Claire opened the car door. Maria stopped her. Pierre brushed against her.

'Last night,' Maria said, 'while you were sleeping, I found the man the police were looking for, Rodrigo Paestra.'

Claire's face grew very serious. She waited a second.

'You were drinking again, Maria,' she said.

Pierre didn't move.

'No,' Maria said. 'Just chance. He was on the roof opposite the hotel balcony. I drove him about eight miles from here, on the road to Madrid. I said I'd be back at noon. He lay down in the wheat. I don't know what to do, Pierre. Pierre, I really don't know what to do.'

Pierre took Maria's hand. From the silence that followed her words, Maria realized she had been shouting.

'Please, Maria,' he said.

'It's true.'

'No,' Claire said, 'no. It is not true, I could swear it isn't true.'

Claire pulled away from the car; she was standing straight, looking so majestic that Maria had to lower her eyes.

'I think he doesn't care whether we come or not,' Maria said. 'He just doesn't care. We don't have to go. I think I'd rather we didn't go.'

Pierre tried to smile.

'But it isn't true?'

'It is. The town is very small. He was there, on the roof opposite the hotel balcony. One chance in a thousand, but it's true.'

'You didn't tell us this morning,' Claire said.

'Why didn't you tell us, Maria? Why didn't you?'

Why? Claire walked away from the car with Judith. She didn't feel like waiting for Maria's answer.

'By chance too,' Maria said to Pierre, 'the first time I saw him, you were with Claire on a hotel balcony.'

Maria saw Claire coming back toward them.

'It wasn't until much later, when both of you were asleep, that I was sure it was him, Rodrigo Paestra. It was very late.'

'I knew it,' Pierre said.

People had stopped on the square. They were looking at Claire, who was walking slowly toward the Rover.

'I told you,' Maria went on, 'after we had finished talking. But you had fallen asleep.'

'I knew it,' Pierre repeated.

Claire was with them again.

'So, that's how it is, he's waiting for you?' she asked softly.

All of a sudden she had become very sweet again. She was close to Pierre, closer than ever. Threatening but discreet. Pierre was now paying attention to Maria's story.

'Oh! I don't know,' Maria said. 'I think he doesn't really care.'

'Eleven twenty,' Pierre said.

'I really don't feel like going there at all,' Maria said. 'You do what you want.'

'Where to?' Judith asked.

'Madrid. We could go in another direction.'

Again the policemen were walking around the square, dragging their feet. It was already as hot as at noon, and they were exhausted. The streets were already dried out by the sun. Just two hours and there wasn't a drop of water left in the gutters.

'The car blanket,' Claire said, 'did he use it?'

'Yes. Oh! Before we do anything else I would like a manzanilla. Before anything else.'

She leaned back against the seat and saw them look at each other. Then look around the square for a café that was open. They would always let her drink, they would always protect her in her desire to drink, always.

'Come,' Pierre said.

They went into the café where she had been the day before. The manzanilla was ice-cold.

'Why did you drink the brandy?' Claire asked. 'It's the worst thing for you, brandy, at night.'

'A mad craving,' Maria said.

She ordered another manzanilla. They didn't interfere. Pierre too was thinking of nothing but Rodrigo Paestra. He asked the waiter for a paper. On the front page there was a bad photograph of Rodrigo Paestra. The two other photographs also. Perez. And a very young woman with a round face and dark eyes.

'They had only been married eight months,' Pierre said.

Claire took the paper from him, read it, and threw it on a chair. The waiter came up to them. He pointed at the police.

'Rodrigo Paestra was a friend of mine,' he said—laughing—and he motioned as if to say that they would never find him.

'They didn't catch the man,' Judith said.

Maria ordered another manzanilla.

Pierre did not prevent her from ordering. Ordinarily he would have. He let her drink a third manzanilla. He looked at his watch. Judith was sitting on Claire's lap and watching. The waiter left.

'You said noon?'

'Yes. He even repeated it. He said noon. But without believing it.'

Pierre also had ordered a manzanilla. Maria was having her third. She smiled.

'It's strange and new,' she said.

'Will you tell us, Maria?' Claire asked.

Maria smiled even more. Then Pierre intervened.

'No more drinking,' he said.

He trembled slightly as he took the glass of manzanilla. Maria promised to stop. Claire had forgotten Rodrigo Paestra and again couldn't keep her eyes off Pierre. The sun had reached the arcade. The whole square was now moving into the midday calm.

'They were living the first days of their love.'

Pierre took her hand and held it tightly. But Maria pointed at the town hall.

'His wife is there,' she said. 'And Perez with her. Decency demanded that they be separated in death.'

'Maria,' Pierre cried.

'Yes. I said: the border, perhaps. He didn't answer. What a mess!'

Around her, already, the loneliness brought on by liquor. She still knew when she would have to stop talking. She would stop.

'It's a change though,' she said.

The waiter came back. They stopped talking. Pierre paid for the drinks. Were they going to Madrid? the waiter asked. They weren't sure. They spoke about the storm. Had they been on the road yesterday? They hardly answered and the waiter didn't insist.

'Would you recognize the spot?' Pierre asked.

'I'll recognize it. But what about our vacation?'

'There's no choice,' Pierre said, 'if that is a question. You've placed us in a situation where we no longer have a choice.'

He had said this without bitterness. He smiled. Claire was silent.

'Our vacation,' Maria said, 'when I mentioned our vacation, I was mainly thinking about you. Not about myself.'

'We knew that,' Claire finally said.

Maria got up. She stood in front of Claire, who didn't move.

'It's not my fault,' she whispered, 'it's nobody's fault. Nobody's.

Nobody's. That's what I meant. I didn't choose to see this man on the roof last night. You would have done the same thing, Claire.'

'No.'

Maria sat down again.

'Let's not go,' she stated. 'First of all, we won't be able to hide him, he's enormous, a giant, and even if we could, he cares so little about it, that we'd be doing something completely useless, even ridiculous I would say. There's nothing we can save of Rodrigo Paestra except his skin. Claire, you will get to Madrid. I won't move. Except to go to Madrid.'

Claire was tapping on the table. Pierre had stood up.

'I won't move,' Maria repeated. 'I'll have a manzanilla.'

'Twenty-five to twelve,' Pierre said.

He left the café by himself and walked over to the car. Judith ran after him. Claire watched him go.

'Come, Maria.'

'Yes.'

She took her by the arm. And Maria got up. No, she hadn't had much to drink. She had been drinking a bit too soon after the brandy, but she'd be all right.

'I'll be all right,' she told Claire. 'Don't worry.'

Pierre walked up to her. He pointed at Judith, who was already sitting in the back of the car.

'And Judith?' he asked.

'Oh! She's still so young,' Maria said. 'We'll just have to be a little careful.'

They slowly drove away from the square. The town was quiet. Some policemen had given in to sleep and were lying flat on the balustrades.

'It's easy,' Maria said. 'You take the road to Madrid. There, straight ahead.'

The road to Madrid. The biggest in Spain. Straight ahead, monumental.

This was still the town. A patrol was coming back, empty-handed, in single file. They didn't look at the black Rover. They had seen many others since morning. The foreign registration plates didn't even make them turn their heads.

Not one of them looked at the Rover.

There was a garage. One garage. Maria had counted two.

'On my way out,' Maria said, 'I was worried. When I drove back, I was drunk. But even so I'm going to remember. There was another garage.'

'The road to Madrid,' Pierre said. 'You can't go wrong.'

The other garage. Pierre was driving nearly as slowly as she had during the night.

'Then some kind of a shop, quite large and isolated.'

'There it is. Don't worry,' Pierre said.

He spoke gently. He felt hot. Probably he was afraid. No one turned to look at Claire who kept silent.

The shop. It was open. An electric saw filled the hot air with its noise.

'Then, I think, some very small houses.'

Low houses, children on the porches looking at the cars. They no longer wondered what time it was. It was any time before noon. Soon, after the houses, there was no other shade on the countryside but the fleeting shade of the birds.

The wheat fields weren't any help. No landmarks. Nothing but the wheat fields in the blinding light.

'I drove a long time through these fields,' Maria said. 'Eight miles as I told you.'

Pierre looked at the mileage. He was figuring out the distance they had covered.

'Two more miles,' he said. 'Two more and we'll be there.'

They stared at the landscape, swelling slightly toward the horizon. The sky was evenly gray. Telephone lines were running along the road to Madrid as far as you could see. There were few cars because of the heat.

'Didn't the road turn?' Pierre asked.

She said she remembered a turn, yes, but she hadn't taken it. Then the road was straight up to the side road.

'Everything is going very well,' Pierre said. 'We're getting to the crossing. Look, there, on the left. Look carefully, Maria.'

He must have been speaking so calmly because of Judith. Maybe because of Claire too. Judith was singing, rested and relaxed.

'He died from the heat, it's all over,' Maria said.

The road was climbing slightly.

'Do you remember? Do you remember this climb?'

She remembered. The road was climbing very slightly, up to a crest that was probably hiding a fork, with one road to the left that they would see upon reaching the top of the hill, and more wheat fields, still more and more wheat fields.

'It's silly. It's stupid,' Maria shouted.

'No,' Pierre said, 'not at all.'

The other wheat fields. They looked less even than the previous ones. They were studded with enormous, brightly colored flowers. Claire was speaking.

'Around here,' she said, 'they've started harvesting.'

VII

'It's like hell,' Maria shouted.

Pierre stopped the Rover completely. Judith listened and tried to understand. But they stopped talking and she began to think of something else.

'Look again,' Pierre said. 'Please, Maria.'

The side road went downhill on the left, straight to the bottom of the valley. There was no one on it.

'It's this road,' Maria said. 'The people who are harvesting are far away, half a mile on both sides of the road. They won't reach it before evening. You see, Claire.'

'Of course,' Claire said.

Maria now recognized the road perfectly, its gentle sweep, so gentle, its width, its original way of being buried in the wheat fields, and even its special light. She took the brandy from the car pocket, Pierre stopped her with his arm. She didn't insist, put the bottle back.

'He lay down in the wheat, waiting for noon,' she said, 'over there, probably'—she pointed to an indefinite spot. 'It's so long ago now, where can he be?'

'Who?' Judith asked.

'A man,' Claire said, 'who was supposed to go to Madrid with us.'

Pierre started the car. He slowly drove a few yards on the road to Madrid and then, still slowly, he turned into the side road. Two car tracks were noticeable, intertwined with those of carts.

'The Rover's wheels,' Pierre said.

'You see, you see,' Maria said. 'The shade from the wheat must be down to nothing at this time of the day. He must be dead from the heat.'

The heat was suffocating. The road was already dried out. The tracks of the carts and of the Rover had been carved into it, until the next storm.

'Oh! How stupid,' Maria said. 'It was there. It's there.'

It was a little after noon, just a little. The time agreed upon.

'Don't talk, Maria,' Claire said.

'I'm not talking.'

In the fields various spots stuck out, here and there, from the wide rectangles of wheat, staked out by dirt roads, each one gently sloping down to the valley. They watched the car that was coming toward them, they were wondering what the tourists were doing, if they had taken the wrong road. Standing, interrupting their work, all of them were now looking at the Rover.

'They're looking at us,' Claire said.

'We're going to rest a little on this road.' Pierre said, 'since we didn't sleep last night because of the storm. There were no rooms in the hotel, remember Claire?'

'I remember.'

Judith also looked at the workers. With her four-year-old experience she was trying to understand. Sitting on Claire's lap, she could see all the way into the valley.

Maria could now recognize the spot. In the hollow of the road, the heat didn't move and brought out sweat from every part of their bodies.

'Twenty more yards. Follow the tracks. I'll let you know.'

Pierre moved ahead. The harvesters, still standing, watched them. This road led nowhere. It belonged to their fields. They were surrounding a large rectangular area, in the center of which Rodrigo Paestra had lain down seven hours before. They had started harvesting at the bottom of the valley. They were moving up toward the road to Madrid, which they would reach by the end of the day.

The dirt road was getting more hollow, dipping beneath the level of the wheat fields. Only the heads, the still heads of the harvesters, could be seen.

'I think you should stop,' Maria said.

He stopped. The workers didn't move. Some of them would probably come over to the Rover.

Pierre got out of the car and made a friendly gesture with his hand, to the group nearest to them, composed of two men. A few seconds passed. And one of the two men answered Pierre's gesture. Then Pierre took Judith out of the car, lifted her, and Judith repeated the same greeting after him. When Maria thought of it later, she remembered Pierre's happy smile.

All the workers answered the little girl's greeting. The group of two men and, a little behind them, a group of three women. Their faces changed: they were laughing. They were laughing, making faces because of the sun: like ripples on the water, that can be seen from far away. They were laughing.

Claire didn't leave the car. Maria got out.

'It's impossible for him to get out of the field now,' she said.

Pierre pointed out to Maria several carts at the bottom of the valley. Half way down, between these carts and the road to Madrid, there were still more carts and horses.

'In half an hour,' Pierre said, 'they're going to eat in the shade of the carts. And, hidden by the wheat, they won't see us at all.'

A voice from the car.

'In half an hour, we'll be dead from the heat,' Claire said.

She again had Judith with her. She was telling her a story, while following Maria and Pierre with her eyes.

They had gone back to work. The wind that came from the valley, full of wheat dust, tickled their throats. And this wind was still balmy, it had blown through last night's storm.

'I'm going there,' Maria said, 'so I can at least tell him to wait, to be patient.'

She slowly moved away, as if taking a walk. She sang. Pierre waited for her, in the sun.

She sang the song she had been singing for Rodrigo Paestra two hours before dawn. A worker heard her, raised his head, went back to work, failing to understand why tourists had stopped there.

She walked on mechanically and calmly, just as Rodrigo Paestra had, when he had left her at four in the morning. The road hollowed out so much that no one could possibly see her. Except Pierre and Claire.

What could Maria call the time that opened ahead of her? The certainty of her hope? This rejuvenated air she was breathing. This incandescence, this bursting of a love at last without object?

Deep in the valley, there must have been a stream where the storm's luminous waters were still rolling.

She hadn't been mistaken. Her hope came true. Suddenly, on her left, the wheat opened up. She could no longer see them. She was alone with him again. She pushed aside the wheat and walked in. He was there. Over him, the wheat, naively, came back together. It would have done the same over a stone.

He was sleeping.

The colorful carts that had passed by him that morning in the rising sun had not waked him. He was where he had settled down, where he had dropped as if struck by lightning, when she had left. He was sleeping on his stomach, his legs folded, just slightly, like a child's, instinctively looking for comfort away from misfortune. The legs that had carried Rodrigo Paestra through his great misfortune, all the way to this wheat field, had, lonely and courageous, adapted themselves to his sleep.

His arms were around his head, and childishly abandoned like his legs.

Maria called out, 'Rodrigo Paestra.'

She bent over him. He was sleeping. She would carry that body to France. She would take him very far, her miracle, the storm murderer. So he had been waiting for her. He had believed what she had told him in the morning. She felt a desire to slip into the wheat next to his body, so that, on waking up, he would recognize an object of this world, the anonymous and grateful face of a woman.

'Rodrigo Paestra.'

Half bent over him, she called very softly, wishing and at the same time fearing to wake him up. Probably Pierre and Claire could neither see nor hear her. Nor even imagine her.

'Rodrigo Paestra,' she said very softly.

So strong was her pleasure at seeing Rodrigo Paestra again that she thought she was still drunk. Then she thought him ungrateful. He was there, waiting for her to come at the appointed time. Just as you wait for spring.

She shouted more loudly.

'Rodrigo Paestra. It's me. It's me.'

She bent still farther and called him. This time closer, lower.

And when she got so close to him she could have touched him, she noticed that Rodrigo Paestra was dead.

His open eyes were staring at the ground. The spot around his head and on the blades of wheat, which she had taken for his shadow, was his blood. It had happened a long time ago, probably a little after dawn, six or seven hours ago. Next to Rodrigo Paestra's face was his gun, like a toy abandoned by a child overcome by sleep.

Maria got up. She left the wheat field. Pierre was standing on the road. He walked toward her. They met.

'There's no point in waiting,' Maria said. 'He's dead.'

'What?'

'The heat probably. It's all over.'

Pierre stayed motionless next to Maria. They looked at each other without speaking. Maria was the first to smile. A very long time ago, they had looked at each other in nearly the same way.

'It doesn't make any sense,' she said. 'Let's go.'

She didn't move. Pierre left her, went toward the spot she had just left, where the wheat opened up. It was his turn to bend over Rodrigo Paestra. He took a long time to get back. But he walked back to Maria. Claire and Judith were waiting for them, completely silent. Maria picked a grain of wheat, and another, held them, let them go, picked more and let those go again. Pierre was next to her now.

'He killed himself,' he said.

'An idiot. An idiot. Let's not talk about it any more.'

They stayed on the road, facing each other. Each one was waiting for the other to say a word that would serve as a conclusion, a word which didn't come. Then Pierre took Maria by the shoulder and called her.

'Maria.'

From the Rover came another call. Claire. She had forgotten her. It was Pierre she was calling. Pierre answered, motioning. They were coming.

'And the man?' Judith asked.

'He won't be coming,' Pierre said.

Maria opened the back door and asked Claire to sit in front. She would keep Judith with her in the back.

'He's dead,' Pierre whispered to Claire.

'How did it happen?'

Pierre hesitated.

'Sunstroke, probably,' he said.

He started the Rover and began to make a U-turn. It was difficult to manage. He had to drive up on the sides a bit because the dirt road was very narrow. Over his shoulder Pierre could see Maria, who had taken Judith in her arms and was wiping her forehead. She was doing this carefully, as always. Claire, in front, was silent. Maria didn't look at her beautiful neck outlined against the wheat fields.

Pierre had managed the turn. He drove up the dirt road and, while on it, moved slowly. Then came the road to Madrid.

'What are we going to do?' Claire asked.

Nobody answered.

'Am I thirsty,' Judith said.

The road to Madrid. Monumental, straight, on and on. Again the harvesters must have looked up, in the fields, but they couldn't be seen by anyone. Pierre stopped again and turned around, looking at Maria without speaking.

'There is no reason,' she said, 'absolutely no reason why we shouldn't do what we had decided to do.'

'Exactly one-hundred fifty-two miles,' Claire said. 'We can be there before dark.'

Pierre started to drive again. The heat was more bearable because of the speed. It blew away your sweat, made your head less heavy. Judith complained again about being thirsty. Pierre promised her they would stop in the next village. Twenty-nine more miles. Judith still complained. She was bored.

'She's bored,' Claire said.

Then, well before the village, the road changed all of a sudden. First it climbed imperceptibly toward a spot that was very far away. Then it went down, in the same fashion, through a higher, rockier, lunar region. It didn't go down as much as it had gone up; then it became flat and straight again.

'We must have entered Castile,' Claire said.

'Probably,' Pierre said.

Judith once again cried that she was thirsty.

'Judith, if you cry,' Maria said calmly, 'if you cry . . .'

Judith cried.

'I'll leave you on the side of the road,' Maria shouted. 'If you cry, Judith, you'd better watch out.'

Pierre went faster. Faster and faster. The Rover was leaving clouds of dust and gravel behind it. The air was torrid. Claire leaned back, looking at the road ahead.

'There's no point in killing ourselves,' she said.

The wheat fields disappeared. All that was left were stones, heaps of stones, completely discolored by the sun.

Judith stopped crying, huddled against her mother. Pierre was driving faster and faster in spite of Claire's warning. Maria was silent.

'Mummy,' Judith called.

'We'll get killed,' Claire announced.

Pierre didn't slow down. He was driving so fast that Judith was tossed from one side to the other, from the back of the seat to her mother. Her mother reached out to hold her against her hip. And Judith stayed there, whimpering again.

'Pierre,' Claire shouted, 'Pierre.'

He slowed down a little. They reached the end of the plateau and the road started climbing again. On the top, it became flat once more, but this time it was not going to go down again. At the end of the road, there was an amphitheatre of mountains with round summits. As they moved ahead, other mountains appeared, strangely piled up. Now there were mountains on all sides, one on top of the other, some resting on others with their whole weight, white, pink or blue from the sulfides exposed to the sun, jostling each other madly.

'Mummy,' Judith called again.

'Be quiet, that's enough,' Maria shouted.

'She's afraid,' Claire said. 'Judith is afraid.'

Pierre slowed down even more. In the rear-view mirror he saw Maria put her arm around Judith and kiss her, and Judith, who at last was smiling.

They were now travelling at a normal speed. They were only six miles from the village that Pierre had announced. There was a pause, the first since the mood that set in after they discovered Rodrigo Paestra's body in the wheat field, when time had started to rush forward.

'Our rooms,' Claire said a little later. 'Let's not forget to reserve them by phone before this evening. Yesterday we had planned to do this before three.'

Maria let go of Judith, who had now calmed down. Maria became aware of Claire again, and of Claire's beauty which nearly made her cry. Claire was there, her profile outlined against the sky and the sulfurous and milky mountains on the horizon, which marked the progress of their trip and foretold its end that evening, in Madrid. Tonight, Pierre. She had been afraid earlier, when Pierre was driving so fast, that she would die while waiting. Now she had become thoughtful and her fear had been erased as she waited for a room, in Madrid, that very night in Madrid, as she waited to be coiled up against Pierre, that night, in Madrid, naked, in the warm moistness of a room closed to daylight, when Maria would be asleep in a lonely slumber brought on by liquor.

Could she see them already, in their white bed, in Madrid, that night, hiding? Yes, except for Claire's nakedness which she didn't know.

'I'll always love you, Claire,' Maria said.

Claire turned around and didn't smile at Maria. Pierre did not turn. There was complete silence in the Rover. Claire had never shown herself naked to Maria. She would tonight, to Pierre. This was just as ineluctable as the coming of twilight in a while would be. She could read the fate of that night in Claire's eyes.

'Look Judith,' Pierre shouted.

It was the village they wanted to reach. Looking like Rodrigo Paestra's, it moved quickly toward them. Pierre slowed down. His hands on the wheel were beautiful, supple, long, brown, uniquely docile from now on. Claire kept looking at them.

'There's an inn,' Pierre said. 'At the other end of the village.'

The village was already enjoying a peaceful siesta. The inn was surrounded by pine trees, where Pierre had said it would be.

It was a rather old, immense residence, entirely shielded from the heat. There were many cars under the pine trees. A round terrace, looking out on the countryside, was empty.

They hadn't even noticed that it was already lunch time. Everybody was eating. Some of the people they had seen at the Hotel Principal. They recognized one another. Claire smiled at a young woman.

Judith discovered she was hungry and said so.

They felt unexpectedly at ease because of the coolness of the staggered, crowded rooms.

'Was it hot,' Maria said at last.

They were shown to a table that looked out on the pine trees —they could see them through the blinds and discovered, next to the pines, a small olive grove. There was a path between them. Judith was brought some water. Judith drank and drank. They watched her drink. Then she stopped.

Maria was between Claire and Pierre. Surrounded by them. Even they had ordered a manzanilla. Judith was coming back to life and began to move about between their table and the entrance to the inn. Maria was drinking manzanillas.

'It's good,' she said. 'I think I'll drink forever.'

She drank. Claire stretched out on the bench and laughed.

'As you like, Maria,' she said.

She threw a quick, circular glance of happiness around her. The dining room was full. It was summer, in Spain. There were fruity food smells in the air about that time, every day, and they always made you feel somewhat nauseous.

'I'm not at all hungry,' Claire announced.

'We're not hungry,' Maria said.

Pierre smoked and drank his manzanilla. Ever since their trip had begun, he was silent, for long periods of time, between these two women.

Pierre ordered fried shrimp. Maria asked for good, tender meat for Judith. It was promised. They put Judith on a chair piled with cushions, the only one at the table.

'We could have arranged a good life for him,' Maria began, 'and perhaps I would have loved him.'

'Who will ever know?' Claire said.

They laughed together, then were silent, and then Maria went on drinking manzanillas.

Judith was brought some acceptable meat. Then they brought the fried shrimp and olives.

Judith ate well.

'Finally,' Pierre said, looking at his child, 'finally she's hungry.'

'The storm,' Claire said. 'This morning she was hungry too.'

Judith, well behaved, was eating. Maria was cutting her meat. She chewed and swallowed. Maria cut some more. They ate while watching Judith eat so nicely. The shrimps were fresh and hot, cracking under their teeth, smelling of fire.

'You will like this, Pierre,' Claire said.

She had one in her mouth. You could hear her teeth biting into it. Again she was unable to escape her desire for Pierre. She had left her ferociousness behind, she was beautiful again, saved from the menace that Rodrigo Paestra had been, alive. Her voice was like honey when she asked him—her voice was completely transformed—whether he liked it, as much as she.

'They'll find him in a while,' Maria said, 'in about four hours. In the meantime, he is still in the wheat field.'

'You know, to talk about it won't change anything,' Claire said.

'I still feel like it,' Maria said. 'Must you stop me?'

'No,' Pierre said, 'no, Maria. Why?'

Maria drank some more. The shrimp were the best in Spain. Maria asked for more. They were eating more than they had thought they would. And, while Maria was giving in to her tiredness, Claire was coming to life like Judith, and devoured the shrimps. The same shrimps he was eating.

'We had hardly started playing, when the game was lost,' Maria went on. 'Lost games like that make you rationalize endlessly.'

'It would have pleased me very much to save Rodrigo Paestra,' Pierre said, 'I must admit.'

'It wasn't the sun, was it?' Claire asked.

'It was the sun,' Pierre said.

Judith was no longer hungry. She was willing to have an orange. Pierre peeled it for her with great care. Judith followed this with envious attention.

They were no longer hungry. Green shade was seeping through the shutters and blinds. It was cool. Claire had stretched out again, completely, on the bench, where Pierre could see her. He wasn't looking at her, but how could he not be aware of her? She was looking toward the blinds and the olive grove, without seeing it. The reflection of the heat was still dancing in her eyes. Her eyes were violently awake, restless like water. Blue, like her dress, dark blue in the green shade of the blinds. What had happened in the morning at the hotel while she, Maria, was sleeping?

Maria half closed her eyes to see this woman, Claire, better.

But nothing could be seen of Claire except her quivering stare at the blinds. And all of a sudden, Maria's vigilance was discovered and had to stop.

Then Pierre suddenly got up, walked to the door, opened it—in a flash of light—and went out. Ten minutes went by.

'I wish he'd come back,' Maria said.

Claire made a vague gesture: she didn't know where Pierre had gone. She stayed in the same position, her face toward the door, refusing to look at Maria. They were silent until he came back. He was smoking a cigarette that he must have lit on the terrace.

'The air is scorching,' he said.

They made Judith get down from her chair.

'Where were you Pierre?' Claire asked.

'On the terrace. The road is deserted.'

There was a little bit of Manzanilla left in the jug. Maria drank it.

'Please, Maria,' Pierre said.

'At last I'm getting tired,' Maria said. 'But this is my last one.'

'We can't leave yet, in this heat, can we Pierre?' Claire asked. She pointed at Judith. Judith was yawning.

'Certainly not,' Maria said. 'She must sleep a little.'

Judith objected. Pierre took her in his arms and placed her on a large couch in the cool shade at the back of the entrance hall. Judith let him. Pierre walked back toward Maria and Claire. Claire was looking at him, all of him, as he came back. He sat down on the bench. They had to wait for Judith to finish her siesta.

'She's already asleep,' he said—he had turned around to look at his child.

'We would have taken him to France,' Maria went on. 'Maybe he would have become a friend. Who knows?'

'We'll never know,' Pierre said—he smiled—'stop drinking, Maria.'

VIII

'How tired I am,' Maria said—she was speaking to Pierre—'it seems you can fight against anything except this kind of tiredness. I'm going to sleep.'

Maria spoke gently. And Pierre was as used to her gentleness as he had been to her body. He smiled at Maria.

'It's a tiredness,' he said, 'that comes from very far, that has accumulated, and is made of all kinds of things, of everything. Sometimes it makes itself felt. Like today. But you know all that, Maria.'

'One always overestimates one's strength,' Maria said. 'I think I'll sleep very well.'

'You have always overestimated your strength,' Claire said. They smiled at each other.

'It's the liquor,' Maria said, 'that's what it is. And afterwards, the distrust that one feels, but you wouldn't know.'

'I don't know. But we can go on talking like this until evening.'

'Oh no,' Maria said, 'I'm going to sleep.'

She stretched out on the bench. Claire was opposite her.

Pierre turned around to look at Judith.

'She's asleep,' he said.

'You'd think it feasible,' Maria said, 'but she's really too small for such long trips, and in this heat.'

She had taken Pierre's place on the bench. There were many tourists stretched out like her. Some men were on the floor, lying on the rope carpets. The rooms were silent. All the children were asleep and people were whispering.

'I would have taken him travelling, a lot, again and again—she was yawning—'and little by little, day by day, I would have seen him change, look at me, then listen to me, and then . . .'

She yawned again, stretched, and closed her eyes.

'No more drinking for you before Madrid,' Pierre said. 'No more.'

'No more. I promise. I didn't drink enough to . . .'

'To what?' Claire asked.

'To be still more talkative,' Maria said. 'And to feel too desperate about Rodrigo Paestra's desertion. You know how it is, I was planning on starting a big project with Rodrigo Paestra. And now, now it has all collapsed before we even started. That's all. But I didn't drink enough not to admit it. Am I sleepy! I'm sleeping, Claire.'

She closed her eyes. Where were they? She could hear Claire.

'Can we wake up Judith in another half hour?'

Pierre didn't answer. Then just one more time, Maria spoke.

'If you like. As you like. I could easily sleep until evening.'

Pierre said he would call the National Hotel in Madrid to reserve three rooms. He was whispering. He went to call. Nothing happened. Claire must have been there. That sigh near Maria, that smell of sandalwood around her, that was Claire. Maria dreamed she was asleep.

Pierre came back. He had reserved three rooms for the night at the National Hotel in Madrid, he said. They were silent for a moment. Rooms in Madrid for the night. They knew that on reaching Madrid, Maria would want to drink and go from bar to bar. They would have to be very patient. Perfectly synchronized, they both closed their eyes. Shame prevented them from looking at each other in her presence, even if she was asleep. And yet they looked at each other, even though they couldn't. Then closed their eyes again, unable to bear the urgency of their desire. Claire said:

'She's asleep.'

What silence. Claire softly stroked the rough linen covering the couch. As she continued to stroke it, she started scratching it with her nails. Pierre looked on, followed the progress of Claire's caress, saw it stop abruptly, and painfully break loose from the couch and fall back on Claire's blue dress. It was surely she who got up first and walked away from the table. That rustling of the air, hardly noticeable, that crackling of unfolding skirts, that slowness, that languid straightening out of a body, it could only be a woman. She would recognize among a thousand others those resinous whiffs, sweetened by a perfume that had ripened on the skin and become adapted to its breathing, to its sweat, to its warmth in the shelter of her blue dress.

The smell of perfume around Maria subsided just as the wind does. He had followed her. Maria opened her eyes, absolutely convinced. They were no longer there. At last.

Maria closed her eyes again. It was going to happen. In half an hour. In an hour. And then the coupling of their love would be reversed.

She wanted things to happen between them so that she too would be illuminated like them and enter the world she bequeathed them, since the day, in fact, when she herself invented it, in Verona, one night.

Was Maria asleep?

There were, in this inn, in this residence shielded from the summer, a few openings onto the summer. There must have been a patio. Corridors that turn and die at deserted terraces where flowers, each day of that season, were dying too, while waiting for evening. During the day no one went through these corridors, or on the terraces.

Claire knew he was following her. She knew. He had already done so. He knew how to follow a woman he desired, from just the right distance so she would become a little more tense than necessary. He preferred them like that.

Here too, there was no one, because of the deadly heat of the countryside. Would it be there? Claire stopped, at the limit, as he wanted her, of the tenseness that came from his not having joined her yet, from his step, behind her, having remained calm and measured.

He had reached Claire. He had reached Claire's lips. But she didn't want to give them to him.

'We have an hour,' she said, 'before she wakes up. We can rent a room. I can do it, rent it, if it bothers you. I can't wait any more.'

He didn't answer.

'I know her,' she continued, 'I knew she would fall asleep. Did you notice? After four manzanillas, she has already reached that stage, she falls asleep.'

He didn't answer.

'But did you notice it? Please. Did you notice it? Pierre?'

'Yes. Today she isn't sleeping.'

She went up to him and pressed herself against him, from head to toe, from her hair to her thighs, entrusting her whole body to him. They did not kiss.

Liquor makes your heart beat more than usual. Such a long time before evening. Maria slightly opened her thighs where her heart, a dagger, was beating.

'Is it that I've already lost you?'

'My love. How can you? . . .'

She pulled away from him, moved away, farther away. He was alone. When she came back he was still in the same place, nailed to it. She was holding a key in her hand.

'It's done,' she said.

Pierre didn't answer. She had gone by him without stopping. He had heard her say that it was done. She was moving away. He followed far behind her. Then she walked up a dark stairway. Even the maids were still sleeping. Hardly ten minutes had gone by since they had left Maria. She turned around on the stairs.

'I said it was for the siesta.'

They reached the room they had to unlock. He did that. It was a very big room looking out on the olive grove. She was the one who slowed down suddenly, opened the window and spoke.

'What luck. Look.'—and she added, loudly, 'I couldn't wait any more.' He looked, and while they both looked, he dared to start touching her. He kissed her mouth so she wouldn't shout any more.

The heat was still dazzling in the deserted countryside.

Was her heart beating in such an unreasonable way for the very last time? She half opened her eyes. They were no longer there. She closed them again. She moved her legs and put them back on the bench. Then she got up and, through the opened blinds, looked at the same olive grove, petrified by the heat. Then she lay down again, again closed her eyes. She thought she was sleeping. Her heart had become calm. She drank too much. Everybody said so, mainly Pierre. You drink too much, Maria.

The window was exactly in the middle of the wall. The grove was there. The olive trees were very old. No grass around the trees. They were not looking at the grove.

Pierre, stretched out on the bed, watched her take off her blue dress and walk toward him, naked. He would remember later that he had seen her come up to him framed by the open window, against the olive trees. Would he remember later? She had taken off her dress very fast and had stepped over it and here she was.

'You're beautiful. God, how beautiful you are.'

Or perhaps they would not say anything.

Rodrigo Paestra's suicide in the wheat field, early in the morning, was foreseeable. He was uncomfortable, disturbed by the noise of the carts, and by the increasing heat of the sun; the presence, in his pocket, of a weapon that prevented him from stretching out, from falling asleep, made him remember a godsend he had absent-mindedly forgotten up to then: death. Maria was sleeping. She was sure of it. If she tried harder, she would dream. But she didn't try. She didn't dream. She was surprised by the sudden calmness that followed her discovery that she was awake. So she wasn't sleeping.

Pierre got up from the bed first. Claire was crying. Claire was still crying from pleasure when Pierre got up.

'She knows everything,' he said. 'Come.'

Then Claire's crying subsided.

'You think so?'

He did think so. He was standing next to her, completely dressed, while she was still naked. Then he turned toward the window and repeated that they had to leave.

'You don't love me?' she asked.

Her voice sounded gloomy. He told her.

'I love you. I've loved Maria. And you.'

Outside, the landscape had softened. He didn't want to know that she was getting up from the bed. The sun was less vertical. The shade from the olive trees had begun to grow longer, imperceptibly, while they were making love. The heat had weakened a little. Where was Maria? Had Maria been drinking herself to death? Had Maria's regal gift for drinking and dying led her into the wheat fields, far away, laughing, just like Rodrigo Paestra? Where was this other woman, Maria?

'Quick,' Pierre said. 'Come on.'

She was ready. She was crying.

'You no longer love Maria,' she shouted. 'Remember, you no longer love Maria.'

'I don't know,' Pierre said. 'Don't cry, don't cry, Claire. Already an hour since we left her.'

She too looked at the landscape and immediately turned away from it. She put on her make-up, looking in the mirror next to the window. She was holding back her tears.

Maria, dead in the wheat fields? On her face a grin that had been stopped, laughter in full bloom? Maria's lonely laughter in the wheat fields. This was her landscape. Everything was leading back to Maria: the sudden softness of the shade from the olive trees, the heat which suddenly made room for the oncoming evening, the various signs which announced everywhere that the day had passed its prime.

Pierre was at the door, his hand on the knob. She was in the middle of the room. He said he would go down first. His hand was shaking on the knob. Then she cried out.

'But what's the matter? Pierre, Pierre, tell me.'

'I love you,' he said. 'Don't be afraid.'

The tourists had waked her. They all seemed in high spirits when they left. Judith was there, delighted, her hair still flat from the sweat of her siesta, in front of the main entrance, happily holding pebbles from the courtyard. Maria got up and Judith ran up to her.

'I'm hot,' Judith said. And she went away.

They weren't there yet. You could still imagine the weigh of the heat. There was a different kind of light in the inn. The blinds had been raised after their love making.

'I'm going to give you a bath,' Maria told Judith. 'You'll see. In five minutes.'

The head waiter went by. Maria ordered coffee. She waited, sitting on the bench. That's when Pierre arrived.

He came through the dining room. He was standing in front of her.

'I slept so well,' Maria said.

The head waiter brought the coffee and Maria drank it greedily. Pierre sat down next to her, smoked a cigarette and didn't speak. He didn't look at Maria but kept looking at Judith, sometimes Judith, and sometimes the door. When Claire arrived, he moved back a little to make room for her.

'Did you sleep?'

'Yes,' Maria said, 'for a long time?'

'I don't know,' Claire said. 'Everybody has gone. I suppose it was for a long time. Yes.' She added, 'I'm glad you slept.'

'You should have some coffee,' Maria said. 'For once it's good.'

Claire ordered some. She turned toward Maria.

'While you were sleeping we took a walk in the woods behind the hotel,' she said.

'And the heat was terrible?'

'Terrible. But you have to accept it. You know.'

'I've reserved rooms in Madrid,' Pierre said. 'So we can leave whenever you want, Maria.'

'I'll give Judith her shower. And we'll leave for Madrid after that?'

They agreed. Maria took Judith to the shower on the ground floor. Judith went along without objecting. Maria put her under the shower. Judith laughed. Then Maria joined her under the shower. And they both laughed.

'How cool you look,' Claire said when they came back. And she pounced on Judith and embraced her.

Outside it seemed at first that the heat had remained unchanged. But the mood wasn't the same. It was very different from the morning and its anguish. And now the approaching evening brought hope. The workers were back in the fields, harvesting the same wheat, and the pale red mountains on the horizon recalled the spent youth of the morning.

Claire drove. Next to her Pierre was silent. Maria had wanted to stay in the back with Judith. They moved toward Madrid. Claire was driving safely, just a little faster than usual. It was only in that respect that, outwardly, their trip seemed to have changed. There was no point in talking about it, since each one of them had accepted and understood this change.

They drove through Castile until the late hours of the afternoon.

'In an hour and a half at the latest,' Pierre said, 'we'll be in Madrid.'

As they drove through a village, Maria said she wanted to stop. Pierre saw no reason why not. Claire stopped. Pierre lit a cigarette for her. Their hands met and touched. They now had precise memories.

The village was quite large. They stopped near its entrance, at the first café they passed. All the workers were still in the fields. They were the only customers. The café was very large and empty. You had to call to get served. A radio, in the back room, didn't manage to drown out the tireless lisping of the flies on the windows. Pierre called several times. The radio stopped. A man, still young, came out. Maria wanted wine that evening. So did Pierre. Claire wasn't going to have anything. Nor was Judith.

'It feels so good here,' Maria said.

They didn't answer. Judith ran around the room and looked at the paintings on the walls. Harvesting scenes. Under a cart, children playing with dogs. A family, naively solemn, eating a meal in a wheat field, on and on, on all the walls, as far as you could see.

'Just looking at her,' Pierre said, 'you can tell it's getting less hot.'

Maria called her and fixed her hair a little. She was thin, wearing nothing but a tiny bathing suit. She made faces as her hair was being combed.

'She will be as beautiful as you,' Claire said.

'I think so too,' Pierre said. 'She looks exactly like you.'

Maria pushed her back a little to see her better and then let her go back to the wheat on the walls.

'It's true that she's beautiful,' she said.

Maria drank her wine. The man, behind the bar, was looking at Claire. Pierre stopped drinking. They had to wait for Maria to empty the carafe. It was a cheap wine, sour and warm. But she said she liked it.

'Tonight,' she said, 'we could go out. We'll register at the hotel, take a shower, change, and then we can go out, all right? I can leave Judith with a maid as soon as we arrive. All right?'

'Of course,' Pierre said. Maria was drinking again. Pierre was watching the wine in the carafe go down. She drank slowly. They had to wait.

'But you're tired,' Claire answered.

Maria pursed her lips as if the wine, all of a sudden, was not wanted.

'No, at night, never.'

She motioned to the man behind the bar.

'Has there been any news of Rodrigo Paestra since this morning?'
The man thought and remembered. A murderer.
'Dead,' he said.
He raised his hand and placed an imaginary gun against his temple.
'How do you know?' Pierre asked.
'The radio, an hour ago. He was in a field.'
'Already,' Maria said. 'I'm sorry I bothered you with this story.'
'You're not going to start again, Maria.'
'I knew it,' Claire said.
Maria had finished her wine. The man had gone back behind the bar.
'Come, Maria,' Pierre said.
'I had no time to choose him,' Maria said. 'He fell on me. At the border, we would have let him loose in the woods and waited for him, at night, on the banks of a river. Such suspense. He would have come. Had he spent all the time needed to reach the border without killing himself, he wouldn't have killed himself later, after getting to know us.'
'Can't you try to forget him?'
'I don't want to,' Maria said. 'He takes up all my thoughts. It was only a few hours ago, Claire.'
They walked out. Carts were already coming back from the fields. The ones who finished first. They smiled at the tourists. Their faces were gray with dust. There were also a few children, asleep.
'The Jucar valley is beautiful,' Claire said. 'Sixty miles to Madrid. We should be getting to the valley now.'
Pierre was driving. Claire wanted Judith with her. Maria let her. Claire's hands were on Judith. After the village, Maria quickly fell asleep once more. They didn't wake her to see the

Jucar valley, but only when Madrid was in sight. The sun hadn't completely disappeared yet. It was level with the wheat fields. They reached Madrid as planned, before the sun set.

'Was I tired!' Maria said.

'Madrid, look.'

She looked. At first the city moved toward them like a mountain of stone. Then they noticed that this mountain was pierced with black holes bored by the sun, and that its rectangular shapes were spread out geometrically, at various levels, separated by empty spaces that swallowed up the pink light like a weary dawn.

'How beautiful,' Maria said.

She sat up, ran her fingers through her hair, and looked at Madrid surrounded by a sea of wheat.

'What a shame,' she added.

Claire turned around abruptly and, like an insult, uttered:

'What?'

'Who knows? Maybe the beauty.'

'You didn't know?'

'I was sleeping. I just noticed it.'

Pierre slowed down, he had to because Madrid was so beautiful even from that distance.

'The Jucar valley was beautiful too,' she said. 'You didn't want to wake up.'

The hotel was full, like the other. But their rooms had been reserved.

They were able to get something to eat for Judith, who was very tired.

The rooms were still warm with the heat of the day. The shower was wonderful. Long, brisk, tepid because the heat had penetrated the city to the very depths of its water. Each one of them showered alone.

In her room, Claire was getting ready for her wedding night. Pierre, lying on his bed, thought of this new wedding made sad by the memory of Maria.

They had adjoining rooms. Claire, tonight, in the fulfillment of her desire, would not be able to scream.

Judith was asleep. Claire and Maria were getting ready, each for her own night. Memories of Verona came back to Pierre. He got up from his bed, left the room, and knocked at his wife's door. He felt an urgent taste for a dead love. When he walked into Maria's room, he felt enshrouded in his love for Maria. What he didn't know was the poignant magic of Maria's solitude, brought on by him, and of Maria's mourning for him that evening.

'Maria,' he said.

She had been waiting for him.

'Kiss me,' she said.

There was about her the irreplaceable perfume of his power over her, of his breach of love, of his wishing her well, there was about her the odor of their dying love.

'Kiss me again, again,' Maria said. 'Pierre, Pierre.'

He kissed her. She moved back and looked at him. Judith was asleep. He knew what would come next. Did he know? She moved back toward the wall and kept looking at him, instead of coming closer to him with her usual lack of shame.

'Maria,' he called out.

'Yes,'—she too called out his name—'Pierre.'

Her attitude was one of shame, her eyes lowered on her body. And there was even fear in her voice.

He moved toward her. He placed a finger on his mouth to signal her not to wake up Judith. He was upon her. She didn't stop him.

'Kiss me, kiss me, quick, please, kiss me.'

He kissed her again. And again she moved back, very calmly.

'What can we do?' she asked.

'You're part of my life,' he said. 'I can no longer be content with a woman just for the novelty. I cannot do without you. I know it.'

'It's the end of our story,' Maria said. 'Pierre, it's all over. The end of the story.'

'Be quiet.'

'I'll be quiet. But, Pierre, this is the end.'

Pierre moved up to her, took her face in his hands.

'Are you sure?'

She said she was. She looked at him, horrified.

'Since when?'

'I just noticed it. Perhaps for a long time.'

Someone knocked at the door. It was Claire.

'You're taking so long,' she said—she seemed pale all of a sudden—'Are you coming?'

They went.

A man was dancing alone on the stage. The place was full. There were many tourists. The man danced well. The music took turns with his steps on the bare and dirty floor. He was surrounded by women, in loud, hastily put on, faded dresses. They must have been dancing all afternoon. The height of the summer with its overwork. Whenever the man stopped dancing, the band would play paso-dobles and the man would sing them into a microphone. Plastered on his face, he had at times a chalky laugh, and at times the mask of a loving, languorous, nauseous drunkenness that made an impression on his audience.

In the room, among the others, packed together like the others, Maria, Claire and Pierre were looking at the dancer.

THE AFTERNOON OF MONSIEUR ANDESMAS

Translated by
Anne Borchardt

I have just bought a house. A very beautiful spot. Almost like Greece. The trees around the house belong to me. One of them is enormous and, in summer, will give so much shade that I'll never suffer from the heat. I am going to build a terrace. From that terrace, at night, you'll be able to see the lights of G. . . . There are moments here when the light is absolute, accentuating everything, and at the same time precise, relentlessly shining on one object. . . .

Words heard during the summer of 1960

CHAPTER ONE

He emerged from the path on the left. He came from the part of the hill that the forest covered completely, in the rustling of the small shrubs and bushes which marked the approach to the plateau.

He was a small-sized, reddish dog. He probably came from the hamlets on the other slope, beyond the summit, about six miles from there.

On this side the hill fell away sharply towards the plain.

While he had emerged from the path, moving briskly, the dog suddenly slowed down as he advanced along the precipice. He sniffed at the grey light which covered the plain. In this plain there were crops surrounding a village, this village, and numerous roads leading from it towards a Mediterranean sea.

He didn't immediately see the man who was seated in front of the house—the only house on his route since the distant hamlets on the other side—and who was also staring at this same illuminated empty space, which was at times crossed by flocks of birds. He sat down, panting from fatigue and the heat.

It was thanks to this pause that he realised that his solitude wasn't total, that it was disintegrating behind him because of the presence of a man. The very light and very slow squeaking of the wicker arm-chair on which Mr. Andesmas was seated followed the rhythm of his difficult breathing, and this unparalleled rhythm did not fool the dog.

He turned his head, discovered the man's presence, pricked up his ears. No longer tired, he examined him. He must have known this plateau in front of the house ever since he was old enough to wander over the mountain and find his way on it. But he must not have been old enough to have known an owner of the house other than Mr. Andesmas. This must have been the first time a man had been there, on his route.

Mr. Andesmas did not move, he didn't show any sign of hostility or friendliness towards the dog.

The dog stared at him for a short while in this contemplative way. Intimidated by this meeting and finding himself forced to bear its full burden, he lowered his ears, took a few steps toward Mr. Andesmas, wagging his tail. But he gave up very quickly, his effort not being repaid by any sign from the man, and he stopped short before reaching him.

His fatigue returned, he panted again and left through the forest, this time towards the village.

He probably came to this hill every day, looking for bitches or food; he probably went to the three villages on the west slope, every day, and followed this very long route in the afternoon looking for various godsends.

'Godsends of bitches, of garbage,' Mr. Andesmas thought. 'I'll be seeing this dog again; he has his habits.'

The dog would need water, one would have to give water to this dog, here, interrupt with a mark of comfort his long trips through the forest, from one village to another, as much as possible ease his difficult existence. There is that pond less than a mile from here, where he can also drink, but bad, stale water, thick with the juice of grass. That water must be green and sticky, heavy with mosquito larvae, unhealthy. This dog, so eager for his daily joy, would need good water.

Valerie would give this dog something to drink since he would pass by the house.

He came back. Why? Once more he crossed the plateau overlooking the precipice. Once more he looked at the man. But although, this time, the man waved at him in a friendly manner, he did not come close again. Slowly he left, not to return that day.

With his coloured streak, he had pierced the grey space at the level where birds flew by. However quiet his progression over the sandstone rocks along the cliff, it had nevertheless outlined in the surrounding air, with the dry scraping of his nails on the rocks, the memory of a passage.

The forest was thick and wild. It had few clearings. The only path which crossed it—the dog took it, this time—bent very sharply beyond the house. The dog turned and disappeared.

Mr. Andesmas raised his arm, looked at his watch, saw that it was four o'clock. So, while the dog had been there, Michel Arc started to be late for the appointment they had made together, two days before, on this plateau. Michel Arc had said that a quarter to four was a good time for him. It was four o'clock.

When his arm fell back, Mr. Andesmas changed his position. The wicker arm-chair creaked more loudly. Then, again, it breathed regularly around the body it held. The already blurred memory of the reddish dog faded away and Mr. Andesmas was left alone with the oversize bulk of his seventy-eight years. When motionless, this bulk stiffened easily, and from time to time Mr. Andesmas shifted it, moved it a little in the wicker arm-chair. This way he could bear the waiting.

A quarter to four, Michel Arc had said. But it was still the warm season and siestas probably lasted longer during summer in this region than elsewhere. Mr. Andesmas always took identical medical siestas, in summer, in winter, rigorously. That is why he remembered other people's siestas, deep Saturday siestas, under the trees of village squares, or sometimes amorous siestas in bedrooms.

'It's to build a terrace,' Mr. Andesmas had explained to Michel Arc, 'a terrace that will overhang the valley, the village and the sea. On the other side of the house, a terrace would be useless, but this side calls for one. Although I am ready to spend what it will take to make this terrace beautiful, large and solid, I would like as a matter of principle, of course, and you must understand this, Mr. Arc, an estimate. Since this terrace is something my daughter Valerie wants, I am willing to make a large financial sacrifice. But an estimate is indispensable, you understand.'

Michel Arc understood.

Valerie is going to buy the pond where the dog had rested. That's agreed.

There was no other building in the forest beside the house Mr. Andesmas had just bought. With its yards, it took up the whole surface of the highest of the plateaus which formed a succession of terraces, on the slope of the hill, leap by leap, down to the plain, the village and the sea, so calm that day.

Mr. Andesmas had been living in the village for a year, since he had reached an age sufficiently ripe to make the best of not working and of waiting for death, doing nothing. This was the first time that he had seen the house he had bought for Valerie.

> When the lilacs will bloom my love
> When the lilacs will bloom forever

In the valley, somebody sang it. Maybe siesta time was coming to an end? Perhaps, yes, it was coming to an end. The singing certainly came from the village. From where else could it come? Between this village and the house, newly acquired by Mr. Andesmas for his child, Valerie, there was certainly no other house.

No other, no other but yours. And this one, because it belongs to you is excluded hereafter, from the fate of any other, of any other that could, just as well, instead of yours, have created in the pine forest this white accident of quicklime.

'I bought this house,' Mr. Andesmas had explained to Michel Arc, 'primarily because it is the only one of its kind. Around it, look, the forest, nothing but the forest. The forest, everywhere.'

The road ceased to be passable about a hundred yards from the house. Mr. Andesmas had come by car up to the point where the road ceased to be passable, a clearing with level ground where cars could turn. Valerie had driven him, then she had left. She hadn't got out of the car, she hadn't gone up to the house, hadn't said she wanted to. She had suggested to her father that he wait for Michel Arc and then for her, in the evening, when it would cool off—she hadn't said at what time—she would come to pick him up.

A few days earlier, they had talked together about this road and the possibility of owning it completely up to the pond, of making it private as far as others were concerned, those who weren't friends of Valerie's.

Mr. Andesmas's friends no longer existed. Once they had bought the pond, nobody would come through any more. No one. With the exception of Valerie's friends.

In the heat of the road, she had sung softly:

When the lilacs will bloom my love

He was now sitting in the wobbly wicker arm-chair he had found in a room inside the house. In the heat, energetically, as if the heat were nothing, she had sung:

When the lilacs

He had painfully reached the plateau, walking carefully, as she had advised him, with measured steps. She would have sung the same way in the coolness of an evening or night, in other places, elsewhere. Where wouldn't she have sung?

will bloom forever

While climbing he could still hear her. Then the noise of the car engine had murdered her song. It had become weak, muted; later snatches had still reached him, and then nothing, nothing more. Once he had reached the plateau, nothing more could be heard of her or her song. It had taken a long time. A long time also to settle this body into the wicker arm-chair. When this had been done, nothing, really nothing could be heard any more of Valerie, or of her song, or the noise of the car engine.

Around Mr. Andesmas the forest rose motionless, around the house also, and all over the hill. Between the trees there were heavy thickets which caught all noises, and even the songs of Valerie Andesmas, his child.

Yes, it was that. It was the village waking up from its siesta. Summer was passing, from one Saturday to the next. Tunes danced up all the way to the plateau, sometimes entangled. It was the workers' week-end rest. Mr. Andesmas never worked any more. Others had to rest from prodigious labour. Hereafter, others only, hereafter. Mr. Andesmas waited for them, waited for them to be ready.

The white rectangle of the square was crossed by a group of people. Mr. Andesmas saw only one part of this square. His desire to see all of it wasn't keen enough to get him to rise and walk the ten steps separating him from the ravine from which he could have seen the square, and also, behind the row of green benches, still empty because of the heat, Valerie's black car.

It was a dance.

It stopped.

Behind Mr. Andesmas, at the edge of the quiet pond completely covered with duckweed and protected by enormous trees, were there children now, playing at catching frogs and innocently submitting them to slow tortures which made them roar with laughter? Mr. Andesmas often thought about the youth of this pond, ever since the dog had come by, who must drink there every day, and ever since he had decided to make it private as far as all others were concerned, except for Valerie, his child.

A series of very brief, dry, crackling noises suddenly surrounded him. Wind blew over the forest.

'Already,' Mr. Andesmas said aloud. 'Already. . . .'

He heard himself speak, he started and was quiet. Around him, in soft succeeding waves, the whole forest bent over. This was now an exceptional spectacle in the life of Mr. Andesmas. The whole forest bent over, but differently depending on the height of the trees, their slant, their more or less heavy load of branches.

Mr. Andesmas did not yet move to look at his watch.

The wind died down. The forest again took up its still posture on the mountain. It wasn't evening, but only a chance wind, not yet the evening wind. Down below, however, the square filled up more and more every minute. Something was happening there.

I must talk to Michel Arc, Mr. Andesmas thought clearly. I'm hot. My forehead is covered with perspiration. He must now be over an hour late. I wouldn't have thought that of him. Make an old man wait.

It was a small dance, like every Saturday at that time of the year.

The melody, picked up by a record player, rose from the main square. It filled the void. The one Valerie had been singing lately, the one he heard her sing as she walked through the corridors in their house, the corridors were too long, she said, and she got bored going through them.

Mr. Andésmas listened to the tune, attentively, very satisfied, and his waiting for Michel Arc became less pressing, less painful. From Valerie he knew all the words of the song. Alone, and now incapable of making his ruined body dance, he could still recognise the appeal of dancing, its irresistible calling, its existence parallel to his death.

Sometimes, finding them too long and becoming impatient, Valerie danced in the long corridors of the house; most of the time, as a matter of fact, Mr. Andesmas remembers, except during her father's siestas. The pounding of Valerie's bare feet dancing in the corridors, he listens to it every time, and each time he thinks that it is his heart racing and dying.

Mr. Andesmas began to wait for this unreliable man, patiently.

He listened to the dancing tunes.

From his lost youth there was left this much: he would at times move his feet rhythmically in his black shoes. The sand on the plateau was dry and lent itself well to this game with his feet.

'A terrace,' Valerie had said. 'Michel Arc claims that it is essential to have one. Far away from you. But I'll come, every day, every day, every day. The time has come. Far away from you.'

Perhaps she is dancing in the square? Mr. Andesmas did not know. She had really wanted this house, Valerie. Mr. Andesmas had bought it for her as soon as she had expressed this wish. Valerie says she is reasonable. She says she never asks for anything she doesn't need. Just the pond, she had said, and after that, I'll never ask you for anything again.

It was the first time that Mr. Andesmas had seen this house he had bought for Valerie. Without seeing it, just because she wanted it, he had bought it for her, for Valerie, his daughter, a few weeks before.

As the whole wicker arm-chair creaked, Mr. Andesmas examined the place chosen by Valerie. The house was small but the land around it was flat. One could easily enlarge it on three sides whenever Valerie wanted to.

'My room, you'll see, will open onto the terrace. That's where I shall eat breakfast, in the morning.'

Valerie, in her nightgown, will therefore soon look at the sea, to her heart's content, when she wakes up. Sometimes the sea will be calm as it is today.

> *When our hope will be present each day*
> *When our hope will be present forever....*

Every twenty minutes, approximately, the tune came back, each time more powerful, more devastating, its strength increased by its regular repetition. And the square danced, danced, danced, all of it.

Sometimes, the sea would be foamy and sometimes, even, it would disappear in the fog. At times it would also be purple, swollen, and storms would frighten Valerie from the terrace.

And Mr. Andesmas was afraid for his child Valerie, whose love ruled without pity over his dying fate, that she might be frightened by storms when, in the morning, on this terrace overhanging the sea, she would discover them in their full rage.

Lots of young people must have been in the village square. At the deserted edge of the pond, deserted even by this gallivanting dog, weren't there flowers in full bloom that would fade tomorrow? Valerie would have to go to her pond and look at her flowers. A short-cut would take her there, quickly. You could probably buy this pond, for very little. Valerie was right to want it for herself. Valerie, it seemed, was still laughing at the frogs which swim on the surface of ponds' waters, wasn't she? Valerie, it seemed, still enjoyed holding them in her hand? Still laughed at frightening them in this way? Mr. Andesmas didn't really know any more. Even if the time of torturing them had passed, wasn't she amused by them in other ways, seeing their sprightliness locked up in her hand, and their terror? Mr. Andesmas no longer knew any more.

'Michel Arc asked me to tell you that he'd be here soon,' the girl said.

Mr. Andesmas hadn't seen her come. Maybe he had dozed off as she was approaching. He discovered her all of a sudden, standing on the plateau, at the same distance as the reddish dog. If he had dozed off, was it as she was approaching or even somewhat earlier?

'Thank you,' Mr. Andesmas said, 'thank you for coming.'

The girl, at this respectful distance, examined the massive body, locked in the wicker arm-chair, the massive body she was seeing for the first time. She must have heard them speak of it in the village. Below the very ancient, smiling and bare head, the body was richly covered with beautiful dark clothes, meticulously clean. You could see the immense shape only vaguely, it was very decently covered with these beautiful clothes.

'So, he is coming?' Mr. Andesmas asked in a friendly tone of voice.

She nodded that he would come, yes. She was already so tall that it was only because of the improper way she stared at him that Mr. Andesmas realised she was still a child.

Beneath her black hair, her eyes seemed light. Her face was small, rather pale. Her eyes slowly became accustomed to the sight of Mr. Andesmas. They left him and surveyed the surroundings. Did she know the place? Probably. She must have come here with other children, and even as far as the pond—this pond where very soon she wouldn't come any more—she must have come. This is probably where, before, the children of this village and those of the distant hamlets in the back of the hill must have met.

She was waiting. Mr. Andesmas made an effort, moved in his arm-chair, and took a hundred franc coin out of his pocket. He held it out to her. It was also the way she came up to him and very simply took the coin that confirmed his impression that she was still a child.

'Thank you, Mr. Andesmas.'

'Oh, you know my name,' Mr. Andesmas said softly.

'Michel Arc, he's my father.'

Mr. Andesmas smiled at the child, instead of bowing. She smiled a polite little smile.

'What should I tell him you said?' she asked.

Taken by surprise, Mr. Andesmas looked for something to say, and found this:

'It's still early, after all, but if he could come soon, it would be very kind of him.'

Both of them smiled at each other again, satisfied with this answer, as if it had been the perfect one the child was waiting for and as if Mr. Andesmas had guessed it by wanting to be nice to her.

Instead of leaving, she went to sit on the edge of the terrace-to-be and looked at the chasm.

The music was still coming up.

The child listened for a few minutes and then she played

at taking the hem of her blue dress, pulling it over her folded legs, lifting it again and pulling it again, several times.

And then she yawned.

When she turned towards Mr. Andesmas, he noticed that her whole body started, briefly, and that her hands moved apart and dropped the hundred franc coin.

She did not pick it up.

'I'm a little tired,' she declared. 'But I'm going down to tell my father what you told me.'

'Oh, I've plenty of time, plenty of time, why don't you rest,' Mr. Andesmas pleaded.

When the lilacs will bloom my love

They both listened to the song. With the second verse, the child began to sing also in a thin, uncertain voice, her head still turned towards the chasm of light, completely forgetful of the old man's presence. Although the music was loud, Mr. Andesmas only listened to the child's voice. At his age, he knew how not to make his presence bothersome, ever, to anyone, particularly children. Turned away from him, she sang the whole song, marking the rhythm as you do in school.

When the music stopped, it was replaced by loud noises. Just as when it stopped before, there was the shouting of men and wallowing in it the happy voices of girls. They requested it a second time, but it didn't come back. Silence, near silence, strangely took hold of the square, laughter and shouting almost stopped, having run their course, exhausted, overwhelmed by their own flow. Then the child whistled the tune. It was a sharper, slower whistling than it should have been. She probably wasn't old enough to dance yet. She whistled, with strained application, badly. It pierced the forest and the listener's heart, but the child didn't hear herself. Valerie whistles in the corridors, wonderfully, except during her father's siestas. Where have you learned to whistle so well, my little Valerie? She cannot tell.

When she had reached the end of the song, the child scanned the village square, for a fairly long time, then turned towards Mr. Andesmas, this time without fear. On the contrary, she had a happy look. Perhaps she was then calling for a compliment that didn't come? Perhaps she hadn't forgotten this old man's presence as much as one might have thought? Why such joy? The happy look lasted, fixed, then suddenly it waned until it reached an immobile and unjustified solemnity.

'You whistle well,' Mr. Andesmas said. 'Where did you learn?"

'I don't know.'

She looked at Mr. Andesmas questioningly, and asked:

'Shall I go? Shall I go down?'

'Oh, take your time,' Mr. Andesmas protested, 'take all the time you want, why don't you rest. You've lost your hundred francs.'

Perhaps she was intrigued by so much concern. She picked up the coin, and once again examined the impressive bulk which seemed thoroughly at rest, squeezed into the arm-chair—in the shade of the white wall of the house. Was she hoping to find some sign of impatience in those trembling hands, in that smile?

Mr. Andesmas tried to find something to say to distract

her from this spectacle, but finding nothing, he remained silent.

'But I'm not that tired, you know,' the child said.

She turned her eyes away.

'Oh, you have all the time in the world,' Mr. Andesmas said.

Smiles no longer registered naturally on Mr. Andesmas's face. Except when Valerie would appear in the frame of the french window which opened onto the garden, and when an uncontrolled, animal-like joy would break through, criss-crossing his whole face, Mr. Andesmas only smiled when he seemed to remember that social conventions called for it, and he could only do it with difficulty, pretending just enough to give the impression of being a good-humoured old man.

'You have all the time in the world, I assure you," he repeated.

The child, standing, seemed to be thinking.

'Then, I'll go for a walk,' she decided. 'In case my father comes, I'll go back with him by car.'

'There's a pond, over there,' Mr. Andesmas said, his left arm pointing at Valerie's future forest.

She knew that.

She walked off towards the top of the hill, where the reddish dog had come from. She walked awkwardly on her skinny, nearly shapeless legs, bird's legs, while the old man looked on, smiling with approval. He watched her until he could no longer see anything of her, nothing, not one speck of her blue dress, and then once again he found himself in the state of abandonment whose disconcerting vastness she had only emphasised through her appearance, no matter how discreet.

On the sunny plateau her dress had been very blue. Closing his eyes, Mr. Andesmas rediscovered the exact shade, while he already had difficulty recalling the reddish colour of the dog who had preceded her.

He was suddenly sorry he had encouraged her to leave. He called her back.

'And what is your father doing?' he asked.

While until then her behaviour had been squeamish, but respectful before such old age, she now became insolent. A shout came back, piercing, exasperated, from the forest.

'He is dancing.'

Mr. Andesmas's waiting started again.

Oddly enough it was at first calmer, less annoyed than a moment before.

He stared at the chasm of light. At this altitude the sea was almost the same blue as the sky, he noticed. He got up to stretch his legs and to have a better look at the sea.

He got up, took three steps towards the chasm, filled with a light already turning yellow, and he saw, as he had expected, Valerie's black car, parked under the trees, alongside the green benches of the village square.

And then he walked back to his arm-chair, sat down again, again considered his bulk, in the dark clothes, sunk in this arm-chair, and that was when he got ready to wait still longer for Michel Arc, and, also, for the return of the child, an expected, foreseen return; and it was during this interlude that Mr. Andesmas was to meet the darkness of death.

Having sat back as he was supposed to, ready to accept Michel Arc's delay, reduced through his own free will to a complete tolerance of any disrespect towards himself while at the same time the memory of Valerie, who was so close—her black car was there on the white village square—came back to him, Mr. Andesmas met the darkness of death.

Was it from seeing the child walk on the path, her frail way of stepping on the pine needles? From imagining her solitude in the forest? Her somewhat frightened running towards the pond? Was it from remembering her submissiveness, this devotion to the duty her father had imposed upon her to inform this old man whose sight had sickened her, a devotion which had in the end marvellously exploded into insolence?

Mr. Andesmas thought he was submerged by a desire to love this other child and by his inability to have his feelings follow this desire.

When he recounted this episode in his endless old age, he claimed it was from the little girl's walking off towards the top of this deserted hill, from the exasperating daintiness of her walk which was taking her to this pond where he knew Valerie would no longer go alone, that he felt this desire that day. That day, he wanted one last time to change his feelings in favour of this child who was going to the pond, with an intensity as brutal, as urgent, he said, as the desire, the mortal passion he had felt, years ago, for a certain woman.

But while he wanted this so much, he suddenly recalled the smell of Valerie's hair when she was a child and his eyes closed with suffering at the thought of such impotence, the last in his life. But (was it the forest hiding in its depths flowers he hadn't seen and that a breeze carried to him? Was it the enduring perfume of this other child who had gone, which he hadn't noticed when she was there?), now the memory came back to him of the scented magnificence of his child's hair, and also, in advance, the infernal memory of a blondness which, in this very house would soon, very soon, perfume the sleep of a still unknown man.

An insinuating heaviness slowly penetrated Mr. Andesmas, taking hold of his limbs, of his whole body, and slowly reaching his mind. His hands became like lead on the arms of his chair and his head grew remote even to itself, letting itself be taken over by a discouragement, never experienced before, at the thought of going on.

Mr. Andesmas tried to struggle and to tell himself that this very long wait for Michel Arc, without moving, in this heat, he had to admit it to himself, was disastrous for his health. But it didn't help. The insinuating heaviness was penetrating still farther, deeper, more and more discouraging and unknown. Mr. Andesmas tried to stay its course, to stop its intrusion within him, but it was engulfing him more and more.

It was now ruling over his whole life, settled there, for the time being, a prowler sleeping on its victory.

The whole time it was there and sleeping, Mr. Andesmas tried to love that other child whom he was no longer able to love.

The whole time it was there and sleeping, Mr. Andesmas tried to face the memory of Valerie who was there, down below, in the white village square, and who had forgotten him.

'I'm going to die,' Mr. Andesmas said aloud.

But this time he was not startled. He heard his voice in the same way he had heard it say that the wind was rising, a while before, but it didn't surprise him since it was the voice of a man he didn't recognise, a man unable to love this child at the pond.

He remained there not loving this child whom he would love if he could, and he was dying from not being able to, of a fictitious death which didn't kill him. Someone else loved her, madly, not he but someone who could be he and yet would not be.

He waited for the disappearance of his intense surprise at noticing that he wasn't dying from believing so strongly that he was. Filled with this impossible desire to change his feelings, to love differently, he looked at the trees with all his strength, begging himself to find them beautiful. But they were of no help to him. He imagined this other child, so delightful, who was watching, without being able to see her at the edge of the pond, the imperceptible growth of the grass forcing its way towards daylight, but she was of no help to him. His preference for Valerie, his child, still remained shining and indescribable. That was it.

'That man, how rude he is,' he went on.

In vain. How he tried to get back into this long wait in which he had buried himself long before and which he could so conveniently call his despair! Let Valerie's blondness roam the world, let the whole world look dull, if that's how it should be, next to so much blondness, why should one think about that? Mr. Andesmas thought. While at the same time knowing that one cannot think about it. And, if one could think about it, why should one think about it with this crushing pain and not tenderly? Mr. Andesmas went on thinking, while knowing he was lying, that one could only attempt to think about it with terrible pain.

This young, hatefully young pain lasted, Mr. Andesmas claimed. How long? He would never be able to say. But long enough for him to become, in the end, its willing prey. And his mind, which had never been of danger to him in his lifetime but had, on the contrary, always been praised as the best possible, also put up with this disturbance from its usual course.

Mr. Andesmas agreed never to know any other adventure but the one of his love for Valerie.

'Why wait for Michel Arc, who won't come today anyhow?'

He had spoken aloud again. He had decided to accept speaking aloud. And he had the impression his voice was questioning. He answered himself without fear because, next to the discovery of Valerie's universal blondness, what fear could he experience?

'Who would do it?' he answered himself. 'Who in my place, wouldn't get angry?'

He ventured a glance towards the left, towards the path through which this other betrayed child should soon be arriving, and he stayed that way, sitting straight in his wicker arm-chair, while this child didn't come back from the pond and while the afternoon reached its full measure of yellow, soft sunshine.

Mr. Andesmas fell asleep in this position.

Mr. Andesmas claimed later on that he had, that afternoon, been the victim of a discovery—a penetrating and empty one, he said—which he hadn't had time to make in the course of his life, and which, probably because of his age, tired him more than it should have, but which he felt was nevertheless a very common one, he said. For the sake of convenience and perhaps also because of his failing vocabulary, he called it the discovery of his understanding of his love for his child.

He went on with his speech, of which Michel Arc was the main subject, but he never knew exactly what this speech had been. Vigorous and violent words were pronounced on the plateau during the period that followed his gain of wisdom. He heard them.

He had just caught a glimpse of the delights of this funeral feast in which he had devoured his own guts, prey to a fear that flagrantly went beyond the strength he had left, and probably because of this fear, Mr. Andesmas turned against Michel Arc's negligence.

After which he collapsed into drowsiness opposite the soft, yellow light of the chasm.

In certain places in the valley, above the already-watered crops, there was a thin mist which this soft, yellow light of the chasm dispelled with more and more difficulty.

This day in June was monotonous perhaps, but it was also of a rare perfection.

How long did this respite of Mr. Andesmas last? This also he was never able to say. He said that he dreamt, during all this time, of ridiculous satisfactions related to his previous talks with Michel Arc about the estimate for Valerie's future terrace, facing the sea of all seasons.

Actually, this respite was of short duration, just long enough to let the little girl play near the pond and return. Then she was coming back from the top of the hill.

Until the last moment of his life, Mr. Andesmas remembered the arrival of this other child.

In the forest, at first very far, then closer and closer, the ground was hit by the pounding of a step. But this walk on the dry leaves of the path did not get the better of Mr. Andesmas's sleep. He heard her. He recognised a human presence, which he placed on the southern side of the hill; he even told himself that the child was coming back from the pond but he thought she was still far from the plateau and that he had time to sleep a little more, and instead of getting ready to greet her, he fell asleep again, and so deeply that he soon no longer heard her at all even when she was a few yards from him.

The child returned. Mr. Andesmas, plunged in this beneficial sleep, probably still bent his head in the direction of the path through which she was to come back from the pond.

Did she look at him in silence for a moment? He never knew. Nor how long her walk had lasted. And this sleep.

'Hey, mister,' the child said very gently.

She softly kicked the sand on the plateau.

When he opened his eyes, Mr. Andesmas recognized upon him the immaculate impropriety of a stare already seen. She had come very close to him, not like the first time, and in the sun he saw her light eyes better. He noticed he had forgotten her.

'Well, well, I fall asleep all the time, everywhere, everywhere,' Mr. Andesmas apologised.

The little girl did not answer. She examined him all over with an insatiable, mad curiosity. This time, Mr. Andesmas tried to meet her gaze. But he didn't succeed.

'Michel Arc has not come, you see,' Mr. Andesmas went on.

The little girl frowned and seemed to think. Her eyes left Mr. Andesmas and tried to find something behind him, on the white wall, to discover something they wanted to see and didn't see. Then, her face suddenly expressed a bewildering brutality, it turned inwards through the effort of a nonexistent stare. She was looking at a dream and was suffering. This dream she was looking at could not be seen.

'Sit down, rest,' Mr. Andesmas said softly.

Her face relaxed a little. But her eyes did not recognise the old man when they rested on him again. However she obeyed. She sat at his feet and put her head against the leg of the arm-chair.

Mr. Andesmas did not move.

He counted his breaths, forced himself to make them deeper so as to harmonise them with the calm of the forest and the calm that had taken hold of the child.

Very slowly, she raised towards Mr. Andesmas a narrow, long, dirty hand, displaying the hundred franc coin. She spoke without turning her head.

'I found this on the path,' she said.

'Oh, that's fine, that's fine,' murmured Mr. Andesmas. Had he really seen her just before? His forgetfulness must have been fleeting, must have crushed her for short moments, only to release her again.

She remained silent, her head against the leg of the arm-chair, in the shade of the wall.

Did she close her eyes? Mr. Andesmas did not see her face; only her motionless, half-open hands. In her right hand was the hundred franc coin. So much stillness was choking Mr. Andesmas.

> *When the lilacs will bloom my love*
> *When the lilacs will bloom forever*

She didn't move while the song lasted. When it stopped, she raised her head and listened to the laughter and shouting coming up from the village square. The laughter and shouting stopped, but she remained as she was, her head raised. That was when Mr. Andesmas moved in his arm-chair.

The child burst out laughing:

'Your arm-chair, it's going to break,' she said.

She got up and he recognised a child he had already seen.

'I'm fat,' he said. 'This arm-chair wasn't made for me.'

He too laughed. But she quickly became serious again.

'My father hasn't come yet?' she asked.

'He's going to come,' Mr. Andesmas said hastily. 'He's going to come, you can wait for him if you like.'

Now that she was abandoned by a father who had forgotten her, she stayed there trying to decide, but reasonably, what she preferred to do with her time. Her eyes remained wild, they, too, abandoned by this frenzy which had just before carried her away as she was walking through the forest. She raised her hands towards her face, crossed them over her mouth, and rubbed her eyes as she probably did when waking up.

What game had she played near the pond? It was dried mud that had dirtied her hands. She must have dropped the coin after holding it out to Mr. Andesmas. That's right, her hands had fallen empty, alongside her dress.

'I'm going,' she said.

Then suddenly Mr. Andesmas remembered what Valerie had told him:

'Michel Arc's oldest daughter is not like others. Michel Arc thinks his daughter is not like others. It isn't so serious they say. At times, she forgets everything. Poor Michel Arc, whose daughter is not like others.'

She didn't seem in a hurry to go now that she had decided to do so. Perhaps she felt secure near this old man? Or, equally indifferent to being there or elsewhere, did she prefer to wait for a better idea than the one she had had, of going back?

'Am I to tell my father that you'll wait for him much longer?'

She smiled. Her face collected itself completely. Cunning filtered into her smile as she waited for Mr. Andesmas's reply, and Mr. Andesmas, his cheeks glowing, shouted merrily:

'Well, as long as it is light, I'll wait for Michel Arc!'

Did she hear the answer? Yes. She heard it.

As she was leaving, she saw the hundred franc coin in

the grey sand of the plateau. She looked at it, bent down, and once again took it and showed it to Mr. Andesmas. Her eyes didn't wander off.

'Look,' she said. 'Someone may have lost it?'

She laughed again.

'Yes,' Mr. Andesmas said. 'Keep it.'

Her hand, ready to close, did so with a click.

Again she became dreamy, distracted. She walked up to Mr. Andesmas and held out her left hand, the one that did not hold the coin.

'Later I'll be afraid,' she said. 'I'll say good-bye now.'

Her hand was warm, rough from the mud of the pond. Mr. Andesmas tried to hold it in his but she slipped away, worried; she had the flexibility, the softness of an uprooted weed, even in the motions she provoked. She held out her hand reluctantly, she did this like a very small child, with acquired and accepted disgust.

'Maybe Michel Arc will only come at night?'

She pointed at the chasm where the dance was going on.

'Listen,' she said.

She stayed like this, with this rapt gesture, incomprehensibly. Then the gesture collapsed without reason, or was it that the dance stopped?

'What did you do at the pond?' Mr. Andesmas asked.

'Nothing,' she said.

She left, without making a mistake, by the path the reddish dog had taken, steadily, slowly. Mr. Andesmas made a gesture as if to stop her but she noticed nothing. Then he straightened, looked for a way to detain her, a way to express himself, and, too late, he shouted:

'If you see Valerie——"

She answered something after having already disappeared behind the turn in the path, but she didn't come back.

Mr. Andesmas heard whistling.

He fell back in his arm-chair. He tried to disentangle from the silence of the forest the words the child had pronounced, but he didn't succeed. Did she say she didn't know Valerie? Or that Valerie knew very well that her father was waiting for her? Or something else that had nothing to do with the question he had asked?

The echo of the childish voice floated for a long time, insoluble, around Mr. Andesmas, then, none of its possible meanings having been retained, it moved off, faded, joined the various shimmerings, thousands of them, hanging in the chasm of light, became one of them. It disappeared.

Again Mr. Andesmas found himself alone. Alone waiting for a man without a sense of time. In the forest.

Some day they would have to chop down many trees in this forest, pull out bushes, ravage part of this shapeless denseness, so that air would be able to sweep into it, free, through immense clearings, at last disturbing this monumental jumble.

The weather was so clear that one could see him, if one wanted to, from the village square. His shape was outlined on the site of the future terrace of his daughter, Valerie. Everybody knew about this forthcoming construction. They knew he was waiting for Michel Arc.

As usual he was dressed in a dark suit. Yes, they could see him, distinguish this dark spot formed by his body squeezed into the wicker arm-chair which stood out against the whitewashed wall of the house he had just bought for his daughter Valerie. This spot was getting darker and larger every minute as time went by, and his presence on the bare, sunny plateau was becoming increasingly undeniable. It was so sandy on this side of the mountain; yes, Valerie was certainly able to see him, this father, if she wanted to see him, while he was waiting for Michel Arc. Others could too. He was there, exposed to their eyes, and everyone knew it could only be he, Mr. Andesmas. The purchase of the hill had caused quite a stir in the village. The land bought in Valerie Andesmas's name by her father covered one hundred and ten acres of forest. They had both been living in this village, in the heart of this chasm, for a year, ever since, it was said, he had decided to retire from the business that had taken up his time, having the means to do so, and even more than the means. With this child. Just because of her wish, a few weeks before, he bought her this side of the hill up to the edge of the pond. He was going to buy the pond.

'Ah! That Mr. Arc, ah, that man,' Mr. Andesmas said.

He had grown accustomed to his own voice.

With difficulty he rose halfway, dragged his arm-chair a little farther forward, closer to the edge of the plateau so he could be seen more easily from down below. But he didn't look into the chasm. They were still dancing, if one went by the singing.

He preferred to look at his body spread out in the arm-chair—more spread out than while the little girl was there—and dressed in this beautiful dark material. His belly resting on his knees, it was wrapped in a waistcoat of the same dark material chosen by Valerie, his child, because it was good cloth, a neutral colour, and because a heavy-set man would be more comfortably and safely hidden in it.

Idle, and alone, Mr. Andesmas examined with boredom what had finally become of him. Still nothing came from the path. From where he was now, he could have seen Valerie's parked black car again, if he had wanted to.

But, he later said, for a moment he was unable either to look at this black car of Valerie's, or to think about the child. These memories surrounded him, interlocked, in a coexistence which for a long time made them one in his mind. He knew that he could contemplate neither Valerie's blondness nor the other betrayed child's madness without being equally terrified. Mr. Andesmas did not even look at the trees which also, so innocently, partook of this same inconceivable fate, to exist that afternoon.

Mr. Andesmas looked at himself. And at the sight of himself he found some comfort. It filled him with a secure, irreversible disgust. It was, that evening, the equivalent of the only certainty he had ever known in the course of his life.

It was the wind coming up. It was never Michel Arc.

Time passed and Mr. Andesmas reaccustomed himself to waiting.

He even played with the secret hope that the child might not have returned to the village, that she was still lingering near the plateau; he reaccustomed himself to the thought of her presence there, nearby, and he even hoped for it, and waiting for the reappearance of the child surpassed his waiting for Michel Arc and Valerie.

A hundred franc coin, fallen from her hands, was shining in front of him in the sand. She had dropped it again, again and again.

'She opens her hands and drops things, she can't keep anything. Yet she has some memory. You can't really tell.'

Mr. Andesmas made an effort to pick up the coin, then gave up. And instead of taking it, he pushed it with his foot as far as possible from his sight. But it didn't reach the little thickets alongside the plateau, as he would have liked it to; it travelled a yard in the soft sand and stayed there, half buried.

No, she won't come back today. She must have arrived in the village by now. She went down without difficulty, whistling at times, looking right and left, at the trees and the ground—her legs, so frail and deft, carry her wherever she wants—gathering things, pebbles, or leaves which for her alone, for an instant, have an obscure interest that captivates her. Then she opens her hands, drops her possessions.

'Yet sometimes she remembers having forgotten.'

Was she afraid during her walk? Did she run once or twice? Did she take the wrong path?

'No, the paths, she knows them better than her brothers and sisters, who have all their wits. Why? You tell me.'

At what moment did she remember she had forgotten the hundred franc coin? If she did remember? Then, yes, she would have had to stop on her way, alone on this deserted path, and with sharp regret she must have wondered whether she shouldn't go back to the old man. But she decided against it in the obscure foreknowledge of her madness, she did not make this childish, irrational move, and, on the contrary, she continued towards the village.

Mr. Andesmas made an effort, threw some sand on the

hundred franc coin which he wanted completely out of his sight. He could no longer see it. He sighed deeply as he did after any effort.

He felt somewhat calmer again. If he went down early enough that evening, there'd be a chance of his seeing this child again in the village square.

Mr. Andesmas had forgotten that Valerie often spoke to him about Michel Arc's daughter.

But he never went to the village square. What then?

He sighed, then got over his apprehension. He would manage to find the child. He would ask Valerie for a way to find her. He would give her back her treasure. The waiting for Michel Arc was relegated behind this other waiting, to give back to the child this treasure she had perhaps forgotten.

What an unexpected consequence of his importance, Mr. Andesmas thought; what a new and final responsibility! Would she remember him? Yes. She had looked at him so much just before that if he showed enough friendliness she would make an effort to remember. That rich, idle and very old man whose daughter is Valerie, you know? Yes. She had called him by his name when she had arrived on the plateau.

'She doesn't understand what others understand, and yet she knows and remembers certain things. Whatever she feels like, one might think.'

Shouts of pleasure rose up from the valley. Then dance music covered them over. It was a waltz with lyrics. Well, let them dance, let them dance, as much as they want; they shouldn't have to suffer, while dancing, from having to stop soon because of an obligation towards me.

Was it after arriving in the square, thinking she still possessed those hundred francs, torn between the desire for a bag of chocolates and the obligation to inform her father that Mr. Andesmas would wait for him until dusk, that this child noticed she had lost her treasure? That the memory of what she forgot came back to her?

She made her way towards the square, she was so obedient, so obedient, then through the dancers. There was her father who dances so well. Did she keep herself from crying tears of sorrow?

'Mr. Andesmas said he would wait for you as long as there is light.'

'That's right, my God, that's right!' Valerie exclaimed.

Wasn't it rather as she walked around the square, in search of a bag of chocolates, that she noticed that once again she must have lost the hundred franc coin which she had found near the old man?

Did she cry, in a corner, at being that forgetful?

He would know this evening. This evening. He wanted to know.

'That's right, my God!' Valerie exclaimed. 'How late it is.'

No, the child must not have forgotten the errand her father had asked her to run. She must have looked for the hundred franc coin in the dust of the square. People looked at her with pity. Was she crying?

Then, through the dancers, she went up to Michel Arc. The errand was completed.

'He has nothing better to do after all,' Michel Arc said.

'But he knows nothing about this forest. It is painful to wait.'

No. The child did not remember the errand. The forgotten hundred franc coin, the terrace. She was crying, alone. Her father was dancing with blind pleasure. She was crying, where? Who saw her cry, who?

Mr. Andesmas's waiting once again finally became calm. The sun was still high. Since he had said so, he would wait until evening. He knew the little girl had forgotten the old man.

What could he do but wait? Wait for Valerie's car. He snickered. He was locked up in the forest by Valerie, his child.

From being on this plateau such a long time, he was going to know inside-out the instructions he would give Michel Arc, concerning the shape of the terrace, its dimensions. Their meeting would be short. In a few words he would tell Michel Arc what he thought should be done, up to what point the railings should go on the plateau.

The terrace would be a half-circle, with no angles, it would come within two yards of the chasm of light.

When Valerie comes out of her sleep, her blonde hair is so mussed that it falls over her eyes. It will be through the foliage of her blonde hair that, from her terrace, upon waking, she will discover the sea, this child of Mr. Andesmas.

Had the sun turned? Apparently, Mr. Andesmas noticed. A beech tree, a few yards away from him, swept him with its noble and impressive shade. This shade began to mingle with the shade of the whitewashed wall.

> *When the lilacs will bloom my love*
> *When our hope will be present every day*

A very young voice was singing, slowly. The song lasted a long time. It was played twice in a row.

When it ended, the joy was less violent. Some laughter, and it died down.

Did Mr. Andesmas fall asleep again, after the song?

CHAPTER TWO

Yes, he must have fallen asleep. The shade from the beech tree now covered the whole site of the future terrace. Mr. Andesmas found himself protected by it without at all remembering having noticed any of its progress.

Yes, he must have fallen asleep again, once again.

Now, from the village square, nothing could be seen of him any more. The shade from the tree was denser than the one from the wall, it was vaster and he was right in the middle. It was useless for him to have moved closer to the precipice a moment before. No more, now, no more.

The proof that he had slept was that he managed to distinguish this sleep from the other, the one that preceded it, to disentangle these wonderful and torturing dreams from the other ridiculous ones that came before, and finally to remember that he had discovered the little girl's mad eyes under a blazing sun, as well as the image he had of how she must have dirtied her hands on the muddy edge of the pond.

Still unnoticed by him, the shade kept spreading without a stir, while he felt surprise at having once again surrendered to sleep.

'It will probably take me several days,' Mr. Andesmas said, 'to recover from the strain of such a wait.'

These sentences, spoken aloud in the solemnity of his loneliness, rendered Michel Arc's offence more serious.

Thus, Mr. Andesmas, in order to make this trial more bearable, was trying to lie to himself as to the length and the consequences of Michel Arc's delay.

He was waiting this way, claiming not to be able to understand Michel Arc's rudeness towards him.

Once again, in a soft and polite voice, he spoke this lie told to himself.

'I don't understand. It isn't right of Mr. Arc, it isn't nice to make an old man wait for hours, as he is doing.'

He stopped speaking, somewhat ashamed. He lowered his eyes, then slowly raised them, while examining in dismay the site of the terrace-to-be.

'How can he allow himself to do something like that?'

One of these days, on this terrace, wearing a sumptuous, light-coloured gown, Valerie would be staring at this path, at this time of the evening. Under this beech tree which would preserve the benefits of its shade for anyone who would be there at this time, in the future, in this same season, Valerie would be waiting for someone to come. It would have to be here that this waiting, this waiting of Valerie's would soon take place.

Mr. Andesmas calmly made this remark. He moved back farther on the plateau until he could no longer see anything of the village.

In the square, which he could no longer see, the dancing stopped.

No one was coming yet.

But Mr. Andesmas, who had claimed he couldn't bear waiting in this way, for such a long time, was getting more and more adjusted to this waiting. His strength was returning with the coolness of the late afternoon. So much so that he kicked the white sand on the plateau with his feet, thinking he was thus expressing his anger. He smiled at his dirtying his shoes and at his now ridiculous strength. But it was a way for him to make the hours pass, like any other hours, like those which passed during other afternoons when he waited for dinner time in his garden.

A wind blew over. The beech tree trembled. And in its rustling, the arrival of a woman took place, unnoticed by Mr. Andesmas.

She was in front of him and spoke to him.

'Mr. Andesmas,' she began.

For how long had she been looking at him, she too, while he played in that way with his feet in the sand? Probably a very short time. The time she had needed to come from the path and walk up to him.

Mr. Andesmas rose slightly from his arm-chair and bent forward.

'Mr. Andesmas, I am Michel Arc's wife,' she said.

She had rather long, straight black hair, which fell a little below her shoulders, light eyes which Mr. Andesmas recognised as being the little girl's eyes, very large, larger perhaps than the little girl's. She too wore canvas shoes and a summer dress. She seemed taller than she probably was, because of her slenderness.

She stood facing Mr. Andesmas.

'This contractor you're waiting for,' she repeated once more, 'I'm his wife.'

She sat down at the edge of the plateau, very straight, her head turned towards the arm-chair.

She seemed by nature reserved, neither sad nor depressed, but this stiffness of her body and the expressionless intensity—to the point of perfection—of her eyes on the old man arose from a will to censure which could have been misleading to anyone but Mr. Andesmas. Except when her eyes closed for a few seconds, exhausted from looking at nothing, one could have thought they were that way, vacant. But when her eyes closed, she was beautiful in such a different way, she was so beautiful—that was when her eyes came back to life in the dark night of her eyelids—that Mr. Andesmas understood that Michel Arc's wife was not this woman standing in front of him, that she must have been different, and he feared he would never know her.

Would he ever know the woman who had been Michel Arc's wife?

'You don't go out much,' she said; 'I've never seen you.'

She pointed at the hill.

'This is high up. I'll rest a little.'

Laboriously, Mr. Andesmas lifted himself from his armchair and moved aside.

'Please,' he said.

The woman examined the empty arm-chair, hesitated a moment, then refused.

'Thank you, but I'm all right here.'

Mr. Andesmas didn't insist. He fell back heavily into his arm-chair. The woman stayed where she was, seated at the edge of the plateau, her head this time turned towards the chasm. She was outside the reach of the tree's shade, still in the sun, like her child. Like her child too, she didn't talk. Even though it was likely she had come to bring a message from her husband to Mr. Andesmas, she said nothing. But then, how could one know if she hadn't just come to be silent there, near this old man, rather than elsewhere? If she had not chosen this spot, this witness?

Panic-stricken at again having to break so much silence, Mr. Andesmas looked for words. His hands, clutching the arms of his chair, made the wicker stir with slight continuous cracklings which she didn't hear, still turned towards the chasm of light.

The square couldn't be seen any more from where Mr. Andesmas had retreated forever. Apart from a few unidentifiable sounds coming from the village, but which could have come from any other village, the valley was now calm.

Mr. Andesmas, making a polite effort, extricated himself slightly from his arm-chair, and finally succeeded in speaking to the woman.

'Will Mr. Arc come this evening?'

She turned sharply. He was certain she had found it superfluous to give the reason for her coming.

'Of course, that's why I came,' she said, 'to tell you. Yes, he is coming this evening.'

'Oh, you had to go out of your way,' Mr. Andesmas said.

'No, not at all,' she said. 'It isn't so far. And there was no choice.'

The singing again rose from the chasm of light.

It was still a record player. The singing varied in loudness. It faded and became distant. The woman listened attentively whether it was distant or close. But was she listening?

Mr. Andesmas saw nothing of her but the black and silky cloth of her hair spread on her shoulders, and her bare arms, which connected by her joined hands, hugged her knees. No, she was probably only looking, not listening. Mr. Andesmas thought he could tell that she was watching this side of the village square, the side with trees and benches, the one he saw after the departure of the child for the pond.

'They are starting to dance again?' he asked.

'No, no, it's over,' she said.

Mr. Andesmas calmed down a little. Her voice had been even, flat, when she had answered.

An event was taking place, Mr. Andesmas knew it—which he called their meeting, much later. This event rooted itself very harshly in the arid duration of the immediate, but it had nevertheless to be, it had to be that this time also should pass. To be sure, Mr. Andesmas's surprise barely passed, but it was passing anyway, ageing anyway. Mr. Andesmas claimed to know it from the fact that, little by little, the slight cracklings of his arm-chair occurred less frequently and he soon only heard around his body the reassuring ones, in tune with his difficult breathing.

But then something happened that baffled him at first, then frightened him. One of the woman's shoes fell from her foot, from her raised foot. This foot was bare, small and white next to her sunburned leg. Since the woman was still outside the stately shade of the beech tree, or rather the shade hadn't yet reached her, her foot seemed even more unveiled than it would have in the shade. And her strange attitude seemed even more evident: she didn't budge, didn't feel that her foot had lost its shoe. Her foot was left bare, forgotten.

Mr. Andesmas, in contrast to the preceding moment, felt then the urgent necessity to cut into the woman's thoughts. He remembered. A little girl had come by. And couldn't the memory of this little girl play a role here, between them, breaking down their separation? About this child, who wouldn't agree?

'Had the little girl got back to the village when you left?' Mr. Andesmas asked in a friendly tone of voice.

The woman hardly turned. Her voice was the same as if she hadn't stopped talking since her arrival. But her foot remained bare, forgotten.

'Yes,' she said. 'She told me she had seen you. It was quite a while after she arrived that I had to come to tell you that Michel Arc would be still a little later than he had thought. He had said that he would be half an hour late. An hour had gone by when I left.'

'An hour?'

'An hour. Yes.'

'She hadn't mentioned any time, just a delay, without any details.'

'I thought so,' she said. 'She must have forgotten. You too, it seems.'

The sea was becoming a large, perfectly smooth metallic surface. It was useless to hide from oneself that slower, more stretched-out hours were making way for others, regular like the first hours of the afternoon.

'I have time, you know,' Mr. Andesmas said.

'The child said so to her father. And even that you would wait as long as it was light.'

'That's right.'

He added timidly, still making the same effort to pull her out of her thoughts even if it was going to hurt: 'The child found this on the path. Then she forgot it. I can give it to you. But I'll give it to you right away, otherwise I'll be afraid not to think of it. Here.'

The hundred franc coin the child had lost was buried in the sand. He took another one from his pocket and held it out into the void. The woman did not even turn, her eyes still glued to the chasm.

'It doesn't matter,' she said.

She added:

'Since she didn't mention it to me, she must have already forgotten it. She is still very childish, more than she should be. But it isn't at all serious, it will stop one day.'

Mr. Andesmas placed the new hundred franc coin back in his pocket. His bulk moved in the arm-chair, crumpled up in it. Again the arm-chair creaked.

The woman changed her position. She unlocked her arms from around her knees; without looking she found her shoe with her foot and put it on.

'Of course,' Mr. Andesmas said, 'it isn't serious, not at all serious.'

She didn't answer.

Mr. Andesmas said that he was afraid at that moment that she would get up and return to the village, but if she had done so, he would have asked her to stay. Even though he knew that she would never be able to satisfy his avid curiosity about her, he wanted her near him, that afternoon. Near him, even interminably silent, he wanted her near him, that afternoon.

If he saw her later, during the years that went by between these moments and his death, it was only by chance, when he drove through the village streets. Never did she recognise him or did she deign to recognise him.

On the contrary, instead of leaving, she stayed there and continued speaking in this even voice, and her words leaked out of a long interior monologue, she let them escape at times and whoever wanted to hear them would hear them.

'The music hasn't started again for some time,' she said; 'so the dancing should be completely over, even in the streets around the square where people sometimes dance because of the heat. They must have left already, but they're taking their time, they are coming up slowly. You have to wait a little longer.'

'Oh, I have time,' Mr. Andesmas repeated.

'I know,' she said. 'Everybody knows.'

The spontaneous way in which Mr. Andesmas reassured her, as well as the gentleness of his voice, softened the stiffness of her resolution. The spectacle she offered this remarkably old man would be forgotten forever.

Her voice became somewhat languid. She repeated what her child had said a moment before. But she spoke to the empty chasm.

'I'm going to wait a little; if he comes, I'll go down with him.'

She hid her head in her arms, and for a few seconds her hair covered her face.

'I'm a little tired.'

Not only the similarity of their expressions but also

her childish tone of voice would have indicated, to anyone who might have seen them one after the other as Mr. Andesmas had, that she was the mother of this little girl without any memory of her sorrows.

'Why not wait, why not rest a little more,' Mr. Andesmas said, 'before going down.'

'I have five children,' she said. 'Five. And I am still young as you can see.'

She opened her arms wide, in an embracing gesture. Then her arms fell down and she again took up her stiff, haughty position, in the sun of the plateau.

'Oh, I understand, I understand,' Mr. Andesmas said.

Perhaps the conversation could go on like this, on the basis of the children, of this aspect of her life as a mother; perhaps it could move in this way, cheatingly, along the by-ways of the time then passing.

'The little girl is the oldest?'

'Yes.'

Mr. Andesmas went on in a chatty tone of voice.

'Shortly before her, well, a good twenty minutes before her, a dog came by. A dog, how can I describe him? A reddish dog, I think, yes, reddish brown. Would this dog belong to your children?'

'Why are you asking me that?' she asked.

'Well, like anything else,' Mr. Andesmas said, crestfallen. 'I've been here since two o'clock and I've only seen this dog and the child. So I thought that perhaps. . . .'

'Don't try so hard to talk,' she said. 'This dog belongs to no one. He follows the children. He is harmless. He doesn't belong to anyone in the village, he's everybody's dog.'

The shade of the beech tree was moving towards her. And while they were both silent and while she was still stiffly and with fascination examining the village square, Mr. Andesmas saw, with growing apprehension, this shade of the tree move towards her.

Suddenly surprised by the coolness of this shade, realising that it was later than she thought, would she leave?

She noticed it.

She did see a change taking place around her. She turned, tried to see where this coolness, this shade was coming from, looked at the beech tree, then at the mountain, and finally, earnestly, at Mr. Andesmas, seeking from him a last certainty that she still seemed to be expecting, that she apparently wanted to be final.

'Oh, it's really late,' she sighed. 'How could it already be so late, with the sun like that.'

'And even if Mr. Arc doesn't come tonight,' Mr. Andesmas said gaily, 'I'll come back, perhaps tomorrow or at the end of the week, what does it matter?'

'Why? No, no, he'll come I assure you. What surprises me is how easily time just goes by. But I know he'll come."

She turned towards the valley, then again towards Mr. Andesmas.

'Especially in summer, especially in June,' she added.

Mr. Andesmas had noticed it.

'Anyway, didn't Valerie promise you that he'd come?'

Mr. Andesmas didn't answer right away. During his whole lifetime, it had always been easy to take him by surprise. And the slowness of his movements and of his speech, which had increased with age, caused the woman to misunderstand.

'I asked you, Mr. Andesmas,' she went on, 'if Valerie hadn't promised you that my husband would come this evening?'

'It's Valerie who brought me here,' Mr. Andesmas finally said. 'Yes, she is the one who made the date with Mr. Arc. Yesterday, I think. For the last year she has been taking care of my appointments.'

The woman got up, moved closer to Mr. Andesmas, abandoned her observation of the valley, sat down, there, almost at the old man's feet.

'So, you see,' she said. 'You have to wait longer.'

Mr. Andesmas took the woman's rebuke to heart. She came even closer, hauled herself towards him while sitting, like an invalid, and her voice was as loud as if she were talking to someone who was deaf.

'And you trust Valerie?'

'Yes,' Mr. Andesmas said.

'If she told you that he had promised her he would come, believe me, it is only a matter of patience. I know him just as you know Valerie. He'll keep his word.'

Her voice suddenly became more womanly, it emerged from a well of gentleness.

'You see, when he makes life difficult for people, it's because he can't do anything else. It's when it is beyond his power to do anything else. It's only in this case that he could wrong you. That's how he is, without any ill will, but sometimes it happens that he can't help looking as if he had ill will."

'I understand,' Mr. Andesmas uttered.

'I know you understand. Isn't Valerie like that?'

She was completely curled up. Her slenderness was covered by her hair and her arms. She said with an effort:

'Who, in such a case, wouldn't act that way? Who? Neither you years ago, nor I today.'

Mr. Andesmas recounted later that he was tempted—but was he sure about his past, this old man—to be cruel to this woman so as to protect himself from the cruelty that she, he knew it, would show him. But was this the right, the real reason? Wasn't it rather because this woman, who a moment before had been so fiercely resolved not to let any part of her feelings be seen, was now sitting at his feet in such despondency, in such complete abandonment of her whole body; dominated by her feelings which had suddenly become so tyrannical that they crushed her, there, in front of him, the wife of Michel Arc?

In the old days, when his strength would have allowed him to subjugate her in this way, the old man remembered he would have done so.

He was cruel. It was Mr. Andesmas who was the first to bring up Valerie again.

'Do you know my daughter Valerie?' he asked.

'I know her,' she said.

She straightened up, calmly hoisted herself out of her silence. She spoke about Valerie as she had spoken about Michel Arc a moment before. Mr. Andesmas's cruelty hadn't reached her.

'I've known her for a year,' she stated. 'You came here a year ago, didn't you, nearly to the day? It was a Monday.

An afternoon in June. The first time I saw Valerie Andesmas, your child, was on the day of your arrival.'

She smiled from deep in her well of gentleness at the memory of that afternoon.

Mr. Andesmas also smiled at the thought of that afternoon.

There they were together facing the memory of Valerie a year before, a child.

Smiling, they did not speak.

Then, Mr. Andesmas asked her:

'Your little girl must be about the same age now as Valerie was last year?'

She graciously objected to this subject:

'Let's not talk about my little girl. It'll take her a long time to grow up, a long time.'

Again she was back in last year's month of June with Valerie as a child.

'People said that you had already been here, long before, years ago. They said that you had just retired from business.'

'Well! That was quite a few years before,' Mr. Andesmas said, 'but she wanted to live near the sea.'

'First you bought that big house behind the town hall, then you bought land. And then this house. And more land. They said that you had already come here years ago with Valerie's mother.'

Mr. Andesmas lowered his head, suddenly despondent. Did the woman notice?

'Am I mistaken?'

'No, no you're not mistaken,' Mr. Andesmas said weakly.

'You're very rich. That was known very fast. And people came to sell you land. They say you buy carelessly. You're so rich that you buy land without looking at it.'

'Rich,' repeated Mr. Andesmas, in a murmur.

'One can understand and admit it, you know.'

He buried himself a bit deeper in his arm-chair and he groaned. But the woman went on, imperturbably.

'You're going to buy the pond too?'

'The pond too,' Mr. Andesmas murmured.

'So Valerie will have a large fortune at her disposal?'

Mr. Andesmas agreed.

'But why are you talking to me about my money?' he sighed.

'It's about Valerie that I'm talking to you,' she said smiling, 'you're mistaken. Why are you buying so much land, so much and so much, in this completely careless way?'

'Valerie wants the whole village.'

'Since when?'

'A few months ago.'

'She won't be able to.'

'She won't be able to,' Mr. Andesmas repeated. 'But she wants it.'

The woman put her arms around her knees again and revelled in pronouncing the name.

'Ah, Valerie, Valerie.'

She sighed with pleasure, deeply.

'Ah, I remember it as if it were yesterday,' Michel Arc's wife continued. 'The moving vans stayed in the square all night. They had arrived before you. No one had seen you yet. And the next day, I was standing at my window as

I often do, looking at the square, it was close to noon, when I saw Valerie.'

She got up suddenly and stayed there, standing, very close to Mr. Andesmas.

'It was just before school finished. I was, I remember, on the look-out for my children. Valerie appeared in the square. I was probably the first one to see her. How old was Valerie then?'

'Nearly seventeen.'

'That's right, yes. I was afraid I'd forgotten. So she crossed the square as I was telling you. Two men—they saw her after me—stopped to look at her walking by. She walked, the square is wide, she walked, crossing it, crossing it. She walked endlessly, your child, Mr. Andesmas.'

Mr. Andesmas raised his head and along with the woman he contemplated Valerie's walk, a year earlier, in the light of the village square, when she did not know the radiance of her bearing yet.

'Indifferent to the stares?' Mr. Andesmas asked.

'Oh, if you only knew!'

The air burst in the chasm of light.

While you might have thought they were no longer dancing, they were dancing again.

But neither Michel Arc's wife, nor Mr. Andesmas, remarked upon it.

'Indifferent to the stares, as we were saying,' the woman went on. 'We were looking at her, the two men and I. She pushed aside the curtain of the general store. We no longer saw her during the time she was in there, and yet not one of the three of us moved.'

The shade of the beech tree now reached the chasm. It started drowning in it.

'In the general store,' Mr. Andesmas repeated.

(He started laughing.)

'Oh, I know!'

'Because of the moving vans that had stayed in the square all night, I knew that the people who had bought that big house behind the town hall were going to arrive, any day. Already the name Andesmas had been mentioned. You had bought that house a few months earlier. Everybody knew that the two of you were alone, a child and father, already old, they said.'

'That old, they said?'

'Yes, in the township they were saying that you had had this child very late, from a last marriage. But you know, seeing Valerie so tall, so blonde as you know, I didn't immediately make the connection between your arrival and her existence. Such blondness, I told myself, how beautiful she must be.'

'Ah,' Mr. Andesmas moaned, 'I know, I know.'

'How beautiful she must be, I told myself, but is she as beautiful as one can imagine from her walk, from her bearing, from this hair?'

She took her time, disregarding the old man's waiting. Then she went on in a voice that had become clear, loud, almost declamatory.

'The curtain closed on her hair. And I asked myself who in the town had brought her, who was to join her any minute, now. The two men also seemed astonished and we looked at one another questioningly. Where did she come from? We kept asking ourselves what man owned this blondness. This blondness only, since we had not yet seen her face. You just couldn't imagine so much useless blondness. Well? She took her time to come out.'

She came closer, sat down right next to the old man and this time they looked at each other but only for as long as she spoke, exactly..

'Then,' she said, 'she finally reappeared. The curtain was moved aside. We saw her as she crossed the whole square in the opposite direction. Slowly. Taking her time. Taking the time of those who were looking at her, as if it had been owed her from time immemorial, unknowingly.'

'Unknowingly,' Mr. Andesmas repeated.

Once again they were relegated to that moment when she had seen, completely, fully, forever, the beauty of Valerie Andesmas.

She stopped talking. Mr. Andesmas had sunk back into his arm-chair. From the crackling of the wicker arm-chair under his hands, he noticed once more that he was trembling.

'Mrs. Arc,' he asked, 'if this house has been for sale so often, as I have been told, it is not without reason?'

She smiled, nodded.

'You've made up your mind to say just anything,' she said.

She added, suddenly, seriously:

'But there must be a reason, I suppose, yes.'

The forest became sunny. All its shadows drowned in the chasm of light, too long now for the hill to contain them.

'I have known none of the owners of this house,' she said, 'but it's true that it passes from hand to hand regularly. There are houses like that, everyone knows that.'

She explored its surroundings very quickly and, again, looked at the chasm of light.

'Its isolation probably, in the end,' she said.

'Because,' she went on, at first, couples, for example, might enjoy it?'

'Ah, probably, probably,' Mr. Andesmas murmured.

'And also this light, in summer, so hard.'

'It isn't any more now,' he said. 'Look.'

It wasn't any more. The mist rose, thicker, from the woods and the fields. The sea was tenderly multicoloured.

'Michel Arc had planned to buy it, you see, at the beginning of our marriage,' she continued. 'But your predecessors were living in it. Afterwards, Michel Arc no longer mentioned it. I only saw it once, three years ago when I took the children to the pond. In the summer.'

'Nobody had thought of a terrace? This is the first time?'

'Oh, not at all, Michel Arc had thought of it.'

'Only he?'

'The others? How would I know? Even though you might think, when you see this plateau, that it calls for a terrace, why had no one thought of it before you? If you know why, tell me, Mr. Andesmas.'

'Money?'

'No.'

'Time?'

'Well, perhaps, Mr. Andesmas, time to build it before leaving this house because of its isolation which, as we were saying, becomes unbearable in the end. Don't you think so?'

Mr. Andesmas did not answer.

She turned.

For a short while, she at last saw this bulk, abominably final. He no longer was even tempted to express himself. And at that point, she probably felt some interest in so much past existence. Mr. Andesmas realised this from her half-closed eyes which lingered on him. Later he said he had recognised this to be the woman's greatest virtue, this ability at such a moment, even for just a few seconds, to forget about herself and take an interest in his immense, cold and burnt-out life.

'Her mother left you,' she said very softly, 'and she has had other children since by different men? There was a law suit?'

Mr. Andesmas nodded.

'A very long, very expensive law suit?' she continued.

'I won, as you can see,' Mr. Andesmas said.

She again got up slowly, moved still closer to him. She touched the arm of the chair and, leaning, stood there looking at him.

They were very close to each other: if she had fallen, her face would have struck his.

'You had great hopes for her probably?'

He felt upon him the smell of a summer dress and of a woman's loose hair. Nobody ever came so close to Mr. Andesmas any more, except Valerie. Was the closeness of Michel Arc's wife more important that what she was saying?

'I had no ideas on the subject,' he said in a very low

voice, 'not yet. You understand. No ideas. That is why I may perhaps seem helpless to you.'

He added in a still lower voice:

'I no longer know anything about what I knew before I had this child. And, you see, since I have her, I have no ideas about anything any more, I know nothing but my ignorance.'

He laughed, tried at least, as he had come to laugh now, falsely.

'I am really astounded, believe me, at such a possibility in life. The love for this child that weathers my old age!'

The woman straightened up. Her hand left the armchair. Her voice became more curt, but barely.

'I wanted to talk to someone about Valerie Andesmas,' she said. 'I assure you that you can put up with this inconvenience.'

'I don't know,' Mr. Andesmas complained, 'I don't know if I can.'

'It's better. No one had talked to you about her and now she's grown up, it's better.'

The shade had now spread over the whole plateau. It was already the shade of the hill. The shade of the beech tree and of the house had toppled over completely into the chasm.

The valley, the village, the sea, the fields were still in the light.

More and more numerous flocks of birds escaped from the hill and turned madly in the sun of the void.

The shade spread faster over this house than over those

in the village. Nobody had thought of it yet, neither Mr. Andesmas, nor Valerie. But the woman noticed it.

'Valerie will lose one hour of light here, compared to the village,' she said.

'Mr. Arc hadn't told me that, you see.'

'Did he know it? Even when we thought of buying it for ourselves, he hadn't mentioned it,' she added, 'ten years ago.'

'What hurts is to see the sun so close, there.'

'One has to be here the way we are to notice it. Otherwise who would think of it, before?'

She took several steps on the path, came back, then sat down, as if reluctantly, a few yards from the old man, this time.

'Valerie makes me suffer a lot,' she said.

She spoke in the same tone of voice about the disadvantages of the house, so that one might have thought the whole world in her eyes suffered from a contagious disorder, but only from that.

The pleasantness of a recent past containing pell-mell Valerie Andesmas's crossing the village square, and what followed, and her suffering too, were equal aspects of this disorder.

Again she moved away towards the path with this walk which was the same as her little girl's, a while before, light, a little crooked, only her legs moving, effortlessly, beneath her straight body. And once more, even in the very depth of his old age, Mr. Andesmas was still able to perceive, subdued, dying, but recognizable, the reasons one might have had for loving her. She was a woman who could not help welcoming into her whole body her moods, whether fleeting or lasting. These moods might be languid, gentle, or cruel; the ways of her body would immediately follow in their image.

When she moved back from the path, her walk was sleepy and careful, extraordinarily childish—deceivingly —and one might have thought that she had been tempted, during the minute she spent alone on the path, to leave the calm disaster she was living. Just as her child might have been tempted.

It was when she hadn't yet come back that Mr. Andesmas understood he would have liked to see her again and again, until evening, until night, and that he began to dread Michel Arc's arrival, which would prevent him from seeing her.

He smiled at her.

But she walked by him without looking at him. As she passed on the windy plateau. She dragged the wind behind her. She was speaking about it.

'It's windy. It must be even later than I thought. We have been chatting.'

'Ten past six,' Mr. Andesmas said.

She sat down in the place she had just left. Still far from him.

Had she just noticed this? Or had she noticed it before?

'Valerie's car is no longer in the square,' she announced.

'Ah! You see,' Mr. Andesmas exclaimed.

Once again, the singing rose up, ravaged by the distance. They had turned down the record player earlier than the time before.

'Then I think they won't be long in coming,' she said. 'Both of them are very decent and charming.'

'Yes, they really are,' Mr. Andesmas murmured.

She got up again, again walked towards the path, came back again, still possessed by this occupation, the passionate listening to the forest noises coming from the path. She came back, stopped, her eyes half-closed.

'You can't hear the car coming up yet,' she said.

She listened again.

'But the road is difficult, longer than you'd think.'

She glanced absently at Mr. Andesmas's motionless bulk, buried in his arm-chair.

'You are the only one I can talk to about her, you understand?'

She walked away, came back, walked away again.

Did she realise that Mr. Andesmas never stopped looking at her? Probably not, but even if she knew, this staring would not have distracted her from listening to the forest, to the valley, to the whole countryside, from its most remote horizons up to this plateau. The total impossibility with which Mr. Andesmas was confronted of finding something to do or say to lessen, if only for a second, the cruelty of this frenzy of listening, this very impossibility chained him to her.

He listened like her, and for her, to any noise that might have signalled an approach to the plateau. He listened to everything, the stirring of the closest branches, their rustlings against one another, their jostlings, sometimes, when the wind increased, the muffled bending of the trunks of the huge trees, the gasps of silence paralysing the whole forest, and the sudden and connected reintroduction of its rustling by the wind, the cries of dogs and chickens far away, the laughing and talking all mixed into one conversation by the distance, and the singing and the singing.

> When the lilacs
> ... my love
> When our hope ...

Sharing one outlook, they both listened. They also listened to the strangled sweetness of this song.

The wind mussed her hair each time she came back from the path. It blew more frequently and a little stronger. Tirelessly, each time she returned towards Mr. Andesmas, she would push her hair back with her hand and hold it like this a few seconds, and her bared face became the face of past summers when, swimming next to Michel Arc, she must have been told that she was beautiful, like that, for him, Michel Arc.

Once, the wind was strong enough to blow all of her hair onto her face and, tired of having to make this mechanical gesture once more, of pushing it back, she didn't do it. She no longer had a face, she no longer had eyes. Instead of moving farther on the plateau, she stayed there, on the path, waiting for the end of the gust that had mussed her hair.

The gust ended and once again she made this reasonable gesture. Her face reappeared.

'So much blondness, so much, so much useless blondness, I thought, so much idiotic blondness, what could it be good for? Except for a man to drown in it? I didn't immediately realise who would madly love to drown in that blondness. It took me a year. A year. A strange year.'

The shade started to cover the fields, it was approaching the village.

More numerous, thicker noises rose from the valley.

The path remained empty.

'People are in the streets,' she said.

'You were telling me, Mrs. Arc,' Mr. Andesmas said hastily, 'you were telling me that the curtain of the grocery had been pushed aside.'

'And the car isn't there any more,' she went on. 'And they aren't dancing any more. And it's already too cool to go to the beach.'

She walked towards the old man, slowly. And slowly, she spoke.

'The curtain was pushed aside. I have time, I have plenty of time to tell you. Yes. The curtain was pushed aside. And she crossed the whole square again, indifferent. I already told you. I could tell you again. She appeared. The bead curtain covered her, she freed herself from it. And that day I heard the almost deafening noise, which I was to hear thousands of times, of the bead curtain falling back after her. I could also tell you how, like a swimmer, she pushed it aside, her eyes closed for fear of hurting herself with the beads, and it was after she had gone through the curtain, in the sunlit square that she opened her eyes, with a slightly embarrassed smile.'

'Oh, I see, I see,' Mr. Andesmas exclaimed.

The woman went on even more slowly.

'And, taking her time, she crossed the square.'
The singing began again.
She listened to it without speaking, attentively.
'So,' she said, 'that's the most popular song this summer.'
She started moving towards the path again, came back again, and then, giving up this game, she sat down like a lump where she was. She let her hair be blown by the wind, her unoccupied hands caressed the ground.
'Beauty, we all know it,' she said, 'starting with ourselves. In love, we are told, how beautiful you are. Even when mistaken, who doesn't know what it is to be beautiful and the peace you feel to hear it said, whether as a lie or not? But Valerie didn't, Valerie, when I first knew her, as strange as this may seem, was still very far from guessing how sweet it is to hear this said, how awaited. But without knowing it, she was looking forward to it, she was wondering who, some day, would come to her, speaking these words for her.'
'She crossed the square,' Mr. Andesmas said, 'you had got to that.'
'She was already tall, Mr. Andesmas, your child was already tall, I tell you.'
There was a lull in the village.
Her mouth half-open, in a daze from paying attention, she stopped talking—her eyes were following Valerie's black car on the road along the sea. Mr. Andesmas also saw this car.
She was the one to start talking again.
'It took me a year,' she went on, 'to unravel this enormous problem posed by the wonderful blondness of your

child. One year simply to accept its existence, to admit this event: Valerie's existence, and overcome my fright at the idea that she was still being offered without any reservations, to whom? To whom?'

One could no longer see Valerie's car.

The road along the beach led into the pine forest that prolonged the beach, at the foot of the hill, but to the east, where it was still sunny.

The car had gone beyond the fork in the road that led to Valerie's house.

Again she started pulling her hair back into order after each gust. Mr. Andesmas watched her gesture as much as he listened to her words. This gesture was the same as the one Michel Arc's wife must have always made.

'She already knew it, she already knew it, actually, what you were saying....' Mr. Andesmas moaned.

'One doesn't know it by oneself. No, she did not know it.'

Mr. Andesmas rose from his arm-chair and whispered.

'But she knows it, she knows it.'

The woman, making a mistake, thought this was a question. She answered.

'You shouldn't ask this horrible question,' she said. 'Tomorrow, or tonight, perhaps she will know it?'

Severely she examined the shapeless bulk that was Mr. Andesmas.

'Did you see her car along the beach, Mr. Andesmas?"

'I saw it.'

'Then we know the same thing, both of us, at this moment which is perhaps the very one when she will find out.'

Very quickly she was elsewhere, crucified on this sunny square that Valerie was crossing.

'That first crossing of the square,' she said, 'that morning, by Valerie, so blonde, as you know it, you too, her father, that crossing under new eyes, she didn't pay any attention to it, certainly, and yet she says she remembers it. She claims she raised her head and saw me.'

'But you couldn't not have known that Valerie was my child,' Mr. Andesmas wailed.

'After she had left the grocery, but much later than her crossing, I understood that Valerie was a child. But only afterwards. After having thought about it.'

'She walked out with? With?'

'Yes!' she shouted.

A dull and lengthy laugh shook Mr. Andesmas's body. As for her, she burst out with a high-pitched laugh which stopped half-way in its soaring.

'With chocolates!' she went on. 'She was looking at no one, at no one, in spite of what she now says, just at the bag of chocolates! She stopped a second. She opened the bag and took out a chocolate, unable to wait any longer.'

She looked at the pine forest in which Valerie's car had been swallowed.

'That is how, afterwards, I remembered her as a child. How old was she exactly?'

Mr. Andesmas said it again.

'Over sixteen. Almost seventeen. Two months short. Valerie was born in autumn. In September.'

Mr. Andesmas was overwhelmed with words, he trembled from this unaccustomed flow of words.

'She was still a very little girl because of your love. But

you didn't know that she would very soon, and no matter what you did to prevent it, be old enough to leave you.'

She stopped. And in this silence, provoked by her, the graceful memory of an old suffering slid into Mr. Andesmas's heart.

'But this other little girl, yours?' he moaned.

She now stared at the pine forest which covered Valerie's car.

'Let her be,' she said.

'Where is she? Where could she be?' Mr. Andesmas exclaimed.

'She's there,' she said slowly. 'There. She thinks she's lost something, she's looking in the square. I can see her. She's there.'

Her eyes left the forest, wandered on the plain, moved closer to the village.

'I recognise her by her blue dress.'

She pointed towards a spot Mr. Andesmas could no longer see.

'There,' she said. 'She's there.'

'I can't see her,' Mr. Andesmas complained.

The graceful memory of his old suffering hardly stirred within him, hardly more than the memory of the inconsolable regret for a love barely glimpsed at, and immediately stifled, and with thousands of others, forgotten.

Its mourning was felt only by the very old flesh of this destroyed body. That was all. This time his head was spared the worry of having to suffer.

'She won't find anything,' Mr. Andesmas said. 'Nothing.'

Could she really see her child, who in the sun and the dust of the square was looking for her memory?

'While she is looking,' she said, 'she's not unhappy. It's when she finds that she worries, when she finds what she is looking for, when she remembers clearly having forgotten.'

Slowly she again turned her head, seized by the spectacle of the pine forest and of the sea. The forest remained closed. The sea was deserted.

Mr. Andesmas lost sight of her as suddenly as he had noticed her earlier.

Probably feeling chilly, she suddenly clasped her shoulders.

'Little by little, day after day, I started thinking about Valerie Andesmas, who would soon be old enough to leave you. You understand?'

With careful steps she moved closer to the chasm, not waiting for an answer from Mr. Andesmas. He was afraid she would let go of her shoulders, he thought that once she would let go of her shoulders, nothing would keep her from going a little farther towards the chasm. But she undid this gesture only after turning towards him again. Mr. Andesmas's fear at seeing her move towards the chasm was so violent that one could have thought that his old age, right then, inadvertently was leaving him.

'Are you asleep, Mr. Andesmas? You're not answering me any more?'

Mr. Andesmas pointed at the sea. Mr. Andesmas had forgotten the child forever.

'It is not as late as you think,' he said. 'Look at the sea. The sun is still high. Look at the sea.'

She didn't look, shrugged her shoulders.

'Since they'll come anyway and since the more time passes the closer the time when they'll arrive, why worry?'

Laughter exploded somewhere on the hill.

The woman stood motionless, like a statue, opposite Mr. Andesmas. The laughing stopped.

'It was Valerie's laugh and Michel Arc's,' she exclaimed. 'They are laughing together. Listen!'

She added, laughing herself:

'At what, I'm asking you?'

Mr. Andesmas lifted his numb, neat hands in a gesture of ignorance. She came towards him walking like a weasel, she seemed very gay all of a sudden. Did he want her to leave now? He imagined the plateau deserted once she would have left and then when she moved towards him, he listened with all his strength.

'You want to know it? It's by giving her chocolates that I met her. A sweet tooth, hasn't she, Valerie?'

'Yes, a sweet tooth!' Mr. Andesmas agreed.

He smiled, he couldn't help it, at this memory.

'I'm the one,' she said, 'who taught her to escape during your siestas.'

Mr. Andesmas became encouraging.

'Was it necessary?'

'Yes. She could hardly bear leaving you alone at your age. The only time it was possible was siesta time, your long siestas.'

'This house?'

'Michel Arc showed it to her during a walk.'

'The terrace?'

'It would be an idea, he told her. It would be nice to have a house, so high up on the hill, with a terrace from which to see the coming of good weather, storms, from which to hear all the noises, even those from the other side of the bay, in the morning, in the evening, at night too.'

'They didn't laugh just before as you claimed,' Mr. Andesmas said. 'We haven't heard a car driving up.'

'If they come by way of the pond, they have to walk so far that they would leave the car much farther down and that's why we wouldn't hear it. It doesn't matter actually, we'll know soon.'

Again laughter exploded from another part of the hill. She listened.

'Children perhaps?' she asked. 'It's over by the pond.'

'Yes,' Mr. Andesmas stated.

Her good mood disappeared. She came back to the armchair, very close.

'What do you think?' she asked very softly. 'Is it worth our waiting longer? A while ago I took advantage of your confidence. I told you I was sure they would come, but it isn't true, I'm not sure of anything.'

'I can't go down by myself without running the risk of dying,' he said. 'My child knows this.'

'I hadn't thought of that,' she said.

She laughed at this joke, laughed. He laughed with her.

'I told this to your little girl. I'd wait for Michel Arc as long as there was light. There is still a lot of light.'

'And she told him.'

'Then you see, you see.'

She sat at the foot of the arm-chair like that little girl a while before. One might have thought she wasn't waiting for anything any more. She closed her eyes.

Her hair was against the wicker of the chair, caressing it.

'She refused what I would give her, chocolate at first,' she said. 'As you had taught her. Even chocolates. Many times.'

She repeated wearily:

'Many, many times. Sometimes it made me feel almost discouraged.'

She turned towards him, stared from very close, and Mr. Andesmas lowered his eyes. Who would still look at Mr. Andesmas, except, at some difficult time, this woman, and, a while before, this child?

'You look as if you weren't thinking of anything any more,' she added softly.

'She's my child,' Mr. Andesmas whispered. 'Her memory is within me, even in her presence, always the same and it makes me lazy to think.'

'And yet you listen to me.'

'You're talking to me about her. Was she running off to your garden, during my siestas?'

'When it wasn't too hot to stay there, yes, it was to our garden.'

'I didn't know anything. But it makes no difference to me now, whether I know or not.'

'You certainly are talking all of a sudden,' she said, smiling.

'When I wake up, Mrs. Arc, at my age, from these old

man's siestas that you are talking about, from a sleep thick as glue, with my memories I know that it's a very common joke to believe that it is useful to have had such a long life. I can still imagine Valerie's mornings and evenings, I can do nothing about it. I think that I shall never reach the moment in my life when the image of Valerie's mornings will have left me. I think that I shall die with all the weight, the heavy weight of my love for Valerie on my heart. I think that's how it will be.'

She felt an outburst of tenderness towards him, such as she hadn't felt once until then.

'But Michel Arc is a wonderful man,' she said. 'Don't worry.'

'I don't think I do,' Mr. Andesmas said, 'although perhaps you're right, I might worry without knowing it. Everything gets to my mind in such a blurred way that rather than being worried it may be that I am happy to be with you, feeling I can trust you.'

'Make an effort, keep listening to me,' she begged. 'I swear I know Michel Arc better than anyone. You'll see him in a little while. Make an effort to know him better, I implore you. You'll see what kind of man Michel Arc is.'

'I believe you,' Mr. Andesmas said absentmindedly.

The woman found herself deprived of his attention and felt concerned.

'You're going to fall asleep, Mr. Andesmas, if I keep talking about him?'

'I don't know,' Mr. Andesmas said still absentmindedly.

'What relief to think of her in that closed garden during my siestas, shut up in that garden during my sad sleep.'

'Listen!'

The hill was once again perfectly silent. The shade was spreading over the edge of the sea.

'I thought I heard something,' she said.

Mr. Andesmas later claimed that from that point on he grew weary, that he began to break away from her, even from her, this woman, the last one to come close to him.

'You see, I don't remember that she left me so often at siesta time.'

'But she would come back before you would wake up, Mr. Andesmas. She looked at her watch, always, ten minutes before you got up. And she left, running to your garden, and very gently closed the gate behind her, and ran on to your room. Come, come now, Mr. Andesmas, what are you imagining?'

'I would have noticed, at least once, only once.'

Sadly he shook his head. So did she. Both of them shared the same pity for Mr. Andesmas's situation.

'I believe you now,' she said. 'You have no memory left. You no longer have any memory.'

'Oh, leave me alone,' Mr. Andesmas suddenly exclaimed.

> *When the lilacs will bloom my love*
> *When the lilacs...*

She listened to the song, indifferent to Mr. Andesmas's angry sadness.

'I still have a memory,' she said, 'the memory of that man, Michel Arc, for whom we are waiting. But some day I'll have a very different memory from this one. Some day

I'll wake up far removed from any memory of this moment.'

She added, in a sudden about-face:

'I have made this my duty. You hear?'

He had heard

'Yes, yes,' he said.

'Ah, I can already feel them move into my life, those other men, tens, hundreds of them, new ones, ah! Who will rid me of this memory, and even of the memory of this moment I'm living here in front of you, this difficult, nearly unbearable moment, but which I bear anyway, as you can see, thanks to your courteous presence. Then, I'll be ashamed to have talked to you like this, to have confided to you these temporary difficulties. You'll be dead perhaps?'

He bent his head and looked at the chasm, in his turn.

'I have the impression that you too are saying just anything,' he mumbled.

She turned, facing the chasm that Mr. Andesmas was looking at and shouted about her belonging to Michel Arc.

'Some day, some day, another man will come to me and under his eyes I'll feel the signs of a first desire, a heaviness, a warmth in my blood, that I won't fail to recognise. In the same way. No other man will be able to come close to me then, I won't be able to bear any, not even him, Michel Arc. In the same way as when he——'

Mr. Andesmas interrupted her.

'Valerie crossed the square, a bag of chocolates in her hand. And then?'

She seemed shocked for a second, then her listening to the forest obliterated any amazement within her.

'Don't you know any more how she crosses squares?' she asked offhandedly. 'You have to be told this?'

Mr. Andesmas laughed.

'Well!' he said, 'I probably don't know too well any more.'

'Others will soon know it better than I, and with a fresher memory. All you'll have to do is ask them.'

'Calmly, indifferent to the heat?' Mr. Andesmas insisted.

'Yes, but how must one go about telling you?'

'It's true that she is nice and calm, my little Valerie,' Mr. Andesmas said.

She probably was convinced that she faced a man who no longer counted.

She left him, went towards the path, sat down, and talked to herself, her back turned to him.

'Oh, how difficult,' she said, 'how difficult it is to describe such a simple suffering, a suffering of love. What a wonderful relief it would have been to meet someone to whom I could have talked about it! How can one describe anything to an old man who has left all difficulties behind him except that of dying, that only?'

'Come back over here,' Mr. Andesmas begged. 'You're mistaken. Everything else, everything else makes no difference to me, except your still talking to me. Please, do come back.'

She obeyed reluctantly, went towards him.

'We were so faithfully united,' she said, 'by day and by night, so exclusively, that sometimes, ashamed, we felt regret at seeing ourselves so childishly condemned to being deprived of other encounters, more daring even than ours.'

Mr. Andesmas raised his hand in a dictatorial way and held it out towards her. She refused to take that hand.

'Valerie,' Mr. Andesmas said, 'Valerie.'

'She went by,' she told him, sounding bored, 'in the way you know she had of crossing squares, a year ago, squares and streets she would come upon. Blonde. Hair in her eyes, always. Busy sucking her sweet, looking at the other ones, sorry not to have all of them together in her mouth.'

An immense, fixed smile had spread over Mr. Andesmas's face.

'She has always been like that, my little Valerie.'

At the bottom of the hill, at the exact side from where they had to come, there was the rumbling of a car engine, magnified by an echo.

The woman took the old man's hand and shook it.

'Hey, it's Valerie's car, this time,' she shouted.

Mr. Andesmas didn't stir.

'As old, as crazy as you may be, you have to accept it, Mr. Andesmas. Listen! The car is stopping!'

'You're making up stories,' Mr. Andesmas said.

The car stopped.

There was a moment of silence. And then you could hear a twin pounding of the earth from the exact side, still, where it should have occurred if Michel Arc and Valerie Andesmas or two other people had been coming.

'Your love for Valerie has to grow accustomed to being far from her happiness. Our estrangement, yours and mine, has to be perfect, incomparable. Do you hear me Mr. Andesmas?'

Mr. Andesmas's smile still lingered on his face. He would always remember this face—his own—torn and paralysed by this smile that he could neither justify nor stop.

Mixed with the twin pounding of the steps was the sound of muted, reserved laughter, without banter and yet without gaiety, but which, like Mr. Andesmas's smile, just didn't stop.

The woman listened, then moved closer to Mr. Andesmas with a frightened, animal-like impulse.

'I didn't recognise this laughter,' Mr. Andesmas said. 'I'd say it was the laughter of children going to the pond.'

'They're coming!' the woman said hurriedly. 'They have a different laughter from the one we know, this is their new laughter. When they are together that's how they laugh, I know it! Listen! How slowly they are walking. They are moving reluctantly. How slow they are!'

'How annoying!' Mr. Andesmas whispered.

The woman moved away from Mr. Andesmas. With an exuberance of gestures, she roamed back and forth on the plateau, extravagant, dishevelled, wringing her hands, imprudently walking along the precipice. Mr. Andesmas, occupied only by his attempts to erase this paralysing smile from his face, was no longer frightened.

The shade had reached not only the edge of the sea but the sea itself, almost entirely. Mr. Andesmas thought he had waked from an enormous siesta, several years long.

'How will they learn it?' the woman went on. 'That's the only thing we don't know yet.'

She was searching for words and stated calmly:
'The only thing that will completely escape us.'

Only a thread of light was left between the horizon and the sea. Mr. Andesmas was still smiling.

'How will they tell each other? While the whole village knows, everyone, and while everyone is waiting for that moment.'

'I couldn't care less about what you're saying,' Mr. Andesmas said. 'But go on talking, please.'

'There are only a few minutes left before they get here, look how late it is.'

'They don't know anything?' Mr. Andesmas asked at last.

'No. Nothing. This morning, nothing yet.'

'Not my child Valerie either?'

'No. Neither Valerie nor Michel Arc.'

When the lilacs will bloom my love

'Listen! It's Valerie singing!'

Mr. Andesmas did not answer. Then she walked back towards him one last time, took his hand again, and shook it.

'After she had crossed the square, do you want to know how we met? I suffer so much, I have to tell you. You're so old, you can hear anything?'

'It's your little girl coming up again,' Mr. Andesmas said. 'It was she. I recognized her voice.'

'They'll be here in a few minutes,' the woman implored. 'I won't tell you anything more than what is necessary. I beg you.'

'I won't listen to anything any more,' Mr. Andesmas warned her.

She spoke anyway, her hand on his, in turn shaking it or stroking it, during the few minutes left before the others' dazzled appearance, in front of the chasm filled with an evenly discoloured light.